BERMONDSEY PROSECCO

Chris Ward

Bermondsey Prosecco

Copyright 2014 Chris Ward
All rights reserve
ISBN – 10: 1500100358
ISBN – 13: 1500100353

CHAPTER 1

It had been nine months since Tony Bolton had first been incarcerated in Broadmoor High Security Psychiatric Hospital in Crowthorne, Berkshire and his brother Paul was making his first visit. He had requested a visit before but the hospital had said they felt it would be unwise, so he should wait a few more weeks.

Paul was being driven by his friend and business colleague Duke, and they had made their way onto the M4, heading west out of London; the satnav had said forty-one miles and that it should take one hour and ten minutes. Paul had chosen to visit on a Saturday and had booked a time slot of 2 to 4 p.m. He was a bag of mixed emotions, for as far as he was concerned, brother Tony had been responsible for the deaths of Emma, the unborn baby, Fifi and Dave. However, Paul was very interested to see how Tony was: he had seemed completely insane when he shot the football referee at the Royal Lancaster Hotel in London and Paul had not been surprised that he had been sentenced to an indefinite stay at Broadmoor.

"How much longer Duke?" Paul Bolton asked his friend.

"Traffic's light so maybe fifteen minutes," Duke replied, eyes on the road. "We're coming off at the next junction, then it's a short journey."

Paul had dressed in smart casuals so he was comfortable for the journey but had to keep wiping his sweating hands on his trouser legs. He was beginning to feel very apprehensive and was taking deep breaths to stop himself having a panic attack. Duke could see that Paul was nervous and obviously suffering with his breathing.

"I know how you must feel," the driver told the worried man. "I don't think I could see him—too many bad memories." Duke didn't even like driving to the hospital, let alone the prospect of going inside the place.

"You know who else is in Broadmoor?" continued Duke. "The Yorkshire Ripper—Peter Sutcliffe, the Stockwell Strangler—Kenneth Erskine, plus other murderers, rapists, serial killers. Jesus, what a bunch."

Paul looked serious for a second then said brutally: "Tony should fit in really well, then." They looked at each other and burst out laughing.

Tony Bolton's brother was looking out of the window and noticed the road sign; they had entered Upper Broadmoor Road. "We must be there. Hey, sorry mate, pull over quickly!"

Duke stopped the car and Paul speedily opened the door and puked into the gutter.

"Never should have had that breakfast," he groaned, once he was sitting back in the seat. "Got any mints or anything?"

Duke rummaged in his pocket and brought out a packet of jelly babies and handed them to him.

"What the hell are these?"

"OK, so I like jelly babies."

Paul stuffed a few in his mouth and they helped to take away the foul taste of vomit.

Duke was pulling into the main car park. Paul was thinking about Emma, the baby, Fifi, the copper that Tony had shot and the Greek bloke at the robbery; everything was crowding on top of him. He lowered the window for some fresh air, he couldn't breathe...

"Duke, I don't think I can go in, it's all too much for me." He began to sob.

The other man put a hand on his shoulder. "Take your time Paul, there's no rush."

Paul sat back and tried to collect his thoughts. "Now we are here, I've got to face him. Listen, don't tell anyone you've seen me in this state."

"Only if you promise not to tell anyone I like jelly babies."

They both smiled. Paul looked at his watch: one-forty-five.

"I better get going then." Paul Bolton opened the car door and looked at the sign pointing towards the visitor centre, then he turned back to Duke. "See you in a bit then." He strode off purposefully.

Paul entered the building and made his way to reception.

"Can I help you, sir?" said the man at the desk.

"I have a confirmation to visit a Mr Tony Bolton today at 2 p.m." Paul passed over the document and the receptionist studied it.

"That's all in order sir. Can you please proceed through that door marked Visit Centre and report to reception."

Paul took back the document and headed through the door. It was a short corridor leading into a large room with a number of small cubicles. There was the usual antiseptic smell of prisons and government establishments.

A warder took the document and motioned Paul to one of the cubicles.

"Please remove your watch and empty your pockets," the warder told him.

There was a wallet, a mobile phone, a few coins and his passport. The passport photo was checked against his face.

"These will be kept locked up for you, sir," the man told him. "You can retrieve them before you leave."

Paul was then photographed and his fingerprints electronically scanned. He was then searched very thoroughly, even having to take off his shoes and socks.

Another official told him: "On this first visit you will be meeting with Mr Bolton in the closed visiting suite; that means, you'll be physically separated."

Paul was again getting fretful. Although it was called a hospital, the security was red hot. He could hear keys turning and doors clanging.

"Right, would you follow me please, sir?"

The warder led Paul through a series of doors and they eventually entered a room which appeared to be similar to a bank. There was a glass partition with seats on both sides and with side curtains which gave a small semblance of privacy to each visitor.

"Sit here please sir, and Mr Bolton will be informed you are here."

Paul looked around; he seemed to be the only visitor at the moment. There was a door at the back of the 'patient' side of the room, and suddenly it opened. A warder came in first, followed by Tony.

Christ thought Paul, *he's so thin and he looks a lot older*. Tony was instructed to sit down and he looked at his brother through the glass that separated them.

They studied each other for a few seconds.

"Hello Tony, how are you?" Paul began the conversation.

Tony didn't answer at first, he just stared at Paul.

"So how are you Tony?"

"Not bad at all, thanks for asking."

Paul frowned slightly and thought that this behaviour was so unlike Tony. He gave him a smile. "What's the food like?"

"Not bad at all. Three meals a day and no bills to pay." Tony spoke as if he had memorised every word.

"Are you on medication Tony?"

"Only about a hundred fucking tablets a day. When I walk, I rattle." He laughed.

That explains a few things, Paul reflected, thinking that the laugh hardly seemed natural, as if it was forced; well it was to be expected, banged up in a place like this. *Well*, Paul thought to himself, *it's all his fault.*

Tony whispered something to Paul.

"What was that Tony?"

"I said you've got to get me out of here."

Paul couldn't believe what Tony had just said.

"How the hell could I do that?" Paul whispered back, frowning.

"I'm going to be here for the rest of my life. Paul you have to help me! Please!"

"I really don't know what I can do," Paul said, shaking his head.

Tony was looking at Paul with evil in his eyes and they were now shining like they used to when he was going off on one.

"You better fucking help me Paul. I'm your brother, for God's sake!"

The old Tony is now speaking, thought Paul.

"I don't know."

Suddenly, Tony leapt at the glass and started banging on it with his hands.

"YOU FUCKING CUNT! I'LL GET YOU FOR THIS! I KNOW YOU SET ME UP!" Tony was spitting at the glass and hammering at it with his fists. "I'm going to kill you, you fucking cunt! Great brother you turned out to be!"

Two warders rushed towards Tony and grabbed an arm each. Tony wriggled free and punched one in the face and followed that up with a head-butt. Through the blood and shattered nose the warder was shouting: "Press the alarm! Press the alarm!"

The other warder pulled away from Tony and smashed the alarm button on the wall. Suddenly Paul could hear a high-pitched screeching alarm, but he could do nothing as he was on the visitor side. He then saw Tony take something from his shoe: it looked like a 50p coin but it had a bit of a straight edge that glistened and looked very sharp. Tony moved towards the warder who was next to the alarm, grabbed his collar and pushed him to the floor. He sat on his chest and started to swing the coin back and forth across the warder's face. While the man was screaming, Paul could see deep cuts appearing and blood gushing out of the wounds.

Paul started to shout, "Somebody help!" He opened the door he had come in through and screamed down the corridor, "Help! Help!" He heard a noise and turned round to see that the door on Tony's side of the room had opened and two warders in riot gear were rushing in. The first one took in the situation and immediately smashed Tony on the head with a baton. Tony collapsed in a heap on the floor.

The injured warder was in a terrible way: blood was everywhere and one of his eyes was hanging down his cheek, and his face was a patchwork of deep cuts with flaps of skin hanging off. Paul felt a hand grab his shoulder and pull him towards the exit door. He was manoeuvred through the door and was being virtually dragged down the corridor. He put an arm out to the warder to slow down

"Are you alright sir?" asked the newcomer.

Paul was in shock; he had never expected anything like that to happen. "I'm okay but I need to sit down," he said shakily.

"Let's get you back to reception, you've had a terrible shock."

Fucking shock is right, thought Paul. *Tony's still as mad as ever or worse. He must have fooled the doctors that he was alright to have visitors.*

They reached reception and Paul sat down and rubbed his face with his hands. All he could think of was that he had to get out of there, and he was never coming back; as far as he was concerned, Tony could rot there for the rest of his life.

Paul made for the car park as quickly as he could. Duke saw him approaching and wondered why he was back so quickly. He got out of the car, saying, "Paul, you alright? What's happened?"

"Let's go," Paul snapped. Duke jumped in the car and started the engine as Paul clipped on his seat belt. They headed towards the exit.

"Fucking hell," Paul began, "Tony attacked two of the guards and cut one up really badly."

"What? Is there no security in the place, for God's sake?"

"He's mad. They'll never let him out. He's completely stark, raving bloody mad!"

Duke was shaking his head and thankful that he didn't have to see Tony. They shot back onto the M4 and headed at speed back to London.

CHAPTER 2

It was nine months since Emma and Fifi had been gunned down in the Westfield Shopping Centre in Shepherds Bush, West London. Paul still hadn't got over it and regularly broke down in tears when he thought of Emma, the love of his life, the baby, and poor sweet fifteen-year-old Fifi.

Paul now lived a very quiet life; most of his time was spent running the business, which was now turning over something like fifty million a year. Jack, his business partner, had retired and was enjoying his roses in Chelmsford. They met once a month to look at the books and that was all the contact they had. It was a lonely existence but Paul couldn't even look at another woman whilst he was still in so much pain from losing Emma. He still visited Emma's grave in Kingswood, but only went occasionally now instead of every month. Paul had a terrible fear that he would forget Emma, so had decided that from that time on, the only alcohol he would drink would be the Prosecco that Emma loved so much. At times he only wanted a single glass, often leaving the rest of the bottle to go to waste, but he could afford it, so he didn't care. Every time the bubbly touched his lips he immediately thought of Emma.

Tony was in Broadmoor with an indefinite sentence. His insanity had reached new heights at the Lancaster Hotel, when he had shot and killed the football referee, Cyril Jones. It had taken some planning to get Jones to attend the meeting at the hotel and it showed that Paul could be totally ruthless when he wanted to be. The sane brother could never get over the fact that Tony had caused the deaths of Emma and the baby and had also pulled Fifi in front of himself to take the bullets meant for him.

But fortunately Tony was history now and would never be let out, especially as Jeff Swan at CID Rotherhithe had also arrested and got him convicted for the murders of PC Chris Morgan, who had been on surveillance in the Old Kent Road and Timius Papadikis, at the raid on Arrow Logistics in Plaistow.

Richard Philips had got life imprisonment with a minimum of twenty years for the murder of a man called Monty. The killer was serving time in Wormwood Scrubs, an old Victorian prison in West London. There hadn't been any need to extradite him to Spain for the jumped-up charges of murdering Jim Telfer and Robin Scott. Jeff Swan had thought about arresting Bruce Coyne for those murders but knew that he had been acting in self-defence and would be dead himself, if he hadn't acted as he had.

Paul had formed the partnership with Jack Coombs but Jack had made it part of the agreement that he was retiring and would leave the running of the business to Paul. The latter was happy with that but had insisted that Jack let him run the business as he saw fit, and the main aspects of his changes were to make the business legitimate in all areas.

The changes included plans to immediately stop supplying guns to other villains and to put an end to the practice of introducing drugs into the lives of the girls who worked in the brothels. The main area of contention was the brothels: the money made from them was incredible, but Paul was determined to slowly sell them off and build up the club business in London. He was also totally opposed to the use of girls trafficked from Albania, Slovakia, Romania and Vietnam, which was where a lot of the sex workers they employed were from. He wanted to do something about that as soon as he could.

CHAPTER 3

Detective Constable Jeff Swan and Detective Constable Karen Foster had received commendations for their work on solving the Tower Bridge Road Cop Killer and Arrow Logistics cases, as well as for helping to put Tony Bolton away for life. Jeff wasn't really that bothered, as he was near retirement but he was over the moon for Karen, who still had a long career in front of her. Karen had celebrated by popping over to Torrelominos to see her friend Placido Sanchez. She had arrived back and Jeff was keen to quiz her on the visit:

"Wow Karen, that bit of tan suits you, you look fantastically healthy. So how was your trip?"

"Great thanks," Karen replied. "Beautiful weather, fabulous food, loads of booze and of course, extras."

"I don't want to hear about the extras, thank you!"

"I'm talking about all the free coffees—what were you thinking Jeff?" They both smiled.

"Let's change the subject shall we. I had a meeting with Michael the other day and we discussed new projects."

Karen suddenly became really interested. "That sounds good, give me more please."

"Well, following our recent outstanding success, proving without doubt that the best CID team in the Met is based at Rotherhithe," Jeff said, smiling from ear to ear, "It would seem we have been given a major case and I know it's something very dear to your heart."

"Go on."

"People traffickers. And as we both know, that is mostly women being trafficked for the sex industry."

"As far as I'm concerned, the people involved in that are the scum of the earth," said Karen with feeling. "Well, we'll certainly get the opportunity to do something about these bastards, sooner rather than later."

"I can't wait. When do we start?"

"I started yesterday, so you're behind."

"Where do most of these girls come from?" Jeff asked.

"Albania, Romania, Vietnam, Slovakia, from all over the world. You know the story: they're promised jobs in the catering and hotel industry and then find themselves with no passport, no money and nowhere to stay, it's then sleeping above a sex shop in Soho and fucking twenty johns a day. If they don't co-operate, then they're turned into drug addicts. It's a really shitty business."

Karen had always been emotionally upset by people-trafficking and wanted to get stuck in as soon as possible. "And some of the girls are so young. These men are animals and they need to be caged for a very long time. So where are we with it?"

Jeff looked thoughtful. "Well we've been looking at the brothels run by Jack Coombs and there's a mix of nationalities, a fair number of local girls but a lot from Albania and various other countries."

"So, we're back on the Jack Coombs trail then?"

"Actually, as he told me when we arrested Richard Philips, he has retired; apparently Paul Bolton is now running the show."

Karen couldn't believe what she had just heard. "What? Paul Bolton? Do you mean Mad Tony Bolton's brother?"

"Yes. Hard to believe, isn't it?"

"Well, I always say nothing can surprise me, but this really has." Karen was thinking it would be good to bring down the other brother as well.

Jeff rubbed his hands together. "Let's get some coffee. I'm not sure it will be as good as Placido's but it will be wet and warm."

"Definitely won't be as good as Placido's, that's for certain." Karen smiled and winked at Jeff as they headed off to get coffee.

They grabbed their coffees and sat at a table in the canteen.

"Jeff, I need to understand the trafficking in more detail. What do you know?" Karen began.

"Well, I did read a Met report the other day. I'll give it to you when I've finished."

"So, give me your summary then I won't have to bother reading it."

"OK, lazybones. Did you know there is a UK Human Trafficking Centre?"

Karen looked shocked. "I had no idea, and I doubt if many other people know either. Go on."

"People are trafficked for different reasons. Women to be exploited in the sex industry, for domestic help, cheap labour, and a few even for organ transplants. Why do women get trafficked? Lots of reasons: poverty, they're not educated, they get tricked into thinking that they have a job to go to as a waitress or dancer; some young girls are even sold by their parents."

"God! Sold by their own parents! It beggars belief." Karen was shocked.

"Some of these girls go through hell, the traffickers even turn some of them into drug addicts so they can be easily controlled. Remember, they get their passports taken, they have no money, they don't know the language, they're in debt and they have probably been threatened with violence or the traffickers have threatened to hurt or even kill their families back home. It's a very dirty business."

"How do these women get here?"

"Various routes, depending on where they come from, but most of them end up in Belgium and the Netherlands before coming over to the UK," Jeff explained.

"Where do most of the girls come from?"

"All over the world but the top countries are China, Vietnam, Albania, Romania, Nigeria and all those funny sounding eastern European countries like Latvia."

"It's a massive worldwide problem then," Karen said in exasperation. "Bloody hell!"

"Look, we're only concerned with what's happening in London, that's our limit. We can't do any more than that, so don't let it get inside your head too much or it'll fuck with your brains. At the end of the day, Karen, like most things, it's all about money. A good sex worker can earn between £200 and a £1000 a day!"

"£1000 a day! Wow! I'm in the wrong business. Actually, I take that back, it's not funny." Karen thought for a moment. "Remember, most of these girls are working to pay off debts, and the traffickers like to keep it that way for as long as possible. Jeff, we must do anything we can to help these girls. Even if we only save one girl, I would be happy."

Jeff could see straight away that Karen was already emotionally involved. *I hope it doesn't cloud her judgement*, he thought.

Karen was keen to get involved as soon as possible. "So what's the plan, assuming there is one?"

"We're going to raid two of Coombs's brothels, or I suppose we should say,

Bolton's brothels, now that he's in charge: the one in Peckham and another in Soho. If we get in at peak shagging time, there could be forty-odd girls. It will be very interesting to see who they are and where they come from."

"I can't wait. When are we going in?"

"Got to be Saturday night, about 11 p.m., that's when they're at their busiest."

"Two days away. Anything I need to do?" Karen asked eagerly.

"We'll go through the details with Michael later but I've already geared up for the Soho one, with you doing Peckham."

"Peckham. Wasn't that the one run by Ted Frost? Good, I can't wait." Karen was already thinking of the pleasure she would get from raiding the brothel and closing it down.

CHAPTER 4

Richard Philips was booked into the First Night Centre at Wormwood Scrubs. He had to endure the lecture about how the prison had been built in 1875 and opened in 1891, that the last female prisoner left in 1902 and there were 1,279 inmates, and that the governor was Matthew Kent. But the gist of the lecture was that if you behaved and knuckled down then you could look forward to enhanced levels of visits and association with other prisoners, and if you didn't, life would be very difficult.

The newest lifer of course knew about Wormwood Scrubs; he had friends who had done time so he was roughly aware of what it was like, but doing life was vastly different prospect than getting a sentence of two years and actually only doing one. There was only one thing Richard was interested in and that was getting out. He had said a million times in his life: money could buy anything and if you had enough of it, that would include being sprung from The Scrubs.

Richard had arrived at the Night Centre at Wormwood Scrubs and was introduced to the prison and was then later moved onto A Wing. He was in a multi-occupancy cell with three other prisoners. He did not get the opportunity to speak to them until the next morning.

"Who the fuck are you then?"

Richard woke up and saw a stubble-faced mean looking prisoner looking down at him and talking.

"Richard Philips," he told him. "And you?"

"Never fucking mind who I am. What you in for?"

"Murder, got life. You?"

"None of your fucking business. Got any burn?"

Richard thought he better get a marker down. "None of your fucking business. Now fuck off back under the stone you crawled out from."

The man couldn't believe what he had just heard. He leaned very close to Richard's face and spat out a string of expletives before continuing his tirade: "Look, you want to prove you're tough, fair enough. But you better know my name is Ed spencer, I'm a lifer and I run this block. Do as your told, pay your dues and we'll get on alright. Have I been clear enough?"

"Yeah, you have, thanks for the lecture." Richard then turned over and feigned sleep. Ed looked at him for a couple of seconds and was thinking of beating the shit out of him but decided to leave it, as Richard had only just arrived and was unaware of how things worked in A Block. He went back to his own bed and started a conversation with one of the other inmates.

Richard was happy to keep a low profile until he knew exactly how A Block worked and who was who. There was only one thing he knew for sure and that was that he would be running things very quickly, then he would find a way out of this hell.

Cells were unlocked at 7.45 a.m. in The Scrubs. Richard got up, had a quick shower, got into his new prison uniform and went down for breakfast. He hated the antiseptic smell of prison and the sight of metal everywhere, which gave rise to continuous clanging noises. He avoided talking to anyone. He was going to look, listen and learn, and then he would make his moves. The first thing he needed was some friends and that would not be difficult when you had as much money as he had stashed away.

The new prisoner got his breakfast tray and looked for where to sit. He could see Ed Spencer sitting and stuffing his face and giving him the evil eye. He decided to take the bull by the horns, and sat down at the same table.

Ed and the three other cons were aghast and just stared at Richard. Finally, Ed said, "You've obviously got a death wish. Are you right in the head?"

Richard looked at Ed and spoke very quietly: "Let's go and sit in private. I have a proposition for you."

Why not, thought Ed. "Okay." He got up and went to an empty table across the hall and sat down.

Richard spoke first. "Look, Ed, we don't know each other but if you make a few enquiries you will find out about me. I have friends in here but as yet I have not made contact with them. I have a multi-million-pound business on the outside so I am connected and very rich."

As soon as Richard said he was connected, Ed knew he had to be careful, and then the mention of being very rich piqued his interest even more, and Ed decided that it would be a shrewd move to make friends, rather than enemies, of the newcomer.

"That's all very interesting Richard. So who do you know in here?"

"Joey Tapping and Bob Kean for a start. Those two names alone should tell you I am not bullshitting."

Ed knew Joey and Bob—both career criminals with incredible reputations for extreme violence.

"So, what do you want from me?" Ed asked.

"I need friends in here, I need people who can get me things, I need people who want to make a lot of money and I need people who want to break out with me. Do you want to join me?"

"I can get whatever you want, but what's in it for me?"

"Have you got family who need money? I can arrange for them to be looked after, I can pay a monthly retainer into a bank account of your choice for your assistants and connections. Anything you need, I can provide. Money is no object."

Ed now knew this was the opportunity he had been waiting for: someone who could provide for his wife and kids and make life a lot easier for him on the inside. "Maybe we can help each other Richard, but I don't want to lose face with my crew. You can't be here ten minutes and suddenly take over—that's just not going to happen."

"Fair enough," Richard agreed. "Tell your guys I'm one of your best connections and that I am to be trusted implicitly and if you're not around, then they answer to me. Now, how much does your family need to enjoy life a bit more?"

"Let's start off with three grand a month for my family and five grand for me, how does that sound?"

"Great." Richard held out his hand and Ed shook it. Richard looked towards Ed's friends and saw they were watching intently.

"So is there anything you need straight away?" Ed enquired.

Richard thought for a second. "Yeah. I need a mobile, alcohol and cigarettes."

"Phones are six hundred, burn and alcohol are not a problem, I can get the lot for a grand. Do you want any drugs? It's like fucking Tesco's in here, you can get whatever you want.

"No drugs. OK, fix it as soon as you can. How do I pay?"

"I'll give you an account to pay in on the outside. Oh, by the way if you don't pay, you'll end up with a shank in the guts, and as you may well not be au fait with prison slang, that means some mean bastard will stick a dirty home-made knife in your guts and rip your insides out."

"One other thing Ed: do you have a prison officer onside?"

"Let me explain, Richard. There are twelve or thirteen bosses to each wing and they look after three hundred-and-fifty-odd prisoners; it's a tough job for them and one of the reasons why we stay in our cells so fucking long. Not only that, they're paid shit money and work all sorts of shifts, it's a dog's life and because of that, yes I have managed to get one onside, but that is the jewel in the crown and if you want him to help with anything, it will cost you a fortune."

"It's good to know. You have done well, Ed."

"I've been here five fucking years, that's why."

"Don't worry, you won't be here much longer."

Richard got his mobile, whisky and burns shortly after his meeting with Ed. With a TV in the cell, it made life a bit more bearable.

Now that Richard had his phone, he could talk to the outside world on a regular basis and he did a few things immediately. One was to set up payments for Cathy and Ed Spencer, he then contacted a hit-man in Manchester and took out a contract. Lastly, he organised for someone to locate the homes of two of the A-Block screws and see what family they had. Everything was to be done as a matter of urgency; he needed to get out of The Scrubs as soon as possible before he went completely mad.

He also made enquiries from an old con about escapes in the past from The Scrubs. He found out that they had been few and far between. The most famous escapee was George Blake, a political traitor, in 1966. Apparently, he had sawn through some bars on a landing and escaped over the wall where a car was waiting. There had been two other significant escapes and one was when a prisoner got himself taken to Hammersmith Hospital and armed accomplices grabbed him and escaped. The other was extraordinary: two prisoners escaped while the play *The Mousetrap* was being acted at the prison—this was in 1959.

There was one word that described life in prison more than any other, and that word was *boring*. The monotonous routine took some getting used to and did actually drive some men insane. Richard had made progress and soon there were other things he needed Ed to arrange.

"Morning Richard, what's new?" Ed asked one day.

"There's a couple of things I need doing."

"Shoot." Ed was happy. He had made a hundred quid commission on the last deal he did for Richard.

"I need to get a job that enables me to move round the prison."

"Fucking hell! You don't want much, do you?"

"Is it possible?"

"Anything is possible but it will cost. Have you heard of the 'Jan Wilcox Unit?'"

"No. What's that?" Richard asked.

"Well, it's a unit where prisoners who are considered trustworthy stay."

"And what jobs do they do?" The rookie prisoner was very interested.

"Work in the kitchen, library, as a cleaner, stuff like that."

"Sounds interesting. Where exactly is the unit?"

"Unfortunately, its bang in the middle of the prison, so it might not suit you."

"Hmm, I'll give that some thought," Richard said. "I also need someone who has experience of working with explosives, such as semtex."

"You're in luck. A guy called Matt Collins is the man to speak to. I'll line up a meet," Ed answered.

"We can do that today, then?"

"Yeah, no reason why not."

Association with other prisoners was at 4.30 p.m. until 6. Richard sat down with Matt at 5 p.m.

"Hi Matt, how's tricks?" Richard Philips asked his new acquaintance.

"You know, alright," Matt answered laconically. "Six naked twenty-year-old playgirl models could improve it, but things are OK."

"How long you been in?"

"Two years with another two to do," Matt told him.

"Would you like to get out earlier?"

"Maybe. So, what can I do for you?"

"I want to know about explosives—semtex in particular, as it seems that it's the favourite nowadays."

"The information and ongoing help will cost you," Matt said warily, "but that really depends on what you want me to do."

"I need to get the gear in here to blow a fucking great hole in the wall."

"Are you serious?" Matt was shaking his head. "Bloody hell! Nobody's ever done that before?"

"'Shock and Awe' as the Americans call it."

"OK listen," Matt explained. "Semtex 10 is Czech made, terrorists all over the world use it, and there are good reasons for that. It's a general purpose plastic explosive containing RDX and PETN. It's used in commercial demolition and has some military applications. It's very malleable so can be hidden in various containers. It has a shelf life of five years and if you can get it, you want it without a detectable vapour signature, which nowadays is mononitrotoluene. What else? Well it's red in colour and waterproof. Oh and you need a detonator to set it off."

"How much would we need to blow the wall?"

"About half a pound will blow the entire fucking wall to pieces."

"How could we get it in?"

"I'll have a think about that but it's very pliable so there are many options."

"Set to work on it Matt, we need to move quickly."

Richard was not interested in sawing through bars, he wanted to go out with a bang, blow the wall to fuck, get in a car and zoom off. He now had Ed and his crew on board, plus Matt on the explosives side, so things were coming together. He was happy that anybody wanting to leave would not be adverse to using a bit of violence but he had to be sure he had very strong backup, so asked Ed to provide someone who wouldn't mind blinding a guard if he had to: 'Shock and Awe', American style. Richard was in his element planning the break, and was already looking forward to silk sheets and a session with Julie, the black girl who gave the best blowjob in London.

The man who was masterminding his escape was due to meet up with a guy called Peter Clarke at dinner. Richard looked him over as he approached him: the guy was only about five-eight tall, but built like a fucking tank, with crew-cut hair, plus he had a very menacing look about him.

"You're Peter then?" said Richard as he held out his hand.

They shook hands. "Fucking hell Peter!" said Richard, rubbing his hand. "You nearly broke my fingers!"

"Sorry, but I think a firm handshake is important," muttered Peter. "So, what can I do for you?"

"I'm after someone who's not scared to use a bit of violence if it's needed."

"What for, exactly?"

"I'm leaving early from here and need someone on my shoulder I can totally rely on."

"I want to come with you," Peter Clarke said decisively. "But I need work when we get out and it'll cost you two K upfront."

"What are you in for?"

"I cut a man into pieces and distributed his body all over Kent."

"Great, I'm sure he deserved it."

"Believe me he did," Peter said with a grim smile of satisfaction. "He was shagging my missus. I've got fifteen years to do. I want out."

"OK, Peter, you're in. Where do you want the two K to go?"

"I'll give you the details later. My word is my bond, Richard." Peter held out his hand. Richard laughed and said, "I'm not falling for that again."

"Richard, I insist! Otherwise the deal is not done."

Richard clasped Peter's hand and pressed as hard as he could. Peter squeezed gently and let go.

"Let me know when you want me," said Peter. Then he was gone.

CHAPTER 5

Mary Coombs had never been so happy. She had her beloved Jack at home permanently and was really spoiling him as much as she could. She had never got involved in the business but of course, she had a good idea what he had spent the past thirty years doing.

It was a lovely sunny day and she was walking down the very long garden path towards Jack, who was messing about in one of his three sheds at the bottom of the garden. In her hand was a tray with a cup of tea and a plate of custard creams, Jack's favourite biscuits. Mary dressed in a smart casual way; she would never be seen in less formal clothes, except for when she was actually weeding or planting. She had got halfway down the two–hundred-foot garden when Jack came out of one of the sheds and waved to her. She waved back, transferring the weight of the tray to her left hand. Jack was smiling and looking forward to his tea and biscuits.

She took a few more steps and then stopped. Jack was suddenly running towards her shouting: "RUN MARY! RUN!" He was shaking his arms, indicating for Mary to get back towards the house. Mary was shocked and confused, she couldn't understand what was happening, and she was rooted to the spot.

Then she saw why Jack was running towards her: two men, with their faces covered by black balaclavas, were coming round the side of the sheds and hurtling towards Jack. She dropped the tray, turned and began to run as fast as she could towards the house. Mary was terrified and started screaming for help: the men had obviously not turned up to enjoy the custard creams.

Mary reached the patio at the back of the house and turned. She could see that Jack had been caught, and one of the men was dragging him back to the sheds and the other man was heading towards her. She knew immediately she could not get away. She started shouting, "JACK!" as she ran towards the man approaching her, determined to be as courageous as she could.

"What are you thugs doing in my garden?" she shouted at the man. He took no notice and grabbed her hair and started dragging her back towards the sheds.

"You'll pay for this, believe me!" she screamed angrily.

"Shut it, bitch!" The man gave Mary a slap across the face that nearly knocked her over. She could feel her hair being ripped from her scalp, it was so painful. They eventually reached the sheds and the man threw her into the same one that Jack had been taken to. Jack rushed to comfort her but was smashed in the face with a fist by the other man. Jack and Mary were pushed onto the floor, up against the back wall of the shed.

"Don't fucking talk!" The first man turned to his mate. "Gag him!" The second man grabbed some old cloths and stuffed them into Jack's mouth.

"Now missus, we want to know where the valuables are in the house."

"We don't keep anything in the house, just a bit of cash," Mary told him.

"Where's your fucking jewellery, bitch?" He kicked Mary in the side. Jack tried to move to protect her, but was pushed back with a warning: "Do that again and see what happens."

"It's in a safety deposit box at the bank," Mary told him. "There's some cheap fashion stuff, that's all."

"You mean to tell me you live in this fucking great house and there's no valuables?"

"That's exactly what I am telling you," said Mary stiffly, looking the thug straight in the eye, even though she was quaking inside.

One of the thugs glanced at his mate and nodded. He pulled Mary away from Jack and pushed her into a corner, saying, "If you know what's good for you, don't fucking move."

The 'boss' thug looked at Jack. "Richard sends his regards."

It all happened in a split second. The burglar took a pitchfork from the side wall and rammed it into Jack's right leg. Jack screamed as the guy waited a second and then put all his weight on the handle and pushed as hard as he could. The fork's tines went through Jack's leg and embedded themselves into the wooden floor. Jack continued to scream in sheer agony, while Mary shut her eyes and turned away.

The pitchfork was now standing upright in Jack's leg. The torturer looked around the shed and then picked up a spade. He lifted it high above his head and brought it down hard, sideways onto Jack's left ankle. Bones shattered and blood sprayed everywhere. Jack gave another agonising scream and almost passed out. Mary shut her tear-filled eyes, feeling faint.

"Richard sends his regards," repeated the thug as he swung a half-size garden rake, prongs facing forward. It hit Jack in the shoulder, digging deep into his flesh.

Jack, feeling even more faint, knew he was going to die and managed to whisper hoarsely: "Please let my wife go, she has nothing to do with this."

The attackers were looking at Jack with the pitchfork still in his leg and the rake in his shoulder, appearing as if he was already dead.

The senior man laughed. "We can see you're a bit of a gardener." He then picked up a pair of secateurs and grabbed Jack by the hair, pulling his head up. He firstly cut Jack's nose off, followed by his ears. His screaming was blood-curdling. There was blood flying all over the shed, some hitting Mary. Jack knew he could not last too much longer. Mary couldn't watch and prayed for Jack to die quickly.

"Richard sends his regards," repeated the thug in a monotone. He then proceeded to shove the secateurs into Jack's mouth and started to cut round through his cheek towards the back of his head. He continued cutting all the way round at the other side of his mouth, and the skin and flesh fell to the sides. Jack was still whimpering piteously. The thug then took a claw hammer and smashed it hard into Jack's head. The injured man gave a feeble groan and expired. There was a disgusting smell of urine and shit as Jack excavated his bowels and bladder.

"Good Job," said the second thug. "What about the slag?"

Mary was in total shock and had kept her eyes shut throughout the gruesome killing of her husband. She was petrified that they were going to start on her.

The senior thug looked at her and turned to his mate. "Give her a seeing to for starters and then we'll decide."

Mary cowered into the corner but the man was strong. He pulled her out and shoved her face-forward against the side table.

"Stick your arse up bitch, you might even enjoy it!"

The creature then lifted her skirt and ripped her underwear off. He splayed her legs, and he opened his trousers and took out his erect cock. He roughly pushed it hard into her vagina and started pumping. After a short while, he withdrew and pushed it forcefully into Mary's anus. Mary was in terrible pain but had almost lost all feeling due to shock. This continued for some time until the man came fully inside her.

Mary fell to the floor in a heap, and the rapist lifted her back up and pushed her back, so she was half sprawled across the table. He then pulled the half-size garden rake out of Jack's dead body, turned it around, and shoved the handle deep into Mary's anus. She screamed as a searing pain coursed through her whole body. He then moved the handle backwards and forwards, getting faster and faster and progressively deeper. Mary hoped she would soon die and join Jack.

He then removed the rake handle and threw it on the floor. "I'm bored," he said to the other man.

"We'll be gone in a minute." Her attacker then reached for a bottle on a shelf, smashed the top off it against the wall, then grabbed Mary, pulled her close and ground the sharp glass edges into her face. He turned to his mate, saying, "The bitch won't forget that in a hurry." He finally spat at her: "Regards from Richard!"

Mary was barely alive. She was drifting in and out of consciousness. She was covered in blood and gore, and searing pain coursed all through her body. She heard the two men leave the shed, she thanked God for it, and suddenly it went very quiet.

Mary knew she had to get medical help or she would die. She could scream but unless someone was in the adjoining gardens no one would hear her—besides, she didn't even have the energy to scream. She cursed herself for not having her mobile phone handy. There was nothing to do but crawl up the garden path to the house.

She started crawling very slowly towards the shed door, feeling the agonising pain scything through her from head to toe. After what seemed an eternity she reached it and crawled over the step and out into the garden. The pain was getting worse and she knew she was losing a lot of blood and was getting weaker by the second. She prayed for the Lord to help her, and then she thought she heard talking.

"Help me please, help!" she croaked as loudly as she could.

"Mary, is that you?" she heard someone shout.

"Yes," she whimpered hoarsely. "Help me. Is that you Liz?" Liz lived next door and had wandered down the garden with her husband Eric, to check on her flower beds.

"Yes. Where are you?" Liz called out.

"Over here, hurry please!" She coughed painfully, aware that she could barely speak.

Liz and Eric hurried down their garden and then peered over the fence. Liz saw Mary, or someone who looked like Mary, lying on the path.

"Oh my God!" She turned to Eric. "Go up to the house. Call an ambulance and the police, quickly!"

Eric looked around fearfully, scared that the madman who had attacked Mary could still be around.

He looked at Liz. "Are you sure? It may not be safe yet."

"Just go quickly!" Liz shouted impatiently.

Eric hurried off. Liz rushed to the bottom of the garden, where there was a fence gate with a latch. She opened it and rushed to Mary who had passed out. Liz cradled Mary's head in her lap.

"It's alright Mary," she tried to reassure the injured woman. "Help will be here very soon."

Liz was shocked to the core. What sort of madman could do something like this? Mary's face was just a jigsaw of deep jagged cuts; she was unrecognisable.

"Mary, try to stay awake. Talk to me!"

One of Mary's eyes opened into a slit. She moaned and whispered, "Thank God you came Liz, I thought I was going to die."

Liz gently squeezed Mary's hand. "Don't worry, everything will be alright, don't worry."

Mary tried to sit up but fell back against Liz and whispered, "Liz, see how Jack is, I think he's dead, he's in the shed."

"I'll go and see, I'll only be a second." Liz gently laid Mary's head down.

Liz took the few steps and entered the shed. She saw Jack and suppressed a scream, turning her face away in fright and shock. Then she slowly turned back and looked more closely.

Jack was, without question, dead. He still had the pitchfork stuck in his leg and the hammer hanging from his head. His face had also been cut to pieces. Liz wanted to make sure and knelt down beside him. She was looking for any sign of life, but there was none. Whoever did this must be inhuman, she thought.

She went back to comfort Mary. "I'm sorry Mary, he's gone."

Mary was beside herself. "How could they do those things to him? He didn't deserve to die like that." She was crying and becoming hysterical, as she was too weak to vent her anger and emotions properly.

"Calm down Mary, hold yourself together. Help will be here any minute." She hugged Mary and started crying herself. Suddenly, she heard noises from the top of the garden.

Two policemen were walking quickly towards them. The policemen took one look at Mary and shuddered. "In the shed," Liz said to the officers. One of them spoke into his phone while the other headed to the shed.

The officer took one look in the shed and his face turned ashen. He hadn't been in the force long and had never seen anything like this before. He turned back to his colleague and stuck a finger in the air and mouthed, "One male dead."

The policeman who was talking on the phone moved away from Mary and Liz. "Yes, one dead male and a badly injured female," he spoke quietly. "Some madman has tortured them beyond belief. It's a miracle the lady is alive."

More officers were called to the scene, roadblocks were set up and one of the Essex police helicopters was launched. Meanwhile, the senior officer on the scene, Danny, knelt down next to Mary.

"Mary, my name is Danny, I'm a police officer. You're safe and an ambulance will be here in one minute and we will have you in hospital very soon. You will recover, don't worry. Who did this?"

Mary was feeling like death but was determined to help as much as possible. "Two men, that's all I can tell you," she gasped.

"Can you give me a description?"

"They were wearing balaclavas, they had northern accents, that's all I know." Then she started coughing and moaning.

"OK Mary, take it easy now, that's fine, well done." Danny glanced up and saw the ambulance crew pushing a trolley stretcher towards them.

"Mary, the ambulance has arrived."

"Thank God," said Mary feebly through the tears that were streaming out of her bloodied, puffy eyes.

The officer turned away and wiped a tear from his own eyes.

Crime scene investigators arrived soon after and started to comb the area for clues. It took hours to investigate the shed until eventually Jack had been bagged up and removed. Mary was rushed to Broomfield Hospital A and E Department and had immediate surgery for internal injuries caused by the rake-handle. Her face was sewn up and she was medicated to control the pain.

Three days later, Mary was just about ready to answer some questions from the police. David Smith was the CID officer assigned to the case. Mary still had the stitches in her repaired face, so she looked pretty awful. But she never ceased to thank God every minute for being alive.

As soon as Paul Bolton heard about the attack, he immediately arranged for Mary to have a private room in the hospital, with a bodyguard outside her door. He then sent to Chelmsford for a world-famous cosmetic surgeon to see what could be done for her face. He also reviewed his own security and added another bodyguard to assist his current minder, Duke.

David Smith arrived at Broomfield Hospital with a female officer, Janet Turner. He always found women relaxed a bit more when there was another woman around. David and Janet made their way to Mary's private room and were shocked to see a huge brute of a bodyguard sitting outside.

David showed the man his badge. "I'm here to see Mary Coombs. Who might you be?"

"I'm employed to keep an eye on Mrs Coombs and make sure she is safe, sir" he said. "She's expecting you. Please go in."

David gave the man a sarcastic 'thank you' look and entered the room. Mary was sitting up and reading a book.

"Hello Mary, is that a good book?"

"Yes, it's all about roses, one of my passions." Mary managed a smile.

"My apologies. I'm David Smith and this is Janet Turner, we're from Chelmsford CID."

"Don't worry, I've been expecting you and I'm sure my friend outside would not have let you in unless you were harmless."

"Yes, who is that chap?"

"A good friend of mine arranged for him to look after me, I told him I didn't need a bodyguard but he insisted. Actually it is comforting to know he's outside and he's quite a big fellow." Mary smiled again, as best she could. "Please sit down."

David and Janet pulled up chairs and did so. Janet pulled out a notebook, ready to take notes.

"So, are you feeling a lot better?" asked David.

"Yes, it's early days but I am getting better. It's only when I think back to Jack, and what happened in the shed." Mary felt tears course down her cheeks. Janet got up and took a tissue from the box on the bedside table and gave it to her.

"I'm so sorry Mary," she said sympathetically, "but we need help to catch these two madmen and put them away in prison for a very long time."

"I understand and I will help as much as I can, but I'm afraid I don't think I can be that helpful."

"It's OK Mary, we realise that. Let me ask the questions and I hope you can answer them as clearly and with as much detail as possible please." Janet put a hand on her arm.

Mary nodded.

"Right, ready?" said David, smiling encouragingly. He took a breath. "Prior to the attack, had you or your husband had any altercation, argument or disagreement with anybody at all?"

"No."

"Can you think of anybody who might have a grudge against you or your husband?"

Mary was now concerned: Paul had told her to be careful what she said to the police. Jack's reputation was at stake, what's more, no one wanted the police sniffing around Jack's past, which would of course, at some point, involve Paul himself. The length of the silence was becoming awkward.

"Sorry Mary, shall I repeat that?" David encouraged her.

"That's not necessary thank you. The answer is no."

"You told the officer at the time of the attack that there were two men involved?"

"Yes, two that I saw."

"And they were wearing balaclavas, so you could not identify them at all?"

"That's correct."

"You said they were Northerners, what made you think that?"

"They both spoke with northern accents. I think I'd be able to recognise a Liverpool, Newcastle or even a Leeds accent. So where does that leave us?"

David immediately said, "Manchester is the most likely. It's the crime capital of the north."

"We'll arrange for you to hear some Mancunian accents and see if you recognise it as being similar to what you heard."

David looked at Janet and nodded. Janet made a note to do so.

"Did the two thugs call each other anything?" he persevered. "A nickname perhaps? Anything like that?"

"Nothing that I can remember."

David looked thoughtful. "I'm not going to gild the lily for you Mary. We haven't got much to go on. We have DNA for the pair of them, but it doesn't match anything on the system. Two men from the north, no descriptions, no nothing. I'm sorry. Do you understand?"

"Yes, I understand. And nothing would give me more pleasure than to see them get what they deserve."

"Look, I guess you would like to rest—"

Before David could finish there was a knock on the door and two men entered the room. One was a very expensively dressed man of medium build and behind him was a huge character, with the physique and bearing of a bodyguard. *Bodyguards everywhere*, thought David. *Strange*.

David looked at the first man. "Hello. I'm David Smith, CID Chelmsford. This is Janet."

Paul held out his hand. "Paul Bolton, friend of the family."

Duke went and sat down at the back of the room.

"I'm guessing you arranged for the extra security outside."

"Yes. Mary has suffered enough. Nobody will ever threaten or hurt her again."

David looked at Paul and got the feeling he was in the presence of someone of importance: he radiated power and strength.

"I'm sure you're right, sir. Did you know Jack Coombs very well?" David asked, looking Paul straight in the eye.

"I did some business with Jack."

"Do you think you may be able to help with our enquiries?"

"I don't think so," Paul said with a dismissive tone. Then he walked to the other side of the bed and hugged Mary lightly, careful not to cause any pain. "Mary, how are you?" he said.

Duke got up and opened the door for the police officers: they were being, as it were, 'shown the door'. As a rule, David would take umbrage at being dismissed in this way, but on this occasion, he took it in his stride. David and Janet went through the door and then had to wait while Duke and the other bodyguard slowly moved out of the way.

As the two police officers walked down the corridor, David said, "Something's going on here. I thought we were going to see some old granny, and we end up surrounded by bodyguards and mafia types. This doesn't add up. We need to do some delving."

David quickened his pace as he wanted to get back to the Nick and do some investigating. *Paul Bolton, we'll start with him*, he thought.

* * *

"So, what did the local constabulary want?" Paul asked Mary.

"Oh, just a few questions. I couldn't really help at all."

Paul was delighted that Mary had kept her mouth shut; he was dealing with this in his own way, and when he found out who was responsible for killing Jack and torturing an elderly woman in her own home, they would regret it. Word was already out in Manchester, Liverpool, Leeds and Birmingham that he wanted the names of these animals and then they would find out what it meant to mess with Paul Bolton or his friends.

"Mary, are you sure you haven't missed anything? Any little thing that could help us?"

"I don't think so."

"Have you got everything you need?" Paul asked her.

Mary looked at the abundance of flowers, chocolates and bottles of juice. "Yes, I think so, although I could—"

"Yes, what?" said Paul with a smile.

"Well, a single malt would be rather nice at bedtime."

Paul laughed and turned to Duke, saying, "Get one of the boys to fetch a bottle, the best, mind."

"What do you want to do when you leave hospital?" asked Paul, serious once more.

"I've already decided. I'm going home."

"Are you sure?"

"Absolutely sure. And don't bother trying to persuade me to go to some bloody home."

Paul held his hands up in surrender. "OK, home it is, but there will be changes. I'll find you a housekeeper and Peter, the chap outside, will stay with you as well. Don't argue, I insist."

"That's good of you Paul. To be honest, I'll be very happy with that. It's such a big house and it will be comforting to know I'm not entirely alone there."

Soon, the single malt arrived, which brought a huge cheery grin to Mary's face.

Paul was more than concerned. He wanted to be free of the violence and free of the need for bodyguards. He still was determined to implement his deep-rooted plan to take the business legit over the coming years.

"Well, I better go then Mary, it's been good to see you. Remember, if you think of anything you can recall, anything at all, you let me know, OK?"

"I will. Thank you for everything, Paul."

Paul turned towards the door and stopped. "As I said, anything you need, let me know."

Mary's friend was halfway through the door when he heard Mary say behind him: "Richard sends his regards."

He took one more step and then turned around and stepped back into the room.

"What did you say Mary?" Paul asked.

"I don't know what I said." She was shaking her head as though trying to shift some secret thought.

"Duke, get the nurse," Paul instructed his bodyguard.

When they were alone he spoke again. "I think you said: 'Richard sends his regards'. What does that mean Mary?"

Mary realised what she had said and why she had said it. "Oh my God! it was him! It was Richard Philips!" She became panicky and agitated. "Oh God! He'll come back for me!" She started to cry. "He's a madman. He'll kill me for sure."

"Mary, calm down," he tried to reassure her. "Richard's in Prison."

"Yes, but the two murderers said 'Richard sends his regards'; they said it while they were torturing Jack, they said it to me as well. He's coming for me! Oh God, you know he's crazy. God help me!"

"Mary, this is important." He looked into her eyes. "Did you tell the police that?"

"No, it just came out now I've remembered it. They must have said it three times: 'Richard sends his regards'."

Yes, Paul calculated, Richard had organised it from prison. The *bastards!* The unspeakable things they did to Jack and Mary: they were real animals.

The nurse arrived, took one look at Mary and tried to calm her down. She then went out and came back two minutes later and gave Mary an injection. Mary quickly settled down and began to nod off.

"Will she be OK, nurse?" Paul asked.

"Of course," the nurse reassured him. "She needs rest more than anything. She's had a very traumatic experience."

"OK, well I'll be off. Please tell her I'll drop in to to see her soon."

Paul left the hospital and was thinking what to do next. Richard Philips had obviously put a contract out on Jack, and Mary had just happened to be there at the time they attacked him. God, another fucking mess to deal with, he thought. He went back to the Den Club and had a steak and a glass of Prosecco. He then called in Duke and Dave Sugar, who was now one of his most trusted advisers.

"Dave," he addressed his advisor. "We have a big problem to sort out. That bastard Richard was responsible for the attack on Jack and Mary Coombs."

"He's inside, isn't he?"

"Yeah, he's in The Scrubs. But he's loaded and money talks. He must have got some boys from up north to do it. Believe me, you don't want to know what they did to Jack and Mary." Paul was looking very thoughtful. "So Richard has sorted Jack. Is he going to come after me next?"

Dave rubbed his chin. "Fuck, it's a serious situation. Richard lost out big time when you and Jack became partners. He's a hard case and I would put money on it that he reckons you owe him a heck of a lot."

"Yeah," Paul followed his logic, "but would he want money? Or would he want to try and get rid of me? I guess we need to find out which it is."

"How the hell are you going to do that?"

"Well of course I'll ask him. What else can I do?" Paul said thoughtfully.

"Ask him?" Dave was incredulous.

"Yeah. I'll visit him and discuss it. Remember, this is business, nothing else."

"Visit him? Are you sure, Paul?"

"Yes, I've decided, and I'll do it as soon as possible, but we will also take some extra precautions. Make sure all the clubs and brothels are on alert and increase security. As for me, I'll be staying here for a few days. Dave, get some more bodies in, I want this place locked down. Make sure the customer searches are done properly and that none of the door team are taking money to let people in."

Paul turned to Duke and went on: "You've seen what those bastards did to Mary Coombs. Well, that's nothing compared to what Jack got. I don't want any of that, so be alert and while you're at it, ask Angus to come over here as well."

Paul turned his attention back to Dave. "So what's the situation with weapons?"

"I'll organise some more so we don't get caught out."

"Good. OK, get to it. By the way, whatever happens with Philips, I want those animals from the north found, and then we'll decide what to do with them."

"OK Paul." Dave went out of the room, leaving Paul and Duke in the office.

CHAPTER 6

It was Saturday afternoon. Jeff and Karen were drinking coffee in the CID offices in Rotherhithe Nick. All the planning had been done for the raids on the Peckham and Soho brothels run by Paul Bolton. Jeff and Karen had been briefing their respective teams and were happy that everyone knew their responsibilities. It was to be a fast: 'get in, secure the premises, get all the working girls and staff into a coach and back to Rotherhithe Nick for questioning'. It was stressed to all that the girls should be encouraged to bring their IDs to prove who they were and where they came from.

"So, you up for this evening?" Jeff asked Karen. He knew exactly what her reply would be.

"You bloody bet I am, I can't wait to get going. Ted Frost is in for a shock. Don't think I'm on some sort of crusade but I want to help any of the girls that don't want to be in this dirty business."

"I agree," Jeff said forcefully. "Keep everything very professional, but if you have a personal reason for doing something like this, it doesn't half help."

They were to hit the two brothels at 11 p.m., their busiest time. The suspected brothel at Soho was above a club in Compton Street. Jeff had sent someone in two weeks before to get the lie of the land.

The club was just a bar with a back door and staircase that led to the upper storey. The back door could well be a steel security door and might need to be smashed down. There was a fire exit from the upstairs rooms at the back of the building and that would probably be where people would try to exit when the raid took place. So Jeff had a comprehensive idea of what would happen once they got in the bar and headed up the stairs.

Jeff and his team of fifteen officers had left Rotherhithe at ten o'clock. They arrived at Compton Street at ten-thirty and went over the plan once more. The idea was for undercover officers to enter the bar over a period of twenty minutes. There were to be six officers in the bar and one was detailed to ask if he could go upstairs. As soon as the back door was opened, the team were to secure it and the uniformed officers would then enter the premises. The undercover officers were all wired and could speak with Jeff, who would be waiting at the end of the street.

The few minutes before a raid were nerve racking, for you could never be sure that some prat wouldn't have a knife or even a gun. The undercover officers had gone in and reported back that it was busy with about thirty punters in the bar, mostly men. They also reported the opening of the back door and men going upstairs. It seemed that there were two guards on the door, one on each side; they were taking no chances and it could be tricky getting in without a fight.

The time eventually arrived and Jeff and his team moved slowly down Compton Street. They were to enter the premises just as the undercover team secured the door. Inside, two of the team followed a punter towards the door that led upstairs.

The security guard opened it and the man took one step through, and at exactly the same time, the two officers rushed the door and slammed into the guard, pushing him away from the door. They then shouted: "POLICE! LEAVE THE DOOR OPEN!" The man on the other side paid no attention and dragged the punter in through the door and went to push it shut.

Mick, one of the officers, jammed his foot between the door and its jamb, and continued to shout: "POLICE OFFICER! MOVE AWAY FROM THE DOOR! NOW!"

Suddenly, uniformed officers arrived and heaved at the door. It opened wide and they rushed through and up the stairs.

Police officers were stationed at the bar entrance and were waiting for anyone who tried to escape via the fire exit out the back. There was pandemonium upstairs, girls were screaming and half-dressed punters were rushing towards the fire exit.

Jeff was sitting at the bar, calmly sipping a very nice four-year-old whisky, courtesy of the bar owner, looking as though he didn't have a care in the world. Uniformed officers eventually gained control and everybody was brought downstairs into the bar. The men and women were separated, taking up residence on the two sides of the room. Sergeant O'Donnell reported to Jeff that the building was secure and that the upstairs rooms were now empty.

"Thank you Jim," Jeff said. "I want the coach brought down. Tell everybody they're going on a nice trip to Rotherhithe. I'm sure they will be very excited about that!"

Soon Jeff heard the uproar when Jim told them they were all going to Rotherhithe Nick. Jeff strolled into the middle of the room. "OK, that's enough! Calm down!" Jeff looked around at the motley collection of individuals that always seemed to typically appear during a brothel raid.

There were of course, scantily clad girls; some of them looked extremely young and most were certainly not British. *Good*, thought Jeff. *We might be able to help some of these girls get home*. The punters were a mixed bag: some very well dressed and some who were right funny looking articles, with at least one tranny, for definite, thought Jeff.

Jeff turned to O'Donnell and said: "Get them on board and let's get going." Jeff made his way to his car, wondering how Rotherhithe Nick was going to cope with forty-two people from this raid alone. He did not notice the black BMW with two hard-looking men watching as he drove away from the bar.

Phone calls had been made to all the other brothels warning them of possible raids and they all closed down very quickly. Ted Frost at Peckham took the call just as the police were swarming into the house. "Too fucking late!" he swore into the phone and slammed it down.

"Hello Mr Edward Frost, I understand you are the owner of these premises?" asked Karen, who had just come into the room.

Ted was watching police officers rushing upstairs. *Fuck*, he thought. *This is bad news*. "Sorry, did you say something?" he asked Karen.

"I said, I understand that you are the owner of these premises, is that correct?"

"Well, I don't know who told you that but it's bollocks. I'm the caretaker."

Karen laughed. "The caretaker! Don't give me that shit. Go and sit down. We'll have a chat later."

She stood to one side as officers brought down girls and punters from the upstairs rooms. She noticed one girl who didn't look very well. Karen said, "Stop!" and the line came to a halt. She took the girl's arm.

"What is your name?"

The girl looked like she was drugged, and had difficulty answering.

"Chau."

"Where are you from, Chau?"

"China," mumbled the girl.

Karen lifted her arm and noticed multiple scabs and needle marks all up the inside of it. "How did you get these?"

Suddenly, Ted Frost appeared. "This girl is not well. She should be at home, I'll get someone to take her."

Karen was seething. "Go and sit down before I really lose my temper," she snapped at the brothel manager.

The female detective turned to one of the social services team, who were attending with the police. "Please, take this lady to hospital immediately, one of my officers will accompany you and stay with her."

Ted Frost, the girls and the punters were loaded onto a coach and were soon on their way to Rotherhithe Nick.

The raids were a great success. Twenty-six individuals from Peckham, eleven of them working girls, fourteen punters and Ted Frost; sixteen girls and twenty-six punters from Soho. The admin was immense and help had to be brought in from Hackney and East Ham.

In the end, statements were taken from the male punters, who gave various reasons as to why they were in one of the two buildings at that time. One said he was attending a fancy-dress party, another swore that he had been kidnapped and held against his will. Most of the punters acted shocked when told that they were being investigated for attending a brothel, and possibly, under-age sex with minors.

When questioned, most of these punters wore a worried expression, then said words to the effect of: "My wife doesn't have to hear about this, does she?" The officers responded by saying that it was possible they would have to attend court. Details were taken from the male punters, then they were all swabbed for DNA, and their fingerprints and photos taken before they were released, pending further investigations. The truth was they would probably never hear from the police again. Ted Frost was put in a cell and he felt like he had been completely forgotten.

The twenty-seven girls were given cups of tea and individually interviewed by police officers and social services personnel. All of the girls went through the same process as the men. Eleven of the girls were then released immediately because they were over twenty-one and had records of arrest for previous prostitution offences. Nine girls were released as they were British and were over twenty-one, although not known to the police. That left seven girls who had no ID and could not prove their age, and they could also have immigration status issues. The girls looked very young, some of them had oriental features. Following their interviews, it soon became abundantly clear that four girls were pleased that they had been picked up by the police.

Translators were brought to Rotherhithe and statements were taken from the girls. It transpired that two of them were sisters: one was sixteen and the other seventeen. They had come to the UK from South Korea, having arranged to work as nannies, and ended up in prostitution. They could give no details of the men who had organised the travel details, or the supposed 'work'.

Apparently, as soon as their plane had landed at Heathrow and they had gone through customs, their passports were taken and they never saw them again. From Heathrow they arrived at the house in Peckham and the next day were entertaining, on average, fifteen men a day. Both girls, Minsue and Jimin, had initially refused to undress and put on the sexy clothes they were given. In the end, both girls were forcibly stripped and repeatedly raped by the men who had initially taken them to the brothel.

It was the most horrific experience both of them had ever faced, made even more ghastly because they had both been virgins. After the rape, they both decided to do as they were told. When asked who the boss at the Peckham brothel was, the two girls replied in broken English that it was Ted Frost.

They were then taken into care by social services. Their parents were contacted and the young women were soon on their way back to South Korea. The other five girls were from Vietnam and had answered an advert for dancers—they had no idea who the men were that had arranged their travel and supposed legitimate employment. They were between twenty-one and thirty and said they wanted to remain in the UK. It was clear that all five did not have permission to stay in the country and were therefore sent to Harmondsworth Detention Removal Centre near Heathrow, prior to them being deported back to Vietnam.

The girl at the hospital, Chau, was drug dependent and had syringe entry points on both arms, thighs and buttocks. Chau had been given regular doses of heroin and had quickly become an addict. She had arrived from China to work in the theatre but had quickly been whisked to Peckham and put to work. She had initially refused to service customers and, like many of the other girls, had been beaten and raped. She had still refused to work, so the men who brought her to Peckham started injecting her with heroin. This went on for some time until she could not function without her fix. She then was forced to start entertaining twenty-odd men a day to ensure she got her regular fix. She was now in Newham Hospital Drug Dependency Unit and had a police officer permanently stationed outside her door.

Ted Frost was brought out of his cell and taken to an interview room, where he sat at the table, accompanied by his solicitor.

Jeff Swan, sitting opposite, began talking to the man he despised: "This interview is being held at Rotherhithe Police Station on September 15th 2013 at 4 p.m. Mr Edward Frost has been arrested under Section 53A of the Sexual Offences Act 2003, namely the owning or managing of a brothel at 21 New Church Road, Peckham. Present today, are DCs Swann and Foster, the duty solicitor Mr Andrew Fox, is also present, representing the accused. Mr Frost has been informed that the interview is being recorded."

Jeff took a deep breath and continued: "Mr Frost, we believe you have been managing the premises at New Church Road as a brothel, offering sexual favours for payment. Would you like to comment on that statement?"

Ted Frost said nothing for about a minute, obviously thinking of what to say to the accusation; eventually he said: "Firstly, I had no idea that place was a brothel. I'm the caretaker, so I do my job and that's it."

Jeff stared at him. "Mr Frost, we have numerous witnesses who have all declared under oath that you were the manager. I should also inform you that you could be jailed for seven years in addition to having to pay a large fine if convicted of the offence. What is your response to that?"

"I can't understand it, honestly. I'm gobsmacked that so many people would lie."

"So you're saying that it's untrue and that you are definitely not the manager?"

"That is so, officer."

"I see. So if you are the caretaker, who is the manager?"

"I have no idea. I go in, I clean and move furniture around and do odd jobs and then I go home."

"I see. So who employed you?"

"I got the job through an agency."

"What's the name of the agency?"

"I can't remember."

Jeff and Karen looked at each other, knowing full well they were not going to get anywhere with Mr Frost.

"Who pays your wages?" Jeff persevered.

"I have no idea. The money is paid into my bank account every month."

"Thank you Mr Frost. This interview is terminated at four-fifteen. Mr Frost will be detained to help further with our enquiries."

An officer took Ted Frost back to his cell.

Jeff and Karen made their way back to the CID office, grabbing a coffee on the way.

"That didn't go particularly well," said Karen.

"No. Well, to be honest, we're wasting our time," Jeff admitted. "The Crown Prosecution Service are not interested in spending months and a small fortune to bring dear old Ted Frost to justice. What we need are the owners, the people who put all the money in their pockets. In other words we want Paul Bolton."

CHAPTER 7

Paul Bolton was sitting in his office in the Den Club in Soho, reflecting on the business and various incidents that had occurred recently. Mary Coombs was back at home. She now had a housekeeper and Peter, the bodyguard, to look after her. The security of Jack's widow was sorted but there was still the matter of finding the two animals that tortured Jack to death and nearly killed Mary. Paul might have accepted it if Jack had been shot in the head and given a quick death, but what they did to him and Mary was beyond the pale.

The next big problem to sort out was Richard Philips. Paul now had two permanent bodyguards, Duke and Tom, just in case Richard had put out a contract on him as well. Paul had got a message to Richard that he wanted to visit and it had been agreed; Paul still had two days to wait until he would be on his way to Wormwood Scrubs. He didn't really want the prison authorities to know he was visiting so he had arranged to be 'someone else' for the afternoon. A new identity had been created for a 'Mr Clarence Doyle', and that was who would be visiting Richard Philips.

Paul's business had suffered as a result of the brothel raids at Soho and Peckham, and Paul was truly sick of lifting stones and finding nasty surprises underneath. The latest was about the girls who had been picked up, and who were well under age and from abroad. It seemed that individual managers had done deals with some traffickers to bring in oriental girls. This was strictly against the rules set down by Paul, and he had swiftly gotten rid of thirty-three such girls from the rest of the clubs. He had been warned that the traffickers would not like this and may well try to reverse his decision. He had already had a phone call from someone purporting to represent the girls, asking to see him, and he had refused. Paul sucked the end of his biro, wondering how long it would take to make all his businesses legit so as to avoid this kind of situation.

He still thought about Emma and the baby; he knew it would take a long time before he could become close to another woman. Sometimes he would just stare into space for minutes and then come to with a jolt.

He had given serious thought to the meeting with Richard Philips. The key to a good outcome was if he could give Richard what he wanted. But did Richard want money? By all accounts, he had a couple of million stashed away. Maybe he wanted his business back and that would be a problem, to say the least. God forbid, he might want Paul dead or maimed for life but if so, he would have already done it, so Paul felt some kind of security. There would be no answers until he had been to see him at The Scrubs, and he wasn't particularly looking forward to that.

Paul had completely forgotten about Tony but there was always that nagging feeling in the pit of his stomach that Tony was his brother and he ought to do something to help him. He sent money to Tony regularly, so he could at least buy extra cigarettes and small luxuries. Paul could not bear to think about Tony's long-term future, as he would probably spend the rest of his life in Broadmoor.

On a personal note, Paul had been out drinking in London clubs, but all that ever happened was that he got drunk very quickly and then got a taxi back to his flat in Chelsea Harbour. He would then look at one or two of his photos of Emma and have a serious crying session. He knew he couldn't carry on like that forever, but thinking of his previous girlfriend still upset him so much.

Thinking of Emma was bad enough, but when he thought of the baby he spiralled into deep traumatic depression, with his only escape being the bottle. He had tried therapy but just couldn't open up to a complete stranger with his innermost thoughts, so that had lasted just one session and he had never gone back.

The other thing he had tried was paying for a prostitute but that had been a complete disaster, since he could not raise as much as a smile, let alone anything else!

He could, of course, have visited any of his clubs and had the pick of a gorgeous bunch of girls but he didn't like staff knowing what he was up to, so he never did that. All in all, he tried to stay as busy as he could at work so he didn't have to think about anything else.

CHAPTER 8

Bujar Dushka was from Tirana, the capitol of Albania, a small city compared to European capitals like London or Paris. It had an urban population of six-hundred thousand. Tirana has had a chequered history through the communist years and now has a market economy. Bujar was a known figure at the strangely named 'Tirana International Airport Mother Theresa'.

He had been a troublemaker since he had hit his teens and had been in trouble with the authorities ever since. Gone were the days of nipping over to Corfu from Saranda on the ferry for a weekend, of drinking and womanising. Now he was seriously involved in people trafficking, 90 per cent of which was importing women for the sex industry to the UK, Germany, France and Spain.

After working for other people for five years he then decided to branch out on his own. He could never forget the first advert he put in the Tirana papers for dancing girls, needed for a new show in London. The response had been incredible: so many gorgeous girls turned up to audition that he couldn't cope with the numbers. As it was, he took five girls to the UK and sold them into a life of degradation and filth. He had made an easy twenty-five thousand pounds on that first deal and since then, he had made a fortune. He never gave a thought as to what happened to the girls, or how the families felt when they never heard from their daughters again. He was a man without scruples, who lived on the misery and suffering of the poor girls he sold into sexual slavery.

This apparent sociopath had started doing business with some of Jack Coombs's brothels in 2010, mostly involving oriental women from China and Vietnam. The home-grown girls in Albania and the Balkans had got wise to the business and were no longer naïve enough to get hooked by the promise of a great life doing an honest job in London or Paris.

Bujar had contacts all over the world and could supply girls from practically anywhere to anywhere. The big bucks were to be made taking girls from poor countries to rich European ones, where prices remained high for good 'quality merchandise'.

Once he had sold the girls to a club or brothel, it was then up to the owners to make sure the girls did as they were told. However he was always happy to lend a helping hand by raping and terrifying girls into submission. The females were at the mercy of the brothel owners, because no passport meant no money. They stayed in brothel accommodation and usually they did not speak the native language. What made it worse was that the victims were mostly from decent backgrounds and loving families, but of course, there were always some who were quite willing and happy to move to Europe and sell their bodies.

"We can't just leave it, we've lost too much money. That fucker has to pay one way or the other," was a common enough sentiment.

Bujar Dushka was pacing round the table and slapping the five men on their shoulders one after the other. He had in his team two other Albanians and three Serbs. They were a formidable team of dangerous lunatics who lived by the gun and had only one thought in life, and that was how to make money.

They all lived together in a house they rented in Chevening Road, Kensal Rise, North West London. The Tube station was a two-minute walk away, which was very handy, and Kensal Rise was one of those nondescript areas that you couldn't really point your finger to and recognise instantly where exactly it was.

On any evening, whoever was in the Kensal Rise premises could be found firstly at the Sacre Coeur Pizza restaurant and later at the Chamberlayne Pub and Steakhouse. They were men of habit and liked what they were familiar with. They were all dressed in jeans and expensive leather jackets: the uniform for traffickers. Bujar thought of women as commodities to be sold to the highest bidder. He had no feelings towards them, for they merely represented dollars to him and that was it.

He had killed, raped and tortured women, turned them into drug addicts, maimed and disfigured them and sold them all over the world. It was a sordid, corrupt immoral way to make a living but he loved it. He loved the fear he instilled in women. Some had physically shit themselves when he had threatened to burn them or inject them with heroine, or kill their children. The men who worked for him were just as bad. They took crap from no one and God help you if you crossed one of them, because they would all come after you.

"There's nothing we can do, we should move on," said Danko Llic, one of the Serbs in his team.

"We've spent a fortune on those girls and I want that money back!" Bujar said, looking hard at the group sitting around the table knocking back tumblers of neat Raki.

"You all want to forget it!" he went on. "Are you fucking mad? There are two things we must do. Firstly, we take the girl back who is in the hospital, and secondly, Paul Bolton will have to pay us, one way or the other."

The others started nodding and as soon as Danko saw the support for Bujar, he agreed and started nodding as well.

"We get the girl first. Mr Bolton has declined to speak to us. Well he will regret that and when we do meet, I promise you that he will regret the day he set eyes on Bujar Dushka."

Bujar grabbed one of the bottles of Raki and filled everyone's glass. He raised his and shouted, "Sukses!" The others joined in with shouts of "Sukses!"

They drained their Raki and sat quietly looking at Bujar, waiting for him to continue. He again filled their glasses and raised his in the air and spoke with a menacing tone: "Paul Bolton do rue diten qe ai doli kunder nesh" (*Paul Bolton will rue the day he came up against us*). They all knocked back the Raki, slamming their glasses on the table in unison.

Bujar once again looked round, making eye contact with his team of devils. "The next step is to get the girl and then we will visit Mr Bolton's club and introduce ourselves." He turned to one of the Serbs. "Adrjana, you will join me on a little jaunt to get the girl, yes?"

"Of course," replied Adrjana. "It will be my pleasure."

They went back to drinking Raki like it was going out of fashion, toasting each other, their families and anyone else they could think of who remotely deserved it.

CHAPTER 9

Richard Philips was happy he now had the team picked who would break out of The Scrubs with him. Ed Spencer—head honcho in A Block, Matt Collins in charge of blowing the wall, and Peter Clarke as his personal bodyguard. Four was perfect: not too many, but enough to get the job done, as long as the plan worked.

Philips had organised a card game in recreation time for the four of them; it was a good way for them to meet and talk without raising suspicion.

"So Matt, is the semtex on site yet?" the organiser of the escape asked.

"No," Matt replied, "but it's all in hand. It will be here next Wednesday."

"How? No, on second thoughts, don't tell me. Just tell me Wednesday night that it's done, yeah?."

"Sure thing Richard."

"Look, we need to get out of here as soon as possible; the restaurant food is so fucking awful I don't know how much longer I can eat in this place." Everybody chuckled. "OK, on to something somewhat more serious. Everything outside is organised. Once the wall's blown, we're picked up by some associates of mine, and off we go. We lay low for a week or two until the dust has settled and then split and go our separate ways."

Matt looked thoughtful. "Why can't we just split as soon as we're outside?"

Richard paused before answering. "Look, I'm going to be straight with you. I want to be sure nobody gets nicked early indoors because that could spell disaster for us all, so we wait a bit of time, and then when the heat's gone down a bit, we move. Does that make sense?" He was looking round at the three others. They all nodded in agreement. "Good. Now, who wants to lose some money playing cards?"

Time passed very slowly in prison. Every day was the same old routine and the only way to fight that was to keep as busy as humanly possible. The big problem was that because of staff shortages, prisoners spent hour upon hour locked up in their cells and only came out for meals. So mealtimes were the highlight of the day; that would be even more the case if the food was half decent, which it wasn't.

Of course, the highlight above everything else was a visit. It could be just the wife, or possibly a visit when the children would come as well. Matt Collins had regular visits from his wife but had asked that his children stay away, since he could not cope with the parting at the end, when they left.

Matt woke up on the Wednesday morning and was already feeling nervous. This was the big day. If it went well, then he could soon be outside. His family lived in a council house in Greenford, West London. It was a small place but was enough for Carole, his wife, and two children, Max and Teddy.

On the Tuesday morning a blue Mercedes pulled up outside the house and a skinny, pale, ill-looking man had come to the front door and rung the bell. Carole answered the door and was handed a parcel. "This is for Matt. Give it to him tomorrow," the man said. The odd looking character then walked back to his car and drove off. Carole shut the door and looked at the large box-like parcel, frowning. She then proceeded to take the wrapping paper off and inside was a box. She looked at it and smiled and then placed it on the table near the door, ready to take the next day.

Next day Carole arrived at the visitor centre and went directly to the reception desk to book in. She showed her passport and it was confirmed that she was Carole Collins and could proceed. She then handed in some items to be given to Matt, and those items would of course be inspected prior to him receiving them.

"Hello Mrs Collins and how are you?" asked the warder.

"Very well, thank you officer."

Carole was then allocated a locker for her handbag, coat and hat. She deposited those items and then moved to the personal search area. She was frisked by a female officer and sniffed by a very nice looking dog, who had been trained to sniff out drugs. Everything was fine and she then proceeded to the final door, which opened into the visiting hall and she passed through. There were rows of tables and chairs and she had been given a table: number 17, which she located quite quickly. Matt was sitting at the table and they smiled at each other.

"Hi Darling how's things?" said Matt

The first few minutes of a visit were always a bit difficult: it came with the territory.

"Everything's fine Matt, thanks." Carol smiled brightly.

"Did you deliver the items to reception?"

"Yes, you should get them later."

"Great." Matt was praying the plan would work.

Matt and Carole chatted about the kids and even managed to laugh a little. The visits lasted an hour but usually went by in a flash. Prisoners were allowed to have two a month, and it wasn't a lot of contact if you wanted to keep your marriage intact. As a rule the couple talked about what the kids were up to, how she was coping with her job and lots of chat about nothing very much. The time came, the whistle went, Carole left, and Matt returned to his cell.

The items left at reception were gathered together and taken to a special room with a plate on the door that read 'Search Room'. Within this room there was a long table and to the side, a set of tools. The designated search officer for that day was Ted Rowland. He ambled into the room and was met by a heap of items that required looking at.

Firstly, a dog who'd been trained to sniff out drugs was brought in and put to work, applying his nose to all the items. This passed without incident and the dog and handler left the room. Ted then commenced to sort out the things and arranged them allocated to individual prisoners, so that all of them could be put into a single container for onward transmission.

There were heaps of underwear, magazines, games, videos and jigsaw puzzles. The good thing was that most of the items were new, so any tampering with the packaging could be spotted quite easily. The newspapers reported about how loads of drugs, mobile phones, cigarettes and booze were getting into prisons, and your average man in the street could not understand how all these proscribed items got past the security systems. Staff shortages on searching and monitoring duty were the main problem and bent prison officers didn't help.

Ted worked diligently through the items until he came to a group of items for a Matt Collins, prisoner number AA6812. Ted moved the underwear across the red line on the table. He then looked at the box which contained Monopoly—the famous board-game involving the sale of London properties—and he put that to one side, not placing it over the red line. A newspaper was then passed over it.

He then picked up the two clogs—special Dutch-style shoes—and looked at them. They had been 'passed' as drug-free by the sniffer dog, but Ted wanted to check them thoroughly, so he took the right clog and pressed and bent it; he was sure that it had not been tampered with and accordingly passed the two clogs over the red line. He had been continually glancing at the Monopoly box, as he couldn't wait to open it; he was sure that he would find something dodgy inside.

Ted finally opened the Monopoly box. Firstly, he looked closely at the metal pieces: there was a train, a shoe, a plane, a ship, a hat and a box. Next, he picked up the green plastic 'houses' and the red plastic 'hotels', smelling them and passing them from hand to hand. He was suspicious, so he moved to the side and picked up a small Stanley knife. He then picked up one of the plastic houses and cut it in half. He did the same with one of the hotels and looked at the pieces, but could see nothing wrong with them. He then picked up the 'Chance' and 'Go' cards but could find nothing untoward about them either. Finally, he looked at the box. After examining that very closely, he passed the game across the red line, packaged up the items marked 'Matt Collins' and moved on to the next items.

At six o'clock that night, a bag arrived at Matt Collins's cell with the items that had been left by Carole.

Matt immediately got a message to Richard, saying: "The goods have arrived."

The explosives expert slipped on his new grey clogs, which were very comfortable and easy to put on and take off. He placed his new underwear in a drawer and put the paper on top of the small cabinet next to his steel-framed bed. He sat on the side of this, took the Monopoly game box and opened it. He touched all the pieces, marvelling at the intricacy of the small items. He read a few of the 'Chance' cards and counted out one thousand pounds of the fake money, laughing to himself as he pretended that it was real.

He then packed up the game, placing everything in its rightful place, perfectly and neatly. He then placed the box of Monopoly at the bottom of his cupboard and sat back on the bed. Matt leaned back and stretched his arms; he then took off his new grey clogs, throwing the right clog to the floor and keeping the left one in his hand. He lifted it up and looked at it closely, then a broad grin spread over his face and he rubbed the clog gently. The clogs had been hand-made and the left one was full of semtex explosives, covered with a plastic shell.

The plan had worked! Luck had been on their side, since the guard had only checked the clog for the right foot, not the left!

The next morning, Matt sat down next to Richard at breakfast.

"Great News Matt. How did you do it?" the latter asked.

Matt looked at Richard and then down at his new clogs.

Richard smiled. "No!"

"Oh yes," Matt replied with a chuckle.

"Brilliant! So what else do you need?"

"The detonator has been organised. That's it, I'm ready."

Richard looked thoughtful. It was now time to decide on the date.

CHAPTER 10

"So Tony. Tell me. Why did you attack the two guards?"

Dr Gary Thompson was sitting across the table from Tony Bolton, conducting one of his weekly assessments.

"I think you have been misinformed Doc. The two guards attacked me for absolutely no reason."

"Guards don't attack patients Tony. They were trying to restrain you and you went berserk and attacked them with a filed coin that was sharpened like the blade of a razor. One of the guards is still in hospital, with severe facial wounds. These guys have a job to do Tony, that's all it is to them, *a job*. That man has a family and will probably be off work for months."

"So you're saying the guards are more important than the patients then?" Tony challenged him.

"No Tony, I'm not saying that at all. What I am saying is that we all have to try and get on with each other, guards and patients alike."

Dr Thompson looked at Tony, waiting for his reply.

"I wish to make a complaint," Tony said woodenly.

"Tony, you have sliced that guard's face and caused serious injuries," the doctor told him, finding it hard to keep his patience. "And you say you want to complain! What exactly are you complaining about?"

"I believe that I am being picked on by the staff, and it's affecting me mentally."

"I will certainly give you a complaint form and you can fill it in. But remember, as I've told you before, you will need to be precise about dates, times, who was present and what happened." The doctor paused, then asked cautiously, "How are you getting on with the new medicine now?"

"I assume you are referring to the serotonin?"

"Yes."

"Well, I don't think about sex as much as I used to, so I suppose it's working."

"Well that's good then Tony," Thompson said, more calmly now.

"When do you think I'll be considered for release, Doc?"

"That's a difficult question to answer and you know it. There may be a lot of ignorant, stupid people in here, but you're not one of them."

"So, you're saying I'll never get out?" Tony said.

"We have had this conversation many times. I have *no idea*, as you well know."

"So, you're saying I'll never get out?"

"Tony, please let's not go round in circles anymore." The doctor was getting exasperated again. "You know you will be in here for a very long time."

"That brother of mine is a complete cunt. Have you met him, Doc?"

"No, I haven't met him. His name is Paul I believe?"

"Yeah, goodie-fucking-two-shoes Paul. We grew up together, very close we were."

"Why do you say *were*? It's not his fault you're in here."

"I was set up." Tony warmed to his theme. "I was taking so many tablets I didn't know what I was doing and I shot the wrong man. He deserved it anyway, but I wouldn't have shot him just because we lost a bloody football match! I thought he was the Greek hit-man who was trying to kill me. After I'd shot him, I couldn't quite work out why he didn't have a scar!"

Tony's mind began to wander and the doctor reflected that it was probable he would never be considered for release.

"So, are you saying I'll never get out?" Tony went on.

"I think you need to rest now Tony. Aren't you tired?"

"Yeah. OK look, next time come prepared. I need to know when I could be considered for release."

"Yes OK Tony, I'll try to find out."

The mad killer was taken out of the meeting area and escorted back to his room, which was really a cell, but marginally more pleasant than the kind of cell you'd find in a normal prison.

He sat in his easy chair and looked around him. He knew very well that they would never release him, so he would have to take some other course of action to get out, but that would be very difficult. He smiled and chuckled to himself, saying, "Nothing is impossible."

CHAPTER 11

Karen Foster drove into the car park at Newham General Hospital in Plaistow and parked up. She didn't bother paying at the 'pay and display' machine, as she was sure they wouldn't ticket a marked police car. It was a miserable day, spitting with rain and windy. She made straight for the main reception and asked where the Drug Dependency Unit was. She then walked through the main concourse to the back of the hospital, where the unit was located.

The female detective walked into a fresh, airy and spacious reception area that smelt and looked more like a home than a hospital. So far so good, she thought to herself. She showed her badge at the reception desk and asked for Chau. She was directed to the first floor, room 104. She found the lift, went up to the first floor, got out and strolled down a long corridor and then turned a corner. She saw a police officer sitting outside a door, reading a book. She approached the uniformed officer who stood up and smiled at her.

"Hello, I'm DC Karen Foster from Rotherhithe," she introduced herself as they shook hands.

"Steve Thomas from East Ham. How you doing?" the officer replied.

"Fine, thanks." She gave the man the once-over and liked what she saw: he was tall, manly and had broad shoulders—not to mention very handsome.

"So, how's the patient?" she asked.

"I'm not an expert but I hear that she's doing very well, but it's better if you ask the doctors for a proper update."

"Can you go and find me the doctor then while I have a chat with Chau?"

"Sure, be happy to." Steve marched off down the corridor and Karen knocked and entered. It was a typical hospital room but with a few homely touches: a couple of easy chairs near the window with a bit of a view, a nice carpet. Chau was sitting in one of the seats, flicking through a magazine. She turned as Karen entered the room.

"Hello Chau, I'm DC Karen Foster. May I come in?"

"Of course, please come," said Chau in broken English.

Karen smiled at Chau and noticed she looked tired and ever so thin. She took her coat off and sat in the chair opposite her.

"So Chau, how are you?"

"Better, much better, thank you."

"I'm so pleased. You're certainly looking much better than when I saw you last time."

"When was that?" Chau asked, looking confused.

"I was at Peckham. I'm the one who sent you here."

Chau looked astonished and burst into tears. She got out of her chair and threw herself into Karen's arms, squeezing her saviour as hard as she could.

"Thank you, thank you," she sobbed, burying her face in Karen's shoulder. "You save my life, oh my God, thank you. *Thank you.*" She continued to hug and sob into Karen's shoulder.

Karen was taken aback but happy. She stroked Chau's hair as though she was her daughter and felt a rush of love for the young, slim oriental woman.

"Don't worry Chau, you are safe now. Nobody will ever hurt you again."

"You promise me, Miss Karen?"

"Yes, I promise." Karen planted a kiss on the girl's forehead.

Chau sat up and moved back to her own chair.

She stopped crying and looked at Karen, whose eyes were misty. Chau got up and gently wiped them with a tissue.

"Miss Karen can we be friends, please?"

Karen was in turmoil; it would be unprofessional to establish a friendship with Chau but she could not help herself.

"Of course, Chau. We are now friends."

Karen heard the door open and turned to see Steve and a lady she assumed was a doctor, come into the room.

Everyone was introduced and chatted for a couple of minutes, then Karen, Steve and the doctor left.

"Let's go to my office," said Doctor Lesley Abbot, leading the way along the corridor. Steve sat down outside Chau's room and went back to his book

Karen and Doctor Abbot went to her office, stopping to pick up a couple of coffees on the way.

"So, how is Chau and when do you think she will be OK to leave hospital?" Karen asked, after the two women were seated either side of a large desk.

"Well, treatment has gone well. You can see she is much better than when she was brought in."

"So, has the detox worked?"

"Yes, to a degree. Coming off heroin is a ghastly experience, whether it's cold turkey or in a controlled medical setting such as this. We have used a synthetic opiate called subutex over the past seven days to wean Chau off the heroin. It's worked well, but long-term, it will be up to her to resist the pressure to go back to it."

Karen glowered angrily. "If I could just get hold of the bastards that did this. Well I intend to. And when I do, believe me, they will regret being born."

"You know what? I believe you, Karen."

"So, when do you think she will be fit enough to come out?"

"There is not much more we can do really," Dr Abbot explained. "She needs to eat and drink well to build up her strength. Where's she going to live?"

"No idea, could be a problem I guess. Leave it with me—I'll get back to you shortly." Karen stood up to leave.

Karen went back to say good bye to Steve and Chau. "Steve, I'll just say good bye to Chau," she told the officer, before pushing the door open. "Chau," she told the oriental woman, who stood up to meet her, "I'm off now. Just one more thing, when you leave here, where are you going to stay?"

Chau's face clouded over. "I do not know. I know sex club at Peckham only." She stared into Karen's eyes with a pleading expression. "I come stay with you, please?"

Karen was taken aback. "Chau, that is not possible! I am investigating the crime. It would be totally inappropriate for you to stay with me."

"What I going to do then?"

"I think I may be able to help. I'll come and see you in a couple of days. Take care, Chau, see you soon."

"OK Miss Karen, I see you soon." Chau smiled happily and hugged Karen.

"See you soon, bye." Karen ducked out of the room.

"Steve, what are you reading?" she asked her new friend.

"*Oliver Twist*. I love the classics."

"I'm impressed."

"What's happening with Chau?"

"She can come out but she has nowhere to go. I'm going to see if we can get her into Witness Protection and put her in a safe house."

"Is she going to court if you catch those bastards?"

Karen gave Steve a withering look. "*When* Steve, not *if*. When we catch those fucking animals! There is no 'if' about it."

"OK, OK, I'm sorry. Yes, WHEN we get the bastards."

Karen was still pissed off at Steve but gave him the benefit of the doubt. "That's better Steve, good. OK, so, I'll see you soon." She smiled, wanting to keep him on her side.

Back in the car, she switched on the siren in order to get back to Rotherhithe as quickly as possible. At the office, she soon found Jeff and asked for a meet. They grabbed more coffee and sat down.

"Jeff, I need to put Chau, the girl at Newham Hospital, into a safe house."

"Why?"

"She's ready to come out of hospital but has nowhere to go. I don't know what else to suggest."

"Hmm, well, will she go to court when we catch the scum that are responsible for this?"

"I think she will."

"Yes, but she could be in a safe house for months, or even years," Jeff pointed out.

"I suppose we could send her back to Vietnam and then bring her back for any court case," Karen reasoned.

"Yeah, but you're thinking she wouldn't come back, aren't you? The Witness Protection Scheme is tough. It's not an easy ride, believe me. I read somewhere there are over a thousand people on Witness Protection. God knows what it must be costing."

"A thousand people? Are there any on our patch?"

"'Course there are," Jeff told her. "But no one is allowed to know who or where. The guys use different computer systems so that bent coppers can't get the information. As for Chau, go through the process; let's see if we can put her on the programme and then take it from there. Meanwhile, we need to find these trafficker bastards so we can put them away."

"Yeah, I couldn't agree more. I'll do the paperwork on Chau."

Karen finished the relevant form-filling and report writing relating to Chau's case and wanted to relax for ten minutes, so she decided to go for a walk. She was praying that the Met would allow Chau into Witness Protection, as she was needed desperately to give evidence against the traffickers. The problem was, they had not made any progress towards even finding out who they were, let alone building a case.

She left the Nick and headed down Lower Road until she was opposite the entrance to Southwark Park. She entered the grassy area and found the nearest clean wooden bench she could find to sit on. It was a bit blustery so she pulled the collar up on her jacket which, at least, helped to keep her neck warmer. She looked around and saw the usual collection of park users: a couple of mums pushing prams. "Crikey," she thought to herself. "That could be me one day, well, certainly not for another couple of years."

There were two older men, who looked as if they were retired, sitting across the way, jabbering on at each other. She was thinking about the next step in the hunt for the traffickers. It was going to be very difficult without any decent leads to go on. She sat back and took a deep breath of fresh air. Then she started coughing and thought perhaps it wasn't so fresh after all. After spluttering for a minute, she got up and strolled back onto Lower Road and headed back to the Nick. She found Jeff sitting, drinking coffee at his desk as usual.

"That won't catch the traffickers, you know," Karen told him.

"What won't?" asked Jeff sharply.

"Sitting around twiddling your thumbs, drinking endless cups of coffee."

"Who rattled your cage today?"

Karen was exasperated. "Well, nothing's happening! We're making no bloody progress!"

"Oh ye of little faith." Jeff picked up a piece of paper from his desk and held it up for her to see. "This is a list of three Albanian men who have been interviewed by the Met over the past year, in connection with selling women to brothels in London."

Karen perked up immediately. "Let me see."

Jeff pulled the paper away from her outstretched hand. "What do you say?"

"Sorry Jeff, I was being a prat."

He gave her the list. She looked at the three names, reading them out loud, pronouncing each name as best as she could: "Adrjana Bardulla, Andrea Gjikokaj and Bujar Dushka. A right weird sounding lot."

"It's a good place for us to start. Even if they're not involved, we can shake them down for more names."

Karen smiled and looked at the three names again. "I look forward to meeting you as soon as possible," she said to herself.

Jeff said, "Check the computer for case notes, get addresses and anything else we have on them."

"Be my pleasure Jeff. Speak to you shortly." Karen was now in a world of her own. She sat down at her desk, turned her computer on and started tapping in the three names.

CHAPTER 12

"I don't know what I'd do without you, Duke!" Paul Bolton said to his friend and minder, sitting next to him in the car.

Duke laughed. "Yes you do. Some other big ugly git would be sitting here driving you to The Scrubs!"

His boss laughed. He had got used to Duke being around and couldn't imagine a time when he wouldn't be.

"This is the second awful visit you have had to do in a short space of time," Duke said.

"Well let's hope it's easier than Tony's visit was. Tony's visit, that was unbelievable! I wonder how that guard is now?"

Paul briefly remembered the visit to see Tony, the guard's skewered face and blood flying in all directions. He hadn't given Tony a thought since that occasion. He still sent money in for him but, as to visiting again in the near future, it was out of the question; not that the authorities would let him have visitors anyway.

The club owner had been thinking about his visit to see Richard Philips for some time. It had to be done to find out what the score was, and also to call him a bastard for what his paid thugs had done to Jack and Mary.

"How much longer?" Paul asked Duke.

"The BBC is on your left."

Paul turned to see Television Centre. "Oh yeah, big place."

"Yeah, there's a load more BBC buildings up the road." Duke continued up Wood Lane, past White City Tube station. "QPR are just down there."

"'Course they are, I remember now, I've been a couple of times," Paul reminisced. "Crap little ground and crap crowds."

Duke hit the traffic lights and went straight ahead, taking the next left into Du Cane Road. "We're there."

They drove past Hammersmith Hospital and saw the imposing Victorian main entrance to Wormwood Scrubs. "Bloody old place isn't it?" commented Paul.

Duke took the next right into Wulfstan Street and parked at the first meter. He turned the engine off and they both sat there, looking straight ahead, without speaking. Duke then took a bag of sweets out of his pocket, opened the top and offered it to Paul.

"I can guess what they are," said Paul, smiling. He stuck his hand in the bag and brought out a handful of jelly babies. "You know what Duke, I even bought some of these myself a couple of days ago; you got me hooked when we went to see Tony." Paul popped a couple into his mouth and shut his eyes. "Yeah, well, better go and get it over with," and he sighed. He opened the car door and stepped out.

"Break a leg Paul!" Duke shouted after him, using the old theatrical phrase to try and cheer him up.

Paul headed back in the direction of The Scrubs' entrance and saw a sign to the Visitor Centre entrance. He took a deep breath and went through the door. He casually glanced around and spotted a camera facing the door, which obviously got a full-face shot of everybody entering. He was not too bothered about this, as his passport and driving licence were perfect original fakes. The club owner, and brother of murderer Tony Bolton, had given his name as a Mr Andrew Turner.

He went through the usual security checks, deposited all his belongings in a locker, remembering to keep the permitted twenty pounds, and proceeded to the Visit Hall. He sat as close as he could to the coffee bar and waited. Five minutes later, a door opened at the far end of the hall and prisoners began to troop in. He saw Richard and put his hand up so that Richard could see him. Paul was feeling a touch nervous but was prepared for anything that Richard had to say.

Paul stuck his hand out, saying, "Richard, how are you?"

Richard shook his hand. "Fine and you?"

"Yeah alright. Coffee and a cake?"

"Lovely, thanks." Paul went to the coffee bar before the big queue formed and was soon back with two lattes and two portions of carrot cake.

Richard grabbed the cake and bit off a big chunk. "Hmm, very nice," He said appreciatively, then slurped down a good mouthful of coffee. "OK, so, what can I do for you, Paul? Although I can guess why you are here."

Paul wanted to get this business over with as quickly as possible.

"What those animals did to Jack and Mary was beyond belief," he told the prisoner, glaring at him. "It was lucky that Mary survived."

Richard looked pensive for a few seconds and said, "I don't give a shit about what they did to Jack, he got exactly what he deserved. As for Mary, sure, I admit they got carried away. I hear it was pretty awful."

"They raped her, buggered her with a rake handle and cut her face up. I'd say that was a bit more than *pretty awful*."

"That's what happens when you give jobs to unskilled people," Richard apologised sincerely. "I'm sorry that happened. Mary was alright."

"I want their names Richard. I'll find them anyway, so you might as well make it sooner rather than later."

"I'll think on that, mate. What's happened to my business?"

"Jack wound it up and we opened a new company as equal partners. Now that Jack's gone, I'm the sole shareholder."

Richard was sipping his coffee and looking straight at Paul. "I want what's due to me, Paul."

"And what exactly is that, Richard?"

"I want one of two things. Either fifty per cent of the company made over to me, or alternatively fifty per cent of the profits with no involvement."

The club owner looked thoughtful. "Remember none of this is personal, Richard, it's just business, and I've done nothing underhand. Jack came to me with a deal which I agreed to. In my book, you losing your share is nothing to do with me."

Richard's face hardened. "I'll be out of here soon, and I'll need to collect what is owed to me."

Paul immediately clocked the *I'll be out of here soon*, but let that pass.

"OK Richard. I don't mind making a gesture."

"Gesture? How much of a gesture?" Richard was suspicious.

"A one-off payment of one million pounds. Cash."

Richard leaned back on his chair. "Life's funny isn't it? Most people would think that to be an incredible offer. But you must be making at least ten million a year net profit, am I right Paul?"

"Well, we have had a few issues. The clubs got raided for a start: Soho and Peckham are closed, and the fucking Old Bill are all over us like a rash. How much do you want, to be happy?"

"Five million cash. Not a penny less."

"I'll think about it." Paul finished his coffee and stood up. "Understand this. I don't want to fall out with you Richard." He stared hard at the other man.

"Remember, it's only money." Richard's words held a warning. "Pay up and we can all get on with our lives. I'll see you soon."

"Yeah, I'll be in touch. Oh, and I want those names, Richard. The ones who hurt Mary so badly."

"I'll think on that." Richard didn't want to give Paul the names, since he might need to use the men again.

Paul left and made his way to the exit. Richard watched him leave and wondered what his visitor would do.

"How did it go?" asked Duke warily as Paul got in the car.

"Very well. He's told me what he wants and I'll give thought as to what I give him, if anything. Let's get back to the club. I've got lots to do."

* * *

It was Wednesday morning at 6 a.m. the day after Paul's visit. Richard was asleep in his cell and was suddenly woken by the key in the lock and the door swinging open. He lifted his head and saw three warders coming into his small living space. "What the fuck do you lot want?" he demanded.

"Get dressed. You're coming with us," one of them told him

"And where exactly are we going?"

"Not we, you. You're going on a nice trip."

Richard was now alert and worried. "Where am I going?"

"Sorry, can't say anything more. Now get dressed."

Richard was escorted to an office within the admin block and was sitting down in front of another warder who he had never seen before.

"So Mr Philips, I understand you're planning an escape?" began his interrogator.

"What sort of rubbish is this?" Richard shouted angrily. "I've no plans to escape. It's impossible to get out of here!"

"In any case we have decided to move you to another facility, which will happen—" He looked at the clock on the wall, "—in about thirty minutes' time."

"This is not on," the prisoner argued desperately. "I refuse to go anywhere. I'm not moving."

"In that case you will be carried onto a prison van and tied to your seat. Think about that." The warder turned to his men. "Take him away."

Richard didn't know it at the time but Ed Spencer and Matt Collins had also been woken early and were also being moved to other prisons. The only reason they were being moved was that they had been seen associating with Richard on a pretty regular basis.

The angry prisoner was taken into the yard and pushed onto a prison van and locked into a cage within it. He was extremely pissed-off, as all his plans had suddenly gone to shit. He couldn't understand how this had happened and who was responsible.

It was one hell of a journey, taking about four hours. The van finally pulled into another prison and Richard was unloaded and taken into a reception room. There was a sign on the wall saying: 'Welcome to HMP Long Lartin'. Richard read it and wondered where the bloody hell he was. He was then taken into an office and told he had been transferred to HMP Long Lartin in Evesham, Worcestershire, as a Category A prisoner. He had also been labelled as an exceptional escape risk.

"This is crazy! I'm no high escape risk!" he spluttered to the warder.

"That's what it says here boyo," the warder told him, "and that means we will be keeping a very careful eye on you."

Richard was shocked and dismayed to say the least. In the next few days, a very different regime to that of The Scrubs was introduced. His cell was searched every other day at different times. He had to wear a bright, high-visibility orange jacket when moving around the prison. And sometimes he had all his clothes taken out of his cell at Lights Out. Escape from Long Lartin seemed impossible and Richard embarked on a period of deep depression that would take a long while for him to emerge from.

* * *

Paul Bolton got the news of Richard's transfer an hour after the man had been driven out of The Scrubs. He was absolutely delighted and treated himself to a bottle of Prosecco with his steak for lunch.

He fully expected Richard to work out it was him who had tipped off the staff at

The Scrubs about his escape plans, but it would probably take him some time.

Ed Spencer and Matt Collins had been moved, purely as a precaution, as they were known to be close associates of Richard. Paul was pleased. Another crisis had been averted and he was sure, with extra warder vigilance, Richard would be in prison for a very long time. Next on his agenda was to find the two bastards who killed Jack and tortured Mary Coombs. Paul still couldn't open the clubs at Soho and Peckham, and, as brothels they were probably finished forever. However, the other eight brothels were still trading well enough.

CHAPTER 13

Bujar Dushka and Adrjana Bardulla were sitting in a stolen Ford Focus outside Newham General Hospital in Plaistow, watching the main entrance. It was nearly 7 p.m. when visiting finished, which was what they were waiting for.

"What is the plan, Bujar?" Bardulla asked.

"Plan!" Bujar replied. "Hah! We go in, we knock the girl out, put her in a wheelchair and walk back out the front entrance! It's all over in five minutes."

Adrjana was not overly impressed with the plan but that was typical Bujar, anyone who got in the way was either shot or maimed for life.

"And If we have to hurt someone, they are very lucky as they are already in hospital." They both laughed loudly as they thought it was so funny.

"Look!" said Bujar urgently.

A large crowd of families were coming out of the entrance.

"Visiting is over," Bujar told his friend. "We wait a few minutes and then go in."

Bujar and Adrjana both took out their Austrian-manufactured Glock 19.9 mm handguns and checked them over.

Bujar looked at Adrjana. "Ready?"

Adrjana nodded.

They got out of the car and headed to the main entrance.

"I want a wheelchair and two white coats," Bujar said.

Adrjana nodded again.

They pushed through the glass doors and moved through the crowd of remaining visitors who were heading out of the hospital. They continued past the reception desk, acting as though they owned the place. Adrjana saw a sign to the laundry and tugged at Bujar's sleeve to guide him to a corridor to the left of Reception. They marched down here and saw numerous cupboards standing open, with bedding and overalls on view. They stopped at one and looked inside. Bujar picked out two white doctors' coats, which they quickly put on.

"That was easy," said Adrjana.

They made their way back to the large reception area and headed towards the back of the hospital. They were walking quickly through long corridors when Adrjana suddenly said, "Wait here." He disappeared down another corridor.

Two minutes later, he came back pushing a wheelchair and with two doctors' stethoscopes hanging around his neck.

"Fucking hell! You're a magician!" marvelled Bujar. "I know where to go now from my recce yesterday."

They now looked like real doctors and no one gave them a second glance as they passed them, even though the identity name tags were missing—people were just too busy to notice. Very soon, they were at the entrance to the Drug Dependency Unit.

"OK Adrjana," Bujar instructed. "No fucking around. We go in, get the job done and get out as quickly as possible."

They pushed through the double doors and headed to the reception desk.

"Which room is a lady called Chau in please?" asked Bujar. "I do not know her surname."

The receptionist studied her computer screen before replying. "Take the lift to the first floor down the corridor and you'll find her room just round the corner," she replied. She then looked more closely at the two doctors. "But just a moment—can I ask who you are please and why you wish to see Chau?"

"You can ask," said Bujar as he whipped out his pistol and hit the receptionist across the head. She crumpled to the floor and there was a sickening loud thud as her head struck the hard surface.

The two Albanians headed straight to the lift, got in and went to the first floor, down the corridor, and were turning the corner when they saw Steve Thomas, the police officer who was guarding Chau's room.

Steve looked up as soon as he heard the noise of the wheelchair, but he relaxed when he saw the two doctors, and stood up to say hello. They got closer to him and he looked at their faces more closely, and noted the absence of name tags on their lapels. He realised something wasn't right.

The police officer put his hand up to stop them. "Excuse me sir, but I have to ask who you are and what you want here?" He had to be polite, because for all he knew they could be real doctors who were just doing their jobs.

"We have come to take Chau for an X-ray," Bujar told him.

Steve again noticed the lack of identity badges. "Can I see your ID please?"

The officer held out his hand expecting to be handed a hospital pass badge. Bujar hit him with the handle of his pistol bang in the middle of his forehead.

The impact was immense. Steve staggered back and crashed to the floor.

In a split second Adrjana and Bujar grabbed Steve's arms and dragged him through the door into Chau's room. The oriental woman recognised her enemies in an instant. She pressed the emergency button and started screaming as loud as she could.

Steve was down but mumbling incoherently.

Bujar turned to Adrjana. "Make sure he doesn't interfere."

Adrjana took his gun out and hit Steve across the back of his head. He could feel and hear the skull shattering. He then turned back to help Bujar with the girl.

"Shut up you bitch!" Bujar snarled, grabbing Chau by the hair and dragging her out of bed. Adrjana leaned over and hit Chau on the jaw with his clenched fist, knocking her out. They dragged her out of bed and pushed her into the wheelchair.

They got out of the door and were in and out of the lift in double-quick time. The two abductors were heading towards the reception when they heard noises. The injured receptionist had been discovered and there were at least two people at the desk, helping her.

So the Albanians took out their guns and held them aloft, aiming at where they thought the danger would be as they turned the corner.

Two nurses were at the reception desk: one was on the phone and Bujar heard her end the conversation, recognising the word 'police'. The other nurse was tending to the fallen receptionist, who Bujar had knocked out earlier. Adrjana shouted at the two nurses.

"Get down! Get down, you fucking bitches!"

The two women were terrified and threw themselves onto the floor. The gunmen then pushed their way through the entrance doors. A hospital security guard appeared. When he saw the guns he immediately backed away and then ran back towards the main hospital reception.

Bujar was getting concerned. "We must hurry, the police will be here very soon."

They burst into a run, pushing the wheelchair as fast as they could. They crashed through the doors into the main reception area, waving their pistols from side to side. The staff and everyone else froze. Bujar and Adrjana burst through the main entrance door at full speed and out onto the pavement wheeling Chau, who was being rocked violently from side to side in the wheelchair.

"Keep moving fast, we are nearly there!" shouted Bujar.

They were running towards the car when suddenly they heard police sirens.

Two police cars were zooming up Prince Regent Lane. They turned into Glen Road, the hospital's address. The pair of vehicles screeched left into the car park and slammed their brakes on.

When the police officers jumped out they immediately came under fire from the two Albanians, who were running and were about twenty yards away from their car. One of the officers returned fire with his Heckler and Koch MP5SF semi-automatic pistol, smashing car windows as the Albanians ran past them.

The pair of chancers reached the car and threw Chau into the back. They jumped into the front and started the engine.

Bujar quickly looked around. "We're blocked in!" he yelled. "Go through the back!"

Adrjana slammed his foot on the accelerator and made for the back of the car park—he quickly realised that their escape was blocked off.

Bujar saw two cars either side of a pedestrian walkway and shouted at Adrjana, "There's a gap!"

Adrjana yelled, "Fucking hell! We could get stuck!"

"Go for it! Otherwise we're dead!"

Adrjana pushed his foot down as hard as he could and drove into the gap. The two wing mirrors were ripped straight off. And there were sparks as they scraped the two cars on either side of them. The noise was deafening but they were through. They bounced off a high kerb, which rocked the car.

Bujar was laughing and rubbing his hands with glee. "Ye Haaa! Let's go baby!"

But he stopped laughing when he saw the wall ten yards away that Adrjana was heading straight for.

"Oh fuck!" The car hit the wall, shattering and scattering bricks and debris in every direction.

"Jesus!" shouted Bujar.

But the car kept going. They were soon out onto Glen road, screeching towards Prince Regent Lane. The signals were red but Adrjana went straight through and turned left. He was on the wrong side of the road, roaring towards more traffic lights. Bujar turned as he once again heard sirens—a police car was fifty yards behind them. He leaned out of the window and opened fire at the driver. The police car skidded as they tried to avoid the bullets, crashing into a parked Audi.

Chau was coming round. She knew she was in a car with the madmen who had originally taken her to Peckham from the airport. Her face hurt badly but she concentrated on what was happening as much as she could. The car was flying round corners and she was being flung around the back of the car. She was terrified but could think of only one thing: she had to get away.

Adrjana reached the lights at the junction with the A13 and slowed down slightly as he veered to the left.

Chau took her chance. She grabbed the handle and pushed the door open. She curled into a ball and leaped out through the gap and onto the road. Bujar turned just in time to see Chau disappear.

"Fucking hell!" he yelled. "The bitch!"

Chau hit the road at speed. She bounced into the air and came down with a thud. She then rolled along the road, burning and cutting her arms and legs until she finally came to a stop. She was in agony but now wide awake, realising that she was lying in the main road.

She looked up and saw a car that was almost on top of her. The scared girl slammed her elbows into the concrete and dragged herself painfully, but as quickly as she could, towards the kerb. The car managed to steer clear, missing her by inches. It was a terrifying experience but she was alive, and that was all she thought about.

The Albanians hit the A13 at seventy miles per hour and Adrjana pushed the speed up to ninety-five in two seconds. They heard more sirens and saw two police cars on the opposite side of the road. They would turn at the Custom House slip road and be after them in about a minute.

"Step on it Adrjana!"

The Ford Focus was now at its maximum speed of about one hundred-and-twenty miles per hour. Adrjana was concentrating like mad as he weaved in and out of traffic, causing chaos to the speed-limit-abiding traffic.

"We won't get away like this, we need to get off this road!"

Bujar was looking in every direction for an escape route. Suddenly he saw the sign 'A406 North Circular Road', and ordered: "Take the next turn-off, and keep left!"

Adrjana took the turn and roared up the North Circular Road. Bujar was looking for something, something he remembered seeing before. They zoomed past Jenkins Lane Sewage Works and the Amenity Centre then past Langdon School on the left. Bujar was still searching. He glanced behind and could not see the police cars but he could faintly hear their sirens. They were not far behind and any second they might hear a helicopter, which would seal their fate.

Still, they sped on. "Take the next left!" Bujar yelled. He wanted to change cars as soon as possible. They turned onto the A124 Barking Road. "Slow down," he told his friend.

"Thank God!" gasped Adrjana.

"We are not safe yet. Take the next left into Napier Road."

Adrjana indicated left and turned.

"Next left."

Adrjana turned into Nelson Street.

"Park up," Bujar told him.

Adrjana pulled into the kerb, parking between two cars outside Nelson Primary School.

"Let's go!" They jumped out of the car and strolled round the corner into Ranelagh Road.

They were halfway down when Bujar stopped. "This will do nicely," he said as they stopped by a fairly old small silver-coloured Peugeot 305. He took a piece of hard tape out of his pocket and slipped it through the side of the window and hooked it onto the locking button. He pulled and opened the door in one movement and jumped in. "Adrjana," he called out, "get in the back and lie down."

Bujar broke open the dashboard and found the wires he was after. Within a few seconds, the engine sprang to life and Bujar pulled out and headed back to Barking Road. He turned left and kept the car at twenty-eight miles per hour. They drove slowly along Barking Road and then suddenly heard sirens behind them. A police car overtook them at high speed and disappeared in seconds.

"I'm sure I'm going to shit myself soon!" shouted Adrjana, looking around apprehensively.

"Don't worry, we are safe. Relax," Bujar said reassuringly.

After a mile, Bujar turned right into Greengate Street; a further mile on and he took a left into Upper Road and found a parking space.

"Thank fuck for that!" said Adrjana as he got out of the small car and stretched his arms and legs.

Then the two Albanians walked to Plaistow station, which took five minutes. They jumped on a train and were in central London within fifteen minutes.

Chau was back in Newham General Hospital receiving much needed care. Although covered in bruises and road burns, she was actually very well considering what she had been through.

Steve Thomas, her police guard, was not so lucky. He was in a coma and it was felt he would probably only have five per cent of brain function. The nurse who had been struck by Bujar had a fractured skull but was not in any serious danger. The police car that crashed in Prince Regent Lane resulted in nothing more serious than both officers receiving whiplash injuries.

"You see the type of people we are dealing with?" said Jeff, shaking his head at Karen.

"I'm going to start carrying a weapon. These men are animals!" she replied.

Jeff and Karen were at Newham General Hospital, visiting Chau and checking on her security. There were now two armed officers outside her door as well as one at the main hospital reception area. Karen had been devastated to hear of Steve Thomas's injuries and Chau had been inconsolable when she had been told.

"Karen, I want the CCTV film from the entire hospital for the past week," Jeff began. "Those guys may well have been here before and I don't want to miss any good images. Also, go over all the film from cameras outside the brothels at Peckham and Soho—you never know, they could have been snooping around and we could get lucky. Compare the new images against the file pics of the three Albanians who were interviewed by the Met last year. I've got a feeling things are going to start swinging our way very soon."

"I'll get on it."

CHAPTER 14

Tony Bolton was sitting in a comfy leather chair in the hospital library, reading a book about the Second World War. He liked the descriptions of violence and enjoyed reading about the huge numbers of casualties. He also read with great interest about how the Nazis gassed and exterminated six million men, women and children.

It was two-twenty and he kept glancing at his watch, because he had a meeting with Dr Gary Thompson at two-thirty. *Ten fucking minutes to go*, he thought. He hated the meetings: the doctor was so fucking boring and he liked to go on and on about the minutest details. And he knew the doc was listening closely to every word he said, looking for reasons—that big word 'reasons'—why he shot the referee at the Royal Lancaster Hotel, why he had a reputation for extreme violence, and why he attacked the guard and cut up his face. Just thinking about that cunt doctor made him want to stick a knife in his eye.

He was woken from his thoughts by a guard saying, "Mr Bolton, Dr Thompson is ready for you now."

"Thank you so much," he replied politely. "It's Tim isn't it?"

Tony liked to know the first names of the guards. It was the first part of building a relationship that one day could be useful.

"Yes it is. Please follow me."

"Of course. We don't want to keep the doctor waiting."

They proceeded to one of the first-floor meeting rooms where Tim opened the door and ushered Tony in.

Tim, on his own, then walked round to the back of the room, opened a secret door in the wall and entered.

He climbed a set of steps and went into a room, one wall of which had a large glass panel that overlooked the meeting room where Dr Thompson and Tony were sitting. Tim sat at the back. There were about eight trainee and junior doctors sitting in the room, watching the action in the room intently. They were all holding clipboards, ready to make notes.

"So how are you Tony?" asked the doctor.

"Very well thank you for asking Doc, and you?"

"I can't complain Tony, nobody listens anyway." He chuckled.

Tony smiled. "I know what you mean Doc."

"Do you Tony? What do you have to complain about?"

Tony wanted to say: *"I'm complaining because you fucking wankers have locked me up in this nuthouse and I don't want to be here, and if I got the chance I'd cut your throat and enjoy watching you bleed to death, you cunt."*

But of course he didn't.

"Look Doc, I realise I've made mistakes. I'm getting treatment now and I'm very thankful for that. I've got no complaints except of course—

Doctor Thompson visibly leaned forward at hearing this.

"—that the portions of the delicious jam roly poly at dinner time are too small."

Thompson leaned back in his chair. "Hmm, well, the caterers do a very good job."

"Doc, do you think I could get a job in the kitchen?" he asked.

"You haven't been here long enough yet Tony. Have you heard from your brother recently?"

Doc Thompson noticed Tony look agitated for a split second.

"I haven't Doc, but he's a very busy man."

"Too busy to remember his brother?" said the doc with some sympathy.

Tony nearly answered too quickly and would have said something he would have regretted.

"He sends me money all the time. It's very kind of him really."

"Yes of course. Are you getting better Tony?"

"Yeah, getting better. Definitely." Tony replied with conviction.

"You do agree you are ill, don't you Tony?"

"I have been ill Doc and, as I say, I am getting better, definitely."

"I've invited one of my colleagues to come in and chat with us. You don't mind, do you?"

This is new, thought Tony. *Two fucking doctors to dance around with.*

"Not at all Doc."

On that cue, one of the trainee doctors from the upstairs viewing room got up and left it, and came downstairs. A few seconds later, the door opened to the meeting room and she walked in.

"Tony, this is Dr Travis."

Doctor Travis was a five-foot-eight-inches tall, slim redhead with a great figure and stunning green eyes. She was wearing a short black skirt and a blue shirt that was a size too small, and which accentuated her very pert breasts.

"Hello Tony." She stuck her hand out and Tony shook it. The feeling of touching a woman sent an electric current through his whole body. Dr Thompson noticed and smiled to himself. This could be fun, he thought.

"Tony, Dr Travis is training and it is very helpful for her to sit in on meetings such as this," Thompson said. "Of course, if you would prefer for her not to—"

Tony didn't let him finish. "Don't be silly Doc, of course I'm happy to help Dr Travis." He turned towards her. "Surely, we can be on first-name terms here, can't we?" He looked at the two doctors enquiringly.

"My name's Sharon," the newcomer replied. "Please call me that by all means." She smiled.

"Thank you Sharon, I appreciate that very much."

Sharon crossed one leg over the other, exposing a flash of thigh. Tony nearly died on the spot as he noticed, but quickly turned back to Dr Thompson.

"So, what shall we talk about now?"

Dr Thompson turned to trainee Sharon. "What would you like to ask Tony?"

Sharon was quick on the cue and looked at the patient. "At what age did you become a violent person?"

Tony didn't like that question and took his time before saying anything. "As I'm sure you've looked at my file, you will have read that I had a very deprived childhood and, without going into huge detail, I was a bit of a nuisance as a teenager."

Dr Thompson burst in: "Bit of a nuisance? Tony you were committing armed robberies at the age of sixteen for God's sake!"

"Yes, as a result of my deprived childhood!" Tony reiterated.

Sharon asked the next question: "Do you get a thrill when you kill someone Tony?"

Good question, thought Dr Thompson.

"Well, for a start, I haven't actually killed that many people."

Sharon quickly replied: "Well, let's see now. There was the policeman in Tower Bridge Road, who was sitting in his car, the Greek man at the robbery in Plaistow, not forgetting the poor referee at the London hotel. And those were only in the last twelve months. Goodness knows how many more people you've killed."

"The referee was a mistake," Tony said grimly. "I thought he was a hired Albanian Special Forces contract killer who was after me."

"Mistake? Is that what you call it?" The woman doctor was shaking her head as though she thought Tony was living in a world of fantasy. "If I remember correctly, the referee got *three* bullets, the one in the middle of the forehead killing him instantly. A mistake? Albanian Special Forces?"

Tony was finding it hard to keep his cool; he counted to ten. "Sharon, the trouble is that you watch too many cops and robbers shows on TV."

Sharon was somewhat indignant at that. "What do you mean by that Tony?"

"Maybe it's not me living in the fantasy world." With that he sat back and smiled at Dr Thompson and Sharon in turn, then he decided to have a bit of fun at her expense. "I expect you're not getting any at the moment and it's making you uptight."

Sharon was thrown off balance and her face turned red. *"What did you say? Not getting any what, exactly?"*

"You know. A big hard cock between your legs. Or up your arse."

Sharon was speechless. Dr Thompson interjected: "I think that's quite enough, thank you Mr Bolton. It was a mistake for us to think you knew the boundaries."

"Sorry Doc, but she's too far up her own arse for her own good."

Sharon had now lost it. "You fucking bastard Bolton! You are a disgusting person and, just in case that twisted brain of yours hasn't worked it out yet, you will rot in here forever."

She stormed out of the room and slammed the door behind her.

Tony laughed. "She's a bit prick-ly. No pun intended Doc."

Sharon made her way back to the viewing room and stomped around for a few seconds before sitting down.

"Tony, that was unfair," Thompson told him. "Sharon's in training."

"I'd like to give her a *certain kind* of training. She's gorgeous."

"Really? Do you find her attractive, Tony?"

"Doc, are you in the real world? She could have any man she wanted. Except me of course."

"And why couldn't she have you, Tony?"

"Because as you know very well Doc, that is not allowed. Anyway, believe me, she couldn't handle it."

From up above, Sharon was looking closely at Tony and imagined him ripping her clothes off and fucking her from behind. She rubbed her eyes and shook her head to break the thought. It worked for a moment, but she found that she was feeling very horny. She looked at Tony again and imagined him naked, with a huge hard-on.

"Well, I think that's enough for today Tony. We will of course catch up again soon."

"OK Doc, see you soon."

Tony was escorted out of the room. As he entered the corridor, he stood to one side as a group of doctors passed by. He saw Sharon amongst them and suddenly felt a hand on his crotch. He was taken aback as he looked her in the eyes. She smiled as she passed him. Now he knew he was going to have her, however long it took: she would be his, one way or the other.

CHAPTER 15

Paul Bolton was born in Guy's Hospital, London, and then lived all his childhood at number 37, Royal Oak Road in Bermondsey, south-east London. He spent most of his youth charging around Leather Market Gardens, a play area which was opposite his house.

The Bolton brothers went to Grange Primary School in Webb Street, regularly truanting, meaning they probably attended every other day. When they transferred to the Sacred Heart Roman Catholic Secondary School in Camberwell New Road, they attended school about once a week.

They left full-time education with absolutely no qualifications and both started work at Bermondsey Scrap Metal Recycling Ltd in Druid Street. Those were what Tony now called the 'good old days', an introduction to drinking, drugs, women and violence. Tony was always the mad one of the pair, which was of course the origin of the nickname he acquired later in life. Although the brothers spent a lot of time together, they were really as dissimilar as chalk and cheese.

Their parents were typical labour-voting Bermondsey residents. Dad was a docker and Mum kept house and looked after the two boys. Dad's dad had been a docker before him as had his father. Paul's granddad had been involved in the great Dock Strike of 1889. The principle demand of these strikers was for the 'docker's tanner', which was six pence (pre-decimalisation pence were worth less than pence today) an hour.

A docker's life at the time was very tough and very badly paid. In the end, they got their sixpence an hour. The docks were badly damaged during World War Two and by the seventies, work was very scarce.

Bolton senior was called Harold and Paul's mother's name was Elizabeth. They were working class and proud of it. A big night out for Harold and 'Liz', as she was known, was to visit the working men's club in Borough High Street on a Saturday night. Harold would sit and drink ten pints of bitter while Liz had one or two sweet sherries. They would then treat themselves to a bag of chips on the way home. Once home, they would climb the stairs, undress and get into their twenty-year-old double bed. Harold would climb on Liz and enter her within five seconds, there would be a bit of grunting, and it would all be over in a minute: the world of female multiple orgasms had not yet made it to Bermondsey!

Paul loved his mum with a passion: she was the beacon of goodness in his life, although she was sometimes very strict. She was the rock of the family and held everything together. If Paul was scared of anything, or just needed some reassurance, he would rush to his mother and wrap his arms around her waist and refuse to let go.

The boys' upbringing was certainly tough and basic, but they always had good food and plenty of it. They had to wear their shoes until they were literally falling apart but so did all the other kids in the neighbourhood.

Paul had a difficult relationship with his father. Harold was very old fashioned and considered kids should keep quiet in the company of adults, unless they were spoken to. He also insisted the kids could never leave the table until they had finished all their food. This wasn't a huge problem as the food was generally good but did, on occasion, see Paul and Tony still sitting at the table at nine o'clock at night.

Tony's brother also took exception to the way his dad sometimes treated his mum: if Harold didn't like the dinner, he had been known to throw the plate at the wall, storm out of the house and go to the pub. This usually resulted in him returning drunk and then giving his wife a good slapping at the slightest provocation. Paul used to lie in his bed crying because he knew he was too small to help his mum.

That was to change as Paul grew up. At the age of fourteen, Paul was still not very muscular but he was strong and wiry, and other kids thought twice before picking on him, and of course there was always Tony in the background and he was a completely different person to Paul.

Tony had started committing serious theft and dealing in drugs at fifteen. He had also given one or two boys serious beatings for as little as just looking at him in way he didn't like. Paul was brighter academically and certainly did not have Tony's propensity for violence. Where Tony would steal money, Paul always looked for the legal way to make it. This was to hold them in good stead later in life, as the two of them together were a real force to be reckoned with.

One thing Paul and Tony loved doing with their dad was going to watch football at the 'Den', the home of Millwall Football Club. When the boys were very young, they used to say they supported Chelsea and Tottenham, and if their dad heard it, he would immediately give them a good whack round the head.

That all changed the day they went to their first live game at the Den. Paul and Tony were hooked. Following that, they went to every match they could. Tony liked the banter with the opposition fans while Paul was always trying to work out what formation the team were playing. Tony went on to become a serious football hooligan and enjoyed nothing better than attacking opposition fans whenever he could, before or after a match.

Although Paul had fumbled around with a couple of girls, his first real girlfriend was Mandy Collins. Paul and Mandy were both fifteen and Paul was madly in love with her. He had been chasing girls for over a year, trying to lose his virginity, and had done everything with girls apart from the sex act itself: because none of the girls he knew would do it with him.

He then went to a party one Saturday and, before long, he was dancing and snogging Mandy. He was a bit shy but she seemed a nice girl and they got on well. Paul had drunk a couple of beers and needed to go for a pee. He was loath to leave Mandy downstairs on her own, as one of his mates could move in while he was gone. He grabbed Mandy's hand and pulled her up the stairs. When they reached the top, Paul stuck his head in one of the bedrooms, which happened to be empty.

"Stay in here, do not let anyone in other than me!" Paul told her, then rushed into the toilet and urinated.

He came out and went back to the bedroom where Mandy was. He opened the door, stepped in, closed it and turned around.

What greeted him was the most incredible sight: Mandy was lying across the bed, she was completely naked, and her legs were up and held apart. Paul was transfixed, he just stared mesmerised at Mandy's hairy bush and thought immediately that this could be it.

He lay down on top of her and kissed her. He felt Mandy's hand expertly undo his belt and pull down the zip on his trousers. He was in heaven, and already had a massive erection. She grasped his cock and moved it slowly up and down. He took her hands in his and settled it between her legs, looking for the way in. He fumbled a few times and she then took hold of his cock and placed it at the entrance to her wet pussy.

Then he heard her whisper, "Push." He did exactly that and felt his cock enter into a warm, wet, tight pussy. He stopped for a second to enjoy the moment, then pulled his cock back and then entered faster and harder. He heard her gasp—he loved that and repeated his thrusting again. He then twisted a bit in order to push his penis in from a different angle, because he had read in a book that was what you were meant to do.

He pushed in again and suddenly gasped: he was coming already! *Shit!* he thought. *Oh God, no condom!*

Then he pulled out and sprayed come all over her stomach and legs. He was so disappointed that it was over so quickly and prayed that Mandy would not spread the word that it had all been completed in a minute. She didn't seem to mind. She took some tissues out of her bag and wiped herself down.

Paul got dressed and ten minutes later they left the party for Mandy to catch the last bus home. As they walked down the street holding hands, he suddenly realised he had a huge hard-on and needed to come again. Thankfully, the bus arrived very quickly. He kissed Mandy and rushed her towards the bus. He waved goodbye and then ran all the way back to the party.

He was feeling so bloody horny he didn't care what the girl looked like, he just urgently needed to fuck someone else. His eye fell on a slightly tubby female called Sarah, who was obviously not with anyone. He danced with her and she clearly had no idea what he had been up to earlier.

The party came to an end and a few people crashed in the lounge. Paul and Sarah cuddled up on the sofa. He tried desperately to get her knickers off but she was just not interested. In the end, she took his cock out and gave him a very nice handjob. Paul was happy and contented. A fuck and a handjob in one night! *Brilliant*, he said to himself.

Paul and Mandy became an item and Paul learned the mysteries of a woman's body, with a very willing Mandy. The next time they had sex it lasted for two minutes instead of one.

His relationship with his father finally came to a head one Saturday night. Harold had been out drinking all day and evening and got back to the house at about midnight. Everybody was in bed sleeping, but that didn't stop him stumbling upstairs into his room, making one hell of a row. He then shook Liz awake and told her he was hungry and that she should get up and make him some food. For Liz, this was a step too far and she told him there was cold ham in the fridge and that if he was hungry he should make himself a sandwich.

The next thing Liz knew was that Harold grabbed her by the arm and started pulling her out of the bed, shouting, "Get down the fucking stairs and make me some food, you fucking slut!"

Liz hit the floor with a bang. She grabbed the side of the bed and held on for dear life. This enraged Harold, who then started hitting Liz in the face, screaming at her to let go. Paul and Tony were asleep in their shared room. Paul woke first and shook Tony awake. They heard the commotion and their mum's screams. They rushed to their parents' bedroom and burst in.

Harold turned to them angrily, yelling: "Get the fuck out of here, you little bastards!"

Paul looked at Tony and they both decided in that split second what they were going to do. Tony jumped at Harold and grabbed his arms. Paul rugby tackled his legs and they both held him tightly on the floor. Liz got up and backed away from the melee.

"If you two don't get off me this second, you're really going to regret it!" Harold snarled. He was fuming. He wrenched a hand free, swung his arm and punched Tony in the face. That was what started the beating that Harold was to receive.

Tony continually smashed his fist into Harold's face while Paul was punching him in the stomach. This went on for what seemed an eternity, probably in fact only a minute or two, and finally Harold lay still. The brothers noticed this and stopped. Blood was pouring out of their father's nose and mouth. Tony and Paul then lifted Harold to his feet and dragged him out of the room and down the stairs. They opened the front door and threw him into the gutter.

Paul shouted after him: "If you know what's good for you, stay away! We don't want you here!" They shut the door and went upstairs to comfort their mother.

They never saw their father again. Rumours surfaced that he had gone to live in Spain, but neither Paul nor Tony could be bothered to find out whether it was true or not.

Tony and Paul then spilt up for a period of time. Tony worked for several scrap dealers and started forging friendships with the criminal element of Bermondsey. Paul had got a job in a club in central London and was learning all the elements of running it, from washing up, to waiting on tables and to counting the cash.

Paul was a natural: he seemed to have that knack of knowing exactly what customers wanted and made sure they got it. He was also good at keeping his fingers on the pulse. Clubs generated huge amounts of cash, and where there was cash, there were always people who wanted some the easy way. Paul knew exactly what was going on in the club, every minute of the late-opening nights. He very quickly became probably the youngest manager of a decent-sized Soho club in London. He was earning good money and enjoying the business buzz. He then invited Tony to join him as security manager; the brothers were back together and looking forward to a good future.

After two years of running the sex-and-drinking club, the owner wanted to retire, and asked Paul if he would like to buy it. There was no way Paul could obtain the finance, but the owner was happy to accept a good deposit and then take a share of the monthly profits. Paul and Tony scraped every penny they could find for the deposit, which amounted to two hundred thousand pounds.

Tony contributed his share on the promise that Paul did not enquire where it came from. Tony's share had in fact come from a bank robbery and his involvement in the Brinks Mat gold bullion robbery. If Paul had known what Tony was up to, he would have been shocked and then he would have gone crazy with worry.

They changed the name of the club to The Den, in honour of Millwall Football Club, and even had footballer John Seasman, a Millwall legend, cut the ribbon at the official opening.

The club did really well. Paul introduced happy hours, stag parties and further innovations that increased numbers by thirty-five per cent, a huge improvement. When you realised that punters were paying four pounds for a bottle of beer and eighty quid for a cheap bottle of champagne, it was no wonder that profits were massive. The Den was just the start. The brothers made so much money they soon opened a second and then a third club. In addition, they had to borrow huge amounts of money, since they liked to own the freehold on the properties and not to have to pay rent. This turned out to be a good move, since property values soared beyond belief over the next few years.

CHAPTER 16

Paul was sending three of his best men up to Manchester to see what they could find out about the thugs that killed Jack and tortured Mary Coombs.

Dave, Pauly and Matt had worked in a few of Paul's clubs. They had also done private work for him of a sensitive nature. Paul trusted them implicitly and felt it was safer to send three in case of trouble. The trio knew each other but not that well, so of course the first thing they did was arrange a get-together in a pub.

The first agreement was that they were now the 'Three Amigos'. They started by knocking back a couple of bottles of Pouilly-Fuisse in the French House in Dean Street. The pub's traditional French feel suited the moment and Matt had chosen it, as he was a bit of a wine buff. They then moved onto the Dog and Duck in Bateman Street where Pauly and Dave were more at home drinking real beer. They downed a few pints and then decided to eat: so they went to Stef's, an Italian Restaurant in Berners street, where they polished off three bottles of Rioja with their Tagliatelle and chickpeas. By the time they left Stef's, they were all a bit the worse for wear. The Amigos then decided to go to a club for a nightcap. They didn't want to go to The Den, which of course would have been cheaper, and ended up in the Barrio Club, drinking whisky and listening to the big band playing.

They all decided to stay the night at the Dean Street Townhouse, a hotel in the heart of Soho. The next morning was a late start for all three. They all had a full English breakfast and wolfed down endless cups of coffee. Eventually the three men decided to walk to The Den for their 11 a.m. meeting with Paul. It was a fresh mild morning and they were fully awake when they arrived at the club.

"Morning guys. How was the night out?" asked Paul.

"Yeah, really good," one replied and the others agreed, grinning at the memory.

"And the food at Stef's?"

Paul was indirectly telling them that whatever they did in Soho, he would hear about it. Dave, Pauly and Matt became less chirpy: they were all miffed that Paul seemed to know their whereabouts the night before, as if he was keeping his eye on them.

"Stef's food was as good as usual," piped up Matt.

"Good," Paul cut the small talk. "Shall we get down to business then? Now you all know what happened to Jack and Mary Coombs. I'm not going to list the injuries but they cut Jack's face up with secateurs, and they used a rake on

Mary… uh… I'll leave the details of what they actually did to her to your imagination. What you need to know is that Jack took a long time to die and Mary was raped and then tortured horribly for at least ten minutes."

Dave hadn't heard the details, and was consequently the most incensed. "These animals need sorting," he muttered grimly. "I hope we're taking weapons," he added, looking at the others and then he turned back to Paul.

"You bet you are," answered Paul. "If those nutcases find out there are people from London in Manchester looking for them, they will try to take you out. Make no mistake, they will not take any prisoners AND they're on home turf, which gives them some advantages." Paul looked at the three men in turn to stress his point. "If you go into a pub asking questions, they'll know you are there within minutes. This is a difficult operation."

"Do we have any leads at all?" asked Matt hopefully.

"In a word, no," said Paul.

Dave was the muscle, Pauly could be a nasty vicious bastard and Matt was devious: a really good mix of talents for the difficult job they had to do in Manchester.

The Three Amigos met at Euston Station to catch the midday east coast train to Manchester Piccadilly, arriving at ten-past-two. They had a couple of beers on the way but that was their limit—they were all very conscious that they were entering dangerous waters and had to be at the very top of their game.

They arrived on time and grabbed a taxi to the four-star Renaissance Hotel in the city centre. Paul had said it was unlikely that "Fucking Batman and Robin are going to enter the Renaissance Hotel, with guns blazing!"

Matt favoured jeans and just a shirt, while Pauly always wore a long dark coat, whether it was summer or winter; Dave wore a blue suit with an open-necked white shirt, and he looked a bit like the TV personality Piers Morgan, the poor sod.

They booked into the hotel and soon met up in the bar for an early pint. No one was in charge as such, but Dave usually spoke first, followed by Pauly and then the final words of wisdom usually came from Matt.

"As I see it, we've got to flush the bastards out and if that means announcing our arrival, so be it," Dave began.

Pauly and Matt look at each other before answering, and then Pauly said, "Eh, you mean like tying a cow to a post and waiting for the lion to turn up? And when it does, you shoot it?"

Matt chipped in: "It could work but we would seriously have to be ready for when they come—there could be five, even ten of them. We could be outnumbered."

They all thought about that for a few seconds.

"And remember," Dave said, rubbing his chin, "Paul said he wanted them alive if possible."

"Jesus! He doesn't want much, does he?" grumbled Pauly loudly.

"Shh, keep it down," said Matt. "We don't want to draw attention to ourselves in here."

"Right, we don't," agreed Dave.

"Whose round is it?" said Pauly, holding up his empty glass.

"You get them in, it's all on Paul's credit card," answered Matt.

"Good," Pauly announced, smiling. "I'm looking forward to a nice Chateaubriand for dinner tonight."

"Pauly, you're always thinking of your bloody stomach," Dave moaned.

"Dave, in case you didn't know, an army marches on its stomach."

"Not that you've been anywhere near the army, eh Pauly!" Dave rejoined.

They all laughed and Pauly went up for the drinks.

"Three pints of lager please, guv," he said to the barman.

"Are you three lads up from London?" the man asked.

"Yeah. What of it?" Pauly glared at him.

"Hey, nothing, mate, nowt at all," the barman protested. "Just making conversation, me. Pretty touchy aren't you?"

Pauly gave the barman one of his *You better keep your fucking mouth shut mate* looks and turned to see what Matt and Dave were up to. Matt was looking at him and raising his hand and lowered it mouthing, "Chill."

Pauly turned to the barman. "Sorry mate, didn't mean to be mouthy. It's just we've been working so hard, see? Left me feeling a bit touchy, you know?"

"No problem pal. What are you doing up here then?"

"We're looking at restaurants to buy."

"Wow! Restaurants, that's brilliant, like to do that myself one day."

"Well, good luck with that. I'm in room 42, OK?" Pauly showed him his room key and took the three pints back to the table.

"Nosy bastard wants to know what we're doing up here," he grumbled to the other Amigos. "He'll want to know how big our cocks are next."

Pauly was distracted as a long legged, slim brunette strolled by. "Hmm, very nice indeed," he said, sniggering and licking his lips.

"None of that on this trip, Pauly," warned Matt.

"Yeah, well, who knows what might happen if only she knew I was here and available." They all laughed again.

Then they had a slap-up dinner with a couple of bottles of wine and finally moved back to the bar. Matt went for a pee and came back out and headed towards reception to get to the bar. He was glancing around and suddenly stopped dead in his tracks, looking at the reception desk, quickly taking a step back so he couldn't be seen. The barman was in the corner, whispering to a hard-looking man who looked to be in his mid-thirties.

Fucking hell! Matt thought. *We've been made already.*

The barman's friend shook the informer's hand and walked to the reception. Matt saw him look around and then walk towards the main entrance. If they knew about it Dave and Pauly would be shitting bricks, he realised. *This is already looking bad*, he thought to himself.

Matt followed the man outside the hotel and saw him get in an Audi Quattro. The lone Amigo then jumped into the first taxi at the rank and said in classic private-dick style, "Follow that car!"

Back in the hotel bar, Dave and Pauly were worried. Where the fuck was Matt, they wondered? Just then, Dave's mobile rang, and when he answered he told the others it was Matt. The quick-witted pursuer then explained what had happened and where he was.

The Audi didn't go far and stopped outside the Old Nags Head pub in Jacksons Row, off Deansgate. Two similarly hard-looking men jumped into the car and they sped off.

In the back of the taxi, Matt was sweating. "Don't let them see we are following them!"

"Don't worry, I've done this before," The taxi driver told him, laughing.

The Audi drove round until it stopped at another pub, The Britons Protection, in Great Bridgewater Street. The three men got out and entered the hostelry. Matt saw them receive a noisy welcome and surmised it must be their local. Good, he thought, progress. "Back to the hotel please," he told the driver, then sat back and his devious brain started to tick over.

"Look they know we are here," said Matt as he sat across from Dave and Pauly back at the hotel. "But can they be one hundred per cent sure why we're here? We now know where their local pub is and can probably eyeball them most nights. We could of course follow them from the pub and find out where they live. So look, we either take them after they come out of the pub, or we locate where they live and take them at home. Or, we could still get them to come after us and then lead them into a trap." Matt had his own ideas of strategy, but wanted to hear what the other two thought before sharing them.

Dave spoke first. "I'm for maximum firepower as they come out the pub. It's the safest way for us."

"Yeah, but Paul wanted them alive," Pauly said quickly.

"Alive *if possible*, was what he actually said," Dave rejoined. "It's bloody dangerous shooting them from a distance, let alone taking them alive, and if we did, how the hell would we get them back to London?"

"I think Paul would be happy to come up here if we could get them," Matt commented. "Hmm." He was thinking hard, examining all the options.

"First thing we do," said Dave, "is disappear. We book out of here, tell that wanker at the bar we're going back to London. We'll book into a quiet hotel just outside the city, then we can at least relax for a minute."

"Good idea," Matt and Pauly both chorused as they nodded.

That evening they told the barman they were leaving early, saying that they had to return to London earlier than expected.

They checked out, noticing that the treacherous barman was standing at the side of the room, watching. They grabbed a taxi and relocated to the Travel Lodge at Birch Motorway Services Eastbound, on the M62. The new hotel was eight miles from Manchester City Centre and it took less than fifteen minutes to get there.

"Well, it's not the Renaissance, is it?" said Matt sarcastically.

"No, but we're a lot safer now," answered Pauly.

Matt was looking intently out of the side of the hotel's entrance, where he could not be seen from the car park.

A taxi had pulled into the Travel Lodge one minute after them. Matt could clearly see the barman from the Renaissance sitting in the back of it. As soon as the taxi pulled away, Matt could see that the shit was talking on his mobile.

"It worked, he's just left," said Matt.

"Good," Pauly muttered with satisfaction. "Now all we have to do it wait for some visitors."

The Three Amigos had booked three single rooms: 22, 23 and 24, on the second floor. They had also booked a further room for a supposed 'colleague' who would be arriving very late. That room was 33 on the third floor, directly above room 23. They carried all their weapons to room 33, took them apart and thoroughly cleaned them, preparing them carefully for action. Matt favoured a Beretta M9 pistol, a favourite of the American military, Pauly used an Austrian manufactured Glock 21 while Dave always carried an Israeli Uzi because of its firepower and relatively small size.

Matt figured that a hit team would come that night, how many exactly, he wasn't sure: he guessed it would be at least five, maybe six. It was gratifying to know that the Manchester hoodlums would be blissfully unaware that they were heading into a trap.

* * *

Graham and Toby Banks had been violent psychopaths from childhood. They liked dishing out violence and being paid to do it: it was like a dream career for them. They didn't care who it was or what they had done, all they wanted to know was how much they would be paid.

They had taken the Coombs job for fifty thousand and it had been easy money. The brothers had really enjoyed torturing Jack and Mary and it had been their best paid job for some time. They had spent the last month enjoying life, which meant drinking in their favourite Manchester pubs and shagging an endless supply of girls who got their kicks by mixing with criminals.

The call from the barman at the Renaissance had come out of the blue. They were extremely interested to learn that three men from London had booked in and there was something 'not quite right' about them. Graham had quickly shot over to the hotel to have a look himself and he agreed that they looked out of place. He only saw Pauly and Dave but some instinct told him that they needed watching. When it was confirmed that they had lied about going back to London and had instead moved to the Travel Lodge, Graham and Toby decided that these guys from London were a problem that needed sorting and needed sorting quickly.

They had all met up in the Britons Protection pub: Graham and Toby plus three of their friends. The Banks brothers had assumed that they would have surprise on their side, so were confident that five men was enough to take care of the trio from London. They were all tooled up with weapons and had a whisky each to warm up. Then they piled into Graham's Audi and were off. It was 11 p.m.

The Manchester contingent pulled into the car park of the Travel Lodge at eleven-twenty and parked over on the east side where it was darkest. They got out the car and made their way to Reception. They rang the bell and waited for a couple of minutes and then an elderly man in uniform arrived from upstairs. The receptionist-cum-night porter, an elderly man called Mr Trent, didn't like the look of the five men at all.

"Good evening," he began, eyeing them warily. "What can I do for you gentlemen?"

Toby tried to make his tone sound friendly. "We've come to see three of our friends, Londoners. We reckon on surprising them."

Mr Trent didn't like the sound of that at all.

"It's a bit late isn't it?" he ventured. "I can call one of them. Who shall I say is here?"

Toby advanced towards Mr Trent with a slight smile on his face. He grabbed the old man by the collar and almost touched noses as he dragged him close.

"What rooms are they in?" Toby demanded.

The old man was scared to death but was brave enough to reply: "I can't tell you that—it's against the rules."

Toby turned towards the other four thugs with a smirk. "Did you hear that boys? It's against the rules."

Then he drew back his fist and smashed Mr Trent straight in the face, breaking his nose. The victim collapsed onto the floor, blood pouring down his chin and onto his shirt.

The attacker squatted down to his level and spoke slowly and clearly: "I'm only going to ask once more and if you don't give me the right answer, I'm going to stick a knife in your eye."

Mr Trent felt the warm trickle of urine dribbling down his leg. "Rooms 23 and

24 on the second floor," he groaned.

"That's better." Toby grabbed hold of Mr Trent's head by the hair and smashed it hard against the floor. It bounced back up and then down finally, as Mr Trent slid into unconsciousness. One of the other guys went into reception and found the box marked 'master keys'; there were three. He took two and gave them to Graham and Toby.

The five men drew their handguns, screwed silencers to the barrels, and headed for the stairs. They climbed to the second floor and tiptoed down the long corridor, following the sign directing them to rooms 20—29. They went on past rooms 20, 21 and 22 and stopped outside 23. Graham pointed at Toby and one other man and then motioned his hand towards room 24. The two men split away from the others and waited outside 24.

Graham and Toby inserted the keys in unison. Graham then nodded decisively, and they burst into the rooms simultaneously, followed by the other gang members. The brothers did not mess about: they pumped bullets into the bed and pillow areas, hoping to decimate their victims' heads and torsos.

But it was soon became apparent that the rooms were empty.

"Shit! What the fuck is going on?" shouted Graham. He emerged into the corridor at the same time as Toby, who was shaking his head. "Fuck! We've been had! The bastards aren't here."

Graham thought for a moment. "Let's go." He started making his way back from the direction in which they had come. They returned to the reception and stopped to plan their next move.

Toby looked at Graham. "What now?"

"I'm not sure," grunted his brother, "but let's get out of here sharpish!"

They all trooped out of reception and headed briskly to the car. They got in.

And as the last back door slammed closed, it happened.

Matt was on the driver's side, Pauly beside him, with Dave in the back. All three held their weapons in front of them and opened fire at the same time. Glass shattered as hundreds of bullets entered the car and hit the occupants.

The three in the back were obliterated by Dave's Uzi and died in the blink of an eye. Graham and Toby took hits but had managed to duck down and were still alive when they were dragged out of the car and thrown to the ground.

"Not so tough now, are you?" asked Dave.

Graham shouted, "FUCK YOU CUNT!"

Dave pointed his Uzi at Graham's head and pulled the trigger. The bone flesh and blood exploded like a melon, pieces flying in all directions.

Matt grabbed Dave's arm and pushed the Uzi down, saying, "That's enough."

Dave calmed down. Pauly was leaning over Toby, assessing his wounds, which he could see were not life threatening.

"This one's going to live," Pauly announced.

Dave was back in control. "We need to move as quickly as possible. Put that piece of shit in the boot."

"What?" shouted Matt.

"I said put that piece of shit in the boot!"

Pauly and Matt lifted Toby, opened the boot, shoved him in and slammed the lid down on top of him. They all got in the car and Graham pulled away.

They were bound for London.

CHAPTER 17

Detective Sergeant Karen Foster had reviewed the arrest reports on the three Albanians and had checked out the addresses they had given. They all turned out to be false, so she was none the wiser in that direction.

Following the incident at Newham General Hospital, Karen was searching through the CCTV cameras to look for any good images of the two assailants who had tried to kidnap Chau. It was a mind-numbing job, because she had to look through hours and hours of footage, but it proved to be rewarding in the end.

Karen had found images of Adrjana Bardulla casing the hospital the day before it had happened. She also had the whole kidnap incident on film, and the men's faces were eminently identifiable. In order to be certain, she cross referenced those images with the pictures from when they were arrested the previous year: they were a perfect match.

Her next job had been to look at all the CCTV from outside the brothels at Peckham and Soho. This was quite a difficult task, but once again turned out to be ultimately rewarding. Two men sitting in a car outside the Soho brothel were identified as Bujar Dushka and Andrea Gjikokaj. The trouble was that simply sitting in a car in a street in London was not a crime, however it was indicative of their links with the place.

However, it looked as if there was nowhere else to go. Karen sat and looked at the screen, thinking there must be *something* else.

And then it hit her: check the car number plate. But no, she thought, it had to be a stolen vehicle, but she checked anyway. She typed in the registration number, NT05SPO, and information immediately came up on the screen. A black BMW, yes, the car matched that. It was registered to a Mr Andrea Gjikokaj.

Karen couldn't believe that the car was *actually registered* to one of the Albanians. She quickly scanned down the screen for an address, finding 32, Chevening Road, Kensal Rise, West London. She immediately rushed to check that address against the false ones the Albanians had given previously. Yes! This was a new address, one they hadn't got anywhere else! Karen's heart was thumping as she thought gleefully that the Albanians might have made a mistake that could cost them dearly.

The excited detective looked around for her friend and colleague, DC Jeff, who was nowhere to be found. She eventually tracked him down in the canteen, stuffing his face with a huge 'fry-up' meal.

Jeff looked up when he saw Karen striding into the canteen. He grabbed his paper napkin and wiped baked-bean sauce off his mouth.

"Jeff, we could have something," she began, sliding into the seat opposite him.

"Yes?" Jeff picked up on her excitement. "Go on for God's sake."

"I checked all the CCTV film. We have a car outside the Soho club on the night of the raid with two of the Albanians sitting in it."

"That's good, gives us a solid connection."

Karen could hardly control her high spirits. "I checked the number plate. You won't believe this, Jeff, but it's registered to Andrea Gjikokaj, one of the Albanians, and gives an address in Kensal Rise."

"Do you really think it could be his genuine address?" said Jeff, looking puzzled.

"Jeff, you told me before, sometimes it's the simplest mistakes that get people caught. We have to check it out as soon as possible."

"Bloody right we do," said Jeff as he sprang up from the table. "Let's go."

They strode back to the CID offices. "Karen, get onto Shepherds Bush Nick in Uxbridge Road," Jeff told her. "See if they have any Intel on the names or the address."

Karen checked with CID at Shepherds Bush but there was no information on the names or the address. Jeff was filling in the forms to apply for a search warrant for the address at Chevening Road.

Once he had finished the form, the detective constable charged out of the office and drove to the magistrate's court, which was five minutes away. Jeff explained the necessity to get the warrant as soon as possible and the paperwork was rushed through to a magistrate who happened to be on a break. The magistrate read the forms and immediately signed the warrant. Jeff was back in the CID office twenty minutes later. He went to look for Karen.

"Right, we need an armed response team and at least ten officers," he told her.

"It's being organised now. Shepherds Bush will supply some, and we'll take three from here with us," said Karen.

"Good, let's get going—we'll take a pool car and put the sirens on."

They set out from Rotherhithe Nick in a marked police car, siren blazing and lights flashing. Jeff and Karen were in the front and the three firearms officers were squashed together in the back. It was eight miles to Shepherds Bush and with the siren on the journey took just twelve minutes.

Karen and her team entered the Nick and booked in. They then met up with the designated team of officers who had been assigned to the operation. In the team there was now Jeff, Karen and ten armed-response officers.

Jeff looked at the maps and decided that there should be three vehicles. The first, with one officer, would park in Wrentham Avenue on the other side of the railway track, opposite the house. Jeff would be in the second vehicle in Kingswood Avenue on the east side of Queens Park, and Karen in the third, in Milman Road, on the west side of the park. The house would be surrounded, but first of all they needed to find out who, if anyone, was in.

When they arrived and parked up, Karen called the other officers to explain that she had stopped a lady delivering local papers and that impersonating her would be a good way to see if anyone was at the address. Jeff agreed. Karen borrowed the lady's coat and took her satchel of papers. She proceeded down Milman Road, pushing the newspapers through letter boxes. She then turned right at the end of the road into Chevening Road.

Her first delivery was for house number 26. Karen strolled back to the pavement. She looked ahead and worked out that their target was the third house from where she was. She could hear some people making noises. She dropped the paper into number 28 and the noise got louder. Karen then walked to the pavement outside number 30 and turned towards the front door. Her mouth was dry. She could hear her heart pounding.

The female detective caught a glimpse of a man in front of 32, who was washing his car. Fantastic, she thought. She popped the paper into the door's letter box, walked back onto the road, and it took twenty paces to reach number 32. She turned into the drive and saw two men: one was washing the car, while the other was sitting on the side wall. Her heart beat faster as she realised that these men were, without question, two of the Albanians they were looking for. The one sitting on the wall she recognised immediately as Adrjana Bardulla. She nonchalantly handed Adrjana the paper.

"Thank you," he said, giving her an admiring look up and down, which turned her stomach.

Karen continued delivering papers past number 32 until she reached the turn into Kingswood Avenue, where she met up with Jeff.

"Two of the bastards are in front of the house washing an Audi. It's perfect," she told him excitedly.

Jeff turned to the squad leader. "Get ten more men down here sharpish, we have to clear the houses on each side of 32."

He turned back to Karen. "What stage was he at with his car washing?"

"What? How the hell should I know?"

"Think! It's important."

"Yeah, OK. Umm... He was soaping the car, using a bucket and sponge."

"We might have a bit more time then before they go back inside. Let's hope he likes to polish the thing afterwards!"

More officers were rushed to the scene, which was now becoming a major incident. Officers went to the back of all the properties adjoining number 32, evacuating all the residents who were in, and then set up roadblocks surrounding Chevening Road, in order to cut off all pedestrians and traffic. Jeff saw a black taxi and told his officers to commandeer it, as an interesting plan was formulating in his head.

The scheme came together very quickly. Three armed officers were crouched down in the back of the cab, and Jeff was the supposed 'customer', with an officer in civilian clothes driving.

The taxi pulled out and turned into Chevening Road. It then stopped between numbers 32 and 30. Jeff could see the two Albanians standing, idly chatting beside the wet car. Jeff got out and pretended to pay the driver and then suddenly coughed.

This was the signal to go.

He swung around, his handgun pointed at the two men. "POLICE!" he yelled. "GET ON THE FLOOR NOW!"

The three armed officers piled out of the back of the cab, their automatic weapons trained on the two men. Simultaneously they were shouting "ON THE FLOOR!" Then they grabbed the two men who had been caught totally unawares and pushed them to the ground.

Backup arrived ten seconds later and soon the whole area in front of the house was crowded with officers. The Albanian people traffickers were then handcuffed and dragged into a police car. Some officers were grouped beside the front door of the house, ready to rush in.

Bujar was upstairs when he heard the shout of: "POLICE!" He rushed to the window and saw the officers aiming guns at Andrea and Adrjana. He rushed to the next bedroom and grabbed an Uzi, ran down the stairs and made for the back of the house, where he saw two police officers outside the back door.

He knew he only had a minute to try and get away. He levelled the Uzi and charged at the back door, shooting at the two officers, who went down in a hail of bullets. Bujar burst out through the back door and sprinted down the small garden, looking out for any other police officers. He wrenched open the fence gate and burst through into Queens Park. He heard a shout "STOP POLICE!" In one fluid movement, he turned and fired at the officer, the bullets ripping into his body, which shuddered before collapsing onto the grass.

Bujar was away, running as fast as he could, scanning to left and right for potential threats. He got to the end of the park and clambered over the fence into Harvest Road. He looked both ways, expecting car-loads of police to be hot on his trail, but he could see none.

Jeff and Karen were just behind some armed officers at the front door when they heard the automatic gunfire. The leading firearms' officer turned to Jeff, saying, "Machine-gun fire! Watch your back."

They crouched, waiting, until Jeff shouted, "He's getting away out the back! Let's go!" The officers kicked the door in and ran into the hall screaming "POLICE!" as loud as they could. They rushed to the back of the house and found the two dead officers, ripped to pieces and covered in blood. The cops moved forward slowly, fanning out and covering every direction with their guns.

Jeff saw the open back fence gate, yelling: "He's in the park! Move!" The detective constable hurtled to the gate and rushed through. *Shit*, he thought. *We're going to lose him.* He turned to one of the officers. "Stop a second. Get vehicle backup. I want all these roads closed off and sealed!"

The officers entered the park and made for the exit at the far end.

Bujar ran across the road and jumped up to look over a five-foot brick wall. He then heard the sirens—police cars were getting nearer. He had no choice but to pull himself up onto the wall and leap over. His feet landed on a grassy wet bank and he span and rolled down the incline, landing in a heap next to some Underground railway lines.

"Fucking hell!" he cursed as he pushed himself up and started running towards a tunnel a hundred yards to his left. He got to the structure, entered it, and felt the darkness envelop him. He stopped just inside, gasping for breath and watching the bank he had just fallen down from. He heard shouting and saw police officers looking over the wall. He then noticed Jeff and Karen who, he assumed, must be in charge. He saw them giving instructions to the men and then running off up the road.

Two officers were looking over the wall but were obviously waiting for something. It was then he heard the dog barking. *Shit!* he thought, *Dogs!* The next second a giant German Shepherd appeared on the wall and jumped down, followed by three police officers. The dog was sniffing the air and then started barking and moving towards the tunnel.

"Fuck!" muttered Bujar to himself. The three police officers advanced towards the tunnel, with the dog in the front.

Should I take them in the open or let them come into the tunnel? Bujar wondered. He had just seconds to make up his mind. He decided to take them in the open. He crouched down and watched the dog warily approaching and sniffing—he must have caught Bujar's odour. The dog started barking furiously and quickened his pace towards the tunnel entrance. The three officers were now concerned, as they thought the escapee could well be in the tunnel and they were sitting targets out in the open. The canine was soon running at full speed towards the tunnel entrance, certain that the man they were after was in there.

Bujar steadied himself as the dog entered the entrance and leaped at him. The sound of machine-gun fire filled the air as the dog twisted in mid-flight as bullets tore into his head and body. He landed at Bujar's feet in a bloody heap.

The three police officers froze for a second. It was their undoing: Bujar ran from the entrance firing, as the unarmed dog handler turned and ran. The other two assumed a crouched position and were about to fire when bullets thudded into them, mostly in the lower abdominal areas. They both went down, shuddering in agony.

Bujar sped past them and took aim at the officer running away. He fired a short burst into his back and saw him fall, lifeless. He turned back towards the tunnel and was about to pump more bullets into the two injured officers but could tell they were both going to die anyway and so left them. The killer was soon back in the tunnel and running for his life when he heard a noise he had been dreading: a Tube train.

It was pitch black. Bujar pushed himself flat, back up against the wall and prayed. The train was speeding towards him, and the noise was deafening as it passed within a foot of his body. He shut his eyes and put his fingers in his ears, but it didn't help. The noise was earth shattering. After ear-splitting seconds of roaring and rattling, the train finally got past him. He then leaned over, took some deep breaths, and ran for the tunnel exit on the other side. He got to the exit and stopped, took a look round outside, and headed to the fence on the left-hand side.

He glanced both ways and then pulled back some broken wires and squeezed through the fence into Brondesbury Road. He then turned right and set off at a normal pace, trying not to draw attention to himself. He then turned left into Donaldson Road and headed north. He continued up past the Paddington Old Cemetery until he reached the junction with Willesden Lane. He turned right and heard police sirens, which seemed to be coming from every direction.

The murderer walked briskly down Willesden Lane and entered Kilburn High Road. He immediately saw and hailed a cruising black cab and jumped into it. "Dunstan Road, off Finchley Road," he ordered, panting.

The cab motored down Cricklewood Broadway, turned right into Cricklewood Lane and was soon in Finchley Road. Bujar was now happy—he could relax for a minute to get his thoughts together. They soon pulled into Dunstan Road and he told the driver to stop at the end of it. He got out, paid and then walked round the corner into Hodford Road. He was soon knocking on number 48. A heavy-set man with a moustache and short beard opened the door.

"Bujar! What a surprise!" the bearded man said. "Come in, come in!"

"Hi Dejan. They got Adrjana and Andrea."

"Shit, that's bad news. Were they hurt?"

"No, they were washing the fucking car."

"Washing the car? Jesus!" said Dejan, shaking his head. "You always have to be ready for trouble."

"Yes, I know it was stupid. We thought we were safe."

"Never think that my friend, it is always a big mistake."

* * *

Jeff and Karen were peering over the wall as the ambulance crews and fire service were attempting to get the three policemen up the bank. Two had died but one was hanging on by a thread.

"What a pile of shit!" Jeff said miserably. "Karen, we fucked up."

Karen was tearful as they pulled the bodies up the bank. "At least we got two of the bastards. But four of ours dead and one terribly injured, it's *so fucking awful*." She was also thinking that it could so easily have been her on the stretcher inside a body bag, riddled with bullet holes, or injured and bleeding buckets of blood.

"Sometimes I hate this fucking job," she added, looking away.

"Let's go, we have work to do," said Jeff, with a steely determination in his voice.

Adrjana and Andrea were in separate cells at Shepherds Bush police station. They both knew they would not see the light of day for a very long time, if ever.

CHAPTER 18

Paul was getting mentally stronger every day and was almost his old self. He still had bad moments but they were getting further and further apart.

It was a particularly nice day and Paul had wanted to get out of the club for a break. He asked Duke to take him to the Westminster area. Duke dropped him outside the Houses of Parliament and went off to find a café for a drink.

Paul strolled around the Parliament building, marvelling at the history associated with the beautiful structure. He then made his way up to Downing Street and stood at the gate for a moment, looking at the famous black door. He then set off towards Trafalgar Square, stopping to stare at the smartly turned out guardsmen on their horses at Horse Guards Parade. Paul was really enjoying himself, being an anonymous person amongst thousands of tourists. He made his way to Trafalgar Square and was admiring Nelson's column when he heard someone speak to him.

"Paul, how are you?"

Paul turned and was looking at a very attractive young lady with a lovely smile. She had long dark hair, a very pretty face and what looked like a slim body under a large baggy jumper and jeans.

He was trying to remember if he'd met her before, but couldn't recognise the girl at all.

"Sorry," he said. "Have we met before?"

"Paul, you don't recognise me?" she asked in surprise. "Seriously?"

"I'm sorry," Paul stammered.

"I'm not surprised. I was blonde last time you saw me and I'm not wearing any make-up. We do know each other very well, believe me. I was so sorry to hear about Emma."

Paul was intrigued but was also getting mildly annoyed.

"Paul, it's *me!*" she told him. "Lexi."

The club owner was shocked. "Oh my God! Sorry, I just didn't recognise you—you look great! And yes, we do know each other very well indeed."

Paul almost blushed when he thought back to the Starlight Club and watching Lexi dance, and also remembered the visits to his flat in Chelsea Harbour. Paul was almost speechless—he couldn't believe his eyes.

"So, what are you doing now?"

"I'm studying for my Masters at uni."

Paul wasn't altogether sure what that exactly meant but it sounded very academic.

"What subject, Lexi?"

"English." Lexi felt so embarrassed when she thought back to the erotic dancing she'd performed at the Starlight Club and the threesomes at Chelsea with Paul and Emma.

"I only ever worked the clubs so I could pay my way through uni. It really was a means to an end."

"I honestly didn't recognise you. I'm so sorry."

"I'm a very different person to the Lexi you knew before, believe me. Only the name's the same."

Paul liked what he saw: a serious and very beautiful young lady.

She interrupted his thoughts: "Look, I've got to go to a lecture." She fumbled in her huge bag, took out a pen and paper and wrote her mobile number on it and gave it to Paul. "I live in Fulham if you would like to, you know, umm, meet up or something."

Paul took the paper. "I would like to meet up again. I'll call you."

Lexi turned and took a few steps, turned back, smiled and waved. Paul hadn't moved. He was watching her walking off. He was remembering the frantic and incredible sensual sex the three of them had enjoyed before. Thoughts of Emma suddenly brought him up short. *Better get on with my acting like a tourist*, he thought.

Paul wandered around for a further half an hour and then decided to call it a day. Duke picked him up and they headed back to Soho, and during the journey Paul was thinking about Lexi and wondering when he should call her.

CHAPTER 19

Tony Bolton had really had enough of the circus that was Broadmoor Psychiatric Hospital. He didn't think he was ill and he had no intention of staying in there for the rest of his life. It seemed as if all of his waking life was occupied by talking to the forensic psychiatrists, social workers, psychologists, psychotherapists, occupational therapists, nurses and security staff.

However, he now had something else to think about. And that delightful something was Dr Sharon Travis, the gorgeous redhead with the sparkling green eyes. Recently he had stopped jerking himself off altogether and put his flagging libido down to his medication. But nothing could have stopped him wanking now, after she had grabbed his balls following the meeting he'd had with Dr Thompson, the first time he'd met her.

He couldn't stop thinking about her or wondering how it could be possible to get her on her own. Something akin to a miracle was needed, he thought.

Tony would have been gratified to know that Sharon Travis had gone home after their brief meeting and pleasured herself mercilessly with her dildo for thirty minutes, all the while imagining that Tony was in charge of the action. She had the hots for him and was thinking exactly the same thing as he was: how she could engineer it so that they could get together?

Sharon seemed to have a split personality: she was good at her job and very professional, but when it came to men she was greedy and voracious. She was a member of various sex clubs in Leeds, Manchester, Liverpool, Bradford and London. She dressed up in outrageous clothes and at the weekends, she thought nothing of having sex with multiple men in a single night.

The problem she had now was how to get that big bastard Tony on his own so that she could fuck the living daylights out of him. It would be difficult, because rules stated a female member of staff could never be alone with a patient. But she was sure that it was certainly not impossible.

Dr Travis thought Tony was an interesting character but lacked gravitas, compared to Peter Sutcliffe—the 'Yorkshire Ripper', or paranoid schizophrenic David Copeland, better known as the infamous 'London Nail Bomber', both of whom were also residents of Broadmoor.

The lady doctor decided that their first liaison would have to be at the weekend when staff numbers were dramatically reduced. Maybe a Saturday night, when there could be some sort of recreational dance or a film show. She consulted the Broadmoor Staff Newsletter and scanned through it, looking for the Saturday night entertainments. Next Saturday there was a film show: 'From

Russia with Love'. Well she wasn't Russian but she could manage the love. Although she much preferred the word 'shag'.

Tony was walking along one of the miles of corridors towards the canteen when he saw Dr Sharon Travis coming towards him. She looked so fucking sexy in that tight black skirt and white blouse that he could feel his cock getting hard, even when she was still twenty yards away.

"Ah, Mr Bolton, how are you?" Sharon asked.

"Hello Sharon," Tony replied. "I thought we were on first-name terms now?"

"Of course we are Tony. I'll see you at the film show on Saturday then." She then marched off, leaving Tony to gape after her. *So it was going to happen at the film show! Shit! I can't wait*, he thought excitedly.

Saturday night came round and Tony had never experienced anticipation like it. He hadn't had a woman in months, and he hoped he was not going to be disappointed. The film shows were held in one of the halls where a large screen was unveiled in front of rows of hard-backed chairs laid out in lines.

The show started bang on 7 p.m. and there must have been thirty-odd patients in attendance—apparently James Bond was a good draw, judging by the larger than average turnout. Tony was sitting on the edge of an aisle next to a large pillar. There were doors at regular intervals around the sides of the hall and one of these was opposite where Tony was sitting. He thought, correctly, that they would all be locked. He kept looking around to see if Sharon was in the hall, but by the interval, she still hadn't turned up. He thought she wasn't coming and sat back to enjoy the film as it restarted for the second half.

Sharon had already looked into the hall to see where Tony was sitting and she was delighted when she saw he was on the end of an aisle near the wall. She casually left the hall and made her way round the side of the building to the door which was opposite where Tony was sitting.

Tony was stretching his neck when he heard a hiss: it came from the door, where he saw the outline of Sharon beckoning him over.

Little did he know, but she had just fucked the key-keeper as a means of getting him to lend her the key for half an hour.

Tony slunk down low in his seat and covered the two feet to the open doorway in a second. He went through it and quietly shut the door behind him.

"So, let's see what you've got Tony," Sharon whispered excitedly as she undid his belt and pulled the zip down on his trousers. He pushed them right down to his feet and his huge erection sprang out from the slit in his underpants.

Mesmerised by his large erect pole, she grasped it, then quickly pushed his underpants down his legs to join the trousers, using the opportunity to press her body up against him. "Oh Tony, this is big!" she declared. "I just love it!" She then knelt down in front of him, took his penis into her mouth and sucked greedily.

Tony moaned in ecstasy.

She broke away to speak urgently, a string of saliva, or Tony's pre-cum, hanging from her lips: "We have to hurry." She was gasping for air, her face flushed and her eyes alight with excitement as she looked up at him. She stood up and turned to face the wall, then lifted up her skirt. Tony saw she had no knickers on and grabbed her arse cheeks with his hands. Standing pressed up behind her, he entered her wet opening hard and fast. She moaned as he started pumping away.

"Harder, *harder Tony!*" she begged, panting faster.

Tony was pumping for all he was worth, wallowing in the ecstatic sensations he hadn't enjoyed for so long now. Then suddenly he found he couldn't stop himself. He came abruptly and with hardly any warning, squirting a massive gush of cum inside her, yelling, "*Ahhhhhhhh!*"

"Sssssh Tony, God, do you want us to get caught?" she hissed urgently.

"Sorry, but it's been such a long time."

"Get back to your seat, quickly."

Tony opened the door an inch and looked in. It was so dark that nobody could possibly see him and he was back in his chair in one second. He relaxed, taking deep breaths, realising that he was out of condition and knackered. He stuck his fingers under his nose and could smell Sharon's wetness on his skin. It was really delicious. Next time, he thought, I will need more time and then of course, even though she may not realise it now, Dr Sharon Travis was going to help him escape from this hell hole.

CHAPTER 20

The Audi pulled into Queen Elizabeth Street at Butlers Wharf, Bermondsey, and halfway along, turned into a disused old warehouse. It was a cavernous area, the size of a football pitch with small rooms, which must have been offices, on both sides. Dave drove the Audi right to the far end of the space and parked up outside one of these little offices. He had to wake Matt and Pauly up as both had been sleeping for hours. They got out, yawning and stretching.

"We better see how that cunt is inside the boot," said Dave, as he went round to the rear of the car. He released the catch and the lid flew open. The stench hit him like a tornado, and Dave stumbled back.

"Fucking hell! That's all we need," he yelled. "He's shit himself!"

They left him for ten minutes while the smell dissipated and then all three went back to have a look at the man. There was blood everywhere but he was wide eyed and awake. Dave took his hands and Pauly grabbed his ankles and they heaved him up and threw him onto the concrete floor. He hit the ground with a sickening thud and crack, as though a bone had been broken.

Toby Banks knew he was going to die. The only thing he prayed for was that it would be quick and as painless as possible.

"What's your name, shitface?" Pauly demanded.

"Water!" Toby whispered hoarsely.

"You didn't give any water to Jack and Mary Coombs, you fucking cunt!" Matt said, and brought his foot back and kicked him in the stomach, which brought a painful gasp from the prone man.

Dave came off the phone, walked across and took Pauly to one side. "Paul's on his way, we're to tidy him up."

"Tidy him up? What the fuck for?" Pauly was incredulous.

"Give him some water and a sandwich from the car."

Pauly and Dave dragged Toby into one of the side rooms and sat him on an old hard-backed chair.

"Just put a bullet in my head for God's sake. Please! Do it now! Let's get it done."

Dave smiled, looking at Toby. "I don't think it's going to be that easy for you son. I just hope you're ready for it."

"God and Jesus help me," Toby said to himself, fearing the worst. "Who are we waiting for then?" he asked feebly, with fear in his eyes.

"Seeing as you're asking, we are waiting for someone who was very close to Jack and Mary and who was distraught at the way you treated them," Dave told him.

"It was nothing personal, just work." *This is getting worse*, Toby thought.

They heard a car and Dave went out to meet Paul. Duke and Paul got out of the car in the company of another man who Dave didn't recognise. Hands were shaken and Paul thanked Dave for doing a good job. He told all three of them they would be getting an envelope very soon. Dave knew that meant cash so he was well pleased. The man with Paul was introduced as Tommy.

"What's his name?" asked Paul, looking at Dave.

"Toby Banks. It was him and his brother who, you know…"

"Yeah, OK, that's good," Paul told him. "So what condition is he in?"

"I think he's got a broken wrist but apart from that, he's OK," Dave explained.

"Well he won't be soon. Let's go." They entered the office.

Paul stood in front of Toby, looking down at him for a few seconds before speaking: "So you're the one who likes to torture defenceless innocent women?"

"Actually," he gabbled urgently, "that was my brother Graham. I was more involved with Jack. Please, it was work, nothing more."

"Yeah, but you seemed to enjoy it a bit too much," Paul said.

"We were well paid."

"Richard Philips is a generous sort of man, eh?"

Paul turned to the man next to him. "Toby, this is Tommy. Tommy say hello."

Tommy looked at Toby and just smiled evilly.

Toby was *really* shitting himself now. *This Tommy geezer looks fucking scary, with a face like one of those Dracula actors*, he thought.

"Let's get started," said Paul loudly.

Tommy went out to the car and came back into the room carrying a box. Toby was now petrified and couldn't take his eyes away from it.

Paul's companion had now assumed command of the room. He looked at Pauly, saying, "You, clean the windows and make a good job of it. Leave one open a couple of inches." Pauly had no idea why he had to do so, but he got some water and started doing as he was told.

"Now strip him," commanded Tommy, looking at Matt and Dave.

Matt and Dave roughly stripped Toby, trying to avoid touching his soiled trousers.

"Hold him tight." Matt and Pauly held his arms behind the chair.

Tommy took out a syringe and without any prevarication, rammed the needle into Toby's arm. The prisoner flinched and tried to struggle. It was a mild sedative which would allow them to do the initial work without too much aggravation.

"Lie him on the floor."

Toby was pushed to the floor, so that he was lying, face upwards.

"Hold him."

Tommy took a hammer and eight six-inch nails out of the box. He then took hold of Toby's left hand and hammered the first nail through the palm into the floorboards. There was a gasp from Toby as he felt the pain shoot up his arm. Tommy then took a second nail and repeated the process with his other hand. He then splayed Toby's feet and did the same thing with a nail hammered into each foot.

Toby was watching all this as it was happening and, because of the sedative, was only feeling part of the pain. But within a few minutes, the effect of the sedative was starting to wear off slowly, around the time when Tommy started work on Toby's feet and legs. He cut slashes and pulled back the skin with a pair of pliers, ripping it off in lengths.

Soon, the feet resembled a piece of meat you would see at the butchers. Tommy worked his way up the legs, stopping at the knees. Toby was now screaming in terrible pain and floating in and out of consciousness. Tommy then slashed deep cuts into Toby's arms, crotch, torso and head.

Paul, Matt, Pauly and Dave were watching the operation. This will be the last time I'll ever authorise something like this, Paul thought to himself, feeling sick. He could hardly watch.

Next, Tommy took a jar of honey out of the box and a small paintbrush. He dipped the brush into the honey and then proceeded to paint Toby's wounds with it. He then trickled honey from his feet spreading out onto the floorboards and did the same thing spreading honey on his head, and allowing it to bleed out onto the wooden floor.

Tommy gathered all his bits together and smiled. "Why don't we go and get some lunch?"

Paul wasn't sure if he could eat anything but he was happy to get out of the room. They all piled into his car and headed off to a café.

Toby was still floating in and out of consciousness. He could feel an excruciating and searing pain and could barely breathe whenever he regained consciousness. He was so traumatised, each time he welcomed the next blacking out. He was lying flat on his back, crucified on the floorboards. He could just about lift his head a little, which he did and looked down.

To his horror he could see one or two ants scurrying around his ankles and then flies started to land on his legs and body. He dropped his head back and felt an itch in his hair and shook his head from side to side which stopped the irritation, but only for a second. He rested for a minute or two and lifted his head again. He stared, wide-eyed as thousands of ants and flies started feasting on the honey that was plastered all over his wounds.

Then he felt an increasing itchiness in his toes, as the ants began to eat their way into his flesh. He didn't realise it at the time but the flies were laying larvae into his wounds—these would become maggots, which in turn would eat at his rotting flesh. His bowels opened and a stream of shit added to the horror all around him.

He closed his eyes and prayed for death. A multitude of insects were now climbing all over his body and face: huge bluebottles, flies and wasps were crawling into his nose, mouth, ears and anus, laying larvae as they dug into the soft flesh. He started shivering and crying, for he knew it would take hours, perhaps even days for him to die while he was being eaten alive by thousands of maggots and insects.

Whilst trying to breathe, he was now swallowing hundreds of insects and flies, resulting in regular bowel excavations until he was virtually swimming in shit. He was trying to spit the insects out of his mouth, but in the end he gave up and decided it might hasten his death if he swallowed as many of them as he could. For the first time in his life, he was praying for the merciful release of death.

Three hours later, Paul and the others returned. Tommy suggested that they should go round the outside of the building and look in through the window, rather than enter the room. Oh, thought Pauly, that's why I had to clean the window. They walked round the side of the building and approached the one clean window in the whole length of the warehouse. As they got closer, they saw hundreds of flies buzzing around and ant trails disappearing off into the distance. Matt, Dave and Pauly stopped short of the room window, while Tommy and Paul kept going and finally looked into the room.

The sight that greeted them was beyond comprehension. Toby's whole body was covered with insects and flies; there must have been hundreds of thousands of them. Every other second, an arm or a leg would twitch and lift up slightly and then Toby would lift his head and spit to evacuate his mouth, then his head would fall back and swarms of flies and other insects would attack his face and mouth once again.

Paul didn't want to be a part of this anymore. He turned to the Three Amigos. "Someone give me a gun," he ordered.

Matt handed him his pistol. Paul opened the window a bit more and took aim at Toby's head. There was an explosion as Paul fired. He shot Toby in the head with three bullets. The flies all rose up like a blanket from Toby's body at the sound of the gun. Paul, Tommy, Matt, Dave and Pauly couldn't get back to the car quickly enough.

* * *

Paul was back in his office and was sipping a glass of his favourite Prosecco. He vowed there and then that he would take his business legitimate whatever the cost. If that meant paying Richard Philips five million, so be it. The brothels would have to go and they would be easy to get rid of. He had already sold his stock of guns that he used to hire out, so that was a step in the right direction.

Clubs. That was where the future was, he realised. Clubs in London. He filled his glass and picked up the piece of paper on his desk, on which was written the name 'Lexi' next to her telephone number. He looked at it for a full minute before putting it down again.

He wanted to call Lexi but he hesitated, feeling confused. Because whenever he thought of Lexi, he would be reminded of Emma. Maybe Emma would be happy if he got together with Lexi, he thought? But, considering it logically, how could Emma be happy when she was dead? His head was a mess again. He cleared his mind and carried on with thinking about who he could sell the brothels to. He would leave early today, but he had one very important call to make. He dialled the number and held the receiver to his ear.

"Mary, it's Paul," he said. "How are you?"

"Oh, hello Paul. I'm very well thank you. It's so nice to hear from you."

"Is Peter looking after you?"

"Oh my goodness, he fusses over me like you wouldn't believe. Between you and me though, I love it and I'm so pleased he's here."

"That's good Mary. Look, I rang with a bit of news. I know you're moving on and trying to forget the past, but I wanted to tell you that those two animals have been dealt with. And I'm talking permanently."

"You know what Paul? I hate to say it, but I hope they suffered for what they did to my Jack."

"Mary, you can be sure that they suffered a great deal. Now, onto happier subjects. The weather's lovely. What are you doing this weekend?"

"You know exactly what I'll be doing: my beautiful roses need a lot of love and attention so I'll be in the garden for two days solid."

"Sounds wonderful," Paul replied, pleased at her attitude. "And remember, if you need anything, please just let me know. Anything at all, OK?"

"I will Paul, thank you so much for calling. Bye."

CHAPTER 21

Chau was completely fed up. The young girl who'd been successfully treated to cure her drug addiction had recovered well, and couldn't wait to get out of Newham General Hospital. The staff were great, even the food was OK, but she just wanted some space so she could begin to get on with her life. The doctors were keen for her to stay in a bit longer but, in truth, there was nothing much wrong with her physically.

Karen had managed to get Chau accepted onto the Witness Protection Scheme with a review after three months, and what would happen then, would depend on how the case against her enemies was progressing. Two of the people traffickers were in custody, with only Bujar Dushka still on the run. Karen could see Chau being in protection for a minimum of twelve months and maybe even longer. The Chinese woman had a stubborn streak and a toughness that belied her tiny stature. She was a determined young lady and when she said she would see the case through to trial, Karen believed that she would.

Chau had packed her small case and was placing it in the boot of Karen's mini. There was an unmarked car behind Karen, with three heavily armed police officers, prepared for any trouble. They set off for the safe house which was on the Isle of Wight. It was a fairly long journey and would also take in a ferry crossing from Portsmouth to Ryde. Karen had managed to swing a four-day pass for the outing and was going to treat it like a mini holiday.

Karen had headed straight down the A13 and onto the M25. They crossed the Queen Elizabeth Bridge and zoomed round to the turn-off for the A3 road to Portsmouth. It was only 11 a.m. and the rush hour had gone so traffic was light, which made a huge difference. They stopped at the Liphook Motorway Services and had a Costa Coffee in the Shell petrol station's forecourt.

From then on, it was all plain sailing all the way to Portsmouth and Karen then followed the signs for the Wightlink Ferry Terminal. They booked in and then sat in the car waiting to board for the twenty-two-minute crossing. The police escort left them and made its way back to London.

Chau was excited. She didn't know where they were going but when she saw the sea she was positively jumping up and down. Karen considered Chau to be a charming and lovely young lady. Eventually they drove aboard the ferry. Karen secured the car and they made their way up to the decks. Chau wanted to see the whole ship and was dragging Karen from pillar to post as she rushed from deck to deck. Finally Chau had seen enough and the two of them went to the restaurant for a snack. Chau became even more excited upon seeing spring rolls on the menu, one of her favourites. She was starving and ordered six.

Karen as usual was watching her weight and stuck to a large latte.

The two women got on really well. Karen found Chau's broken English very endearing and, as Karen was so much taller than Chau, she felt an instinctive desire to be her protector. They arrived in Ryde and they then headed along the road to Cowes. It was a glorious day and driving through the country lanes was exhilarating for Karen and so different from dusty, dirty Bermondsey.

Finally they arrived in Cowes and made for Baring Road. Karen thanked the Lord for satnavs as the their own had directed them to right outside number 32. It was a three-bedroom bungalow with a view out over the sea.

Chau jumped out of the car and ran to the front door. She turned to Karen, saying, "Come on! Hurry, hurry please!"

Karen laughed and quickly opened the front door. Chau ran round, opening the entrance to every room and looking inside. She then shouted excitedly: "This is my room! This is my room!" Karen followed her inside.

"Wow!" Karen said. "Beautiful view from the window."

"Yes, I like see the sea. Oh, I'm so happy!"

"My room's nice as well, but no view for me," said Karen feigning hurt.

"Oh no, you stay here. We share," Chau replied decisively.

Karen looked at the bed. "The bed is too small for both of us. Don't worry, I will be perfectly happy next door."

"Are you sure Miss Karen?"

"Perfectly. And why don't you just call me Karen instead of 'Miss Karen'?"

"OK, Miss... Oh... Karen." And they both laughed as Karen went back to her room to unpack.

By the time they finished unpacking, it was 5 p.m. and both women were hungry. Chau said she would like to cook if that was alright with Karen. The detective was delighted at the prospect of home cooking, so they drove into Cowes town centre and found the local Tesco supermarket. Chau went round the store, slowly filling her trolley with endless products of every type. Karen made sure there were a couple of bottles of red wine. She paid and they made their way back to Baring Road.

Soon, Chau was busy in the kitchen while Karen sat in the lounge sipping a glass of red wine, watching the news on the old television. The aromas coming from the kitchen were incredible: ginger, soy, chilli, and even peanut. Karen was so looking forward to a good hot meal.

In thirty minutes the food was ready and Karen and Chau sat in the small dining room. Karen marvelled at the hot and sour fish soup which was followed by a delicious spicy chicken salad.

"Chau, this is lovely! You must do all the cooking from now on!"

"I love cooking Karen, and I like very much to cook for you. We friends now so I try make you very happy."

Karen picked up the bottle of red and was surprised to see it was empty. "Oh God, I seem to have finished the first bottle."

"Open other bottle. After all you on holiday, Miss Karen."

"Well, just one more glass then." She went to the kitchen and returned with the opened bottle.

Chau jumped up. "We go in lounge and be comfortable."

They sat next to each other on the sofa and Chau lifted her legs and placed them on Karen's lap. "You do not mind Karen? I stretch for a minute."

"No, I don't mind at all." Karen then took one of Chau's tiny feet and started gently massaging it.

"Oh, that *lovely*, Karen." Chau stretched back in ecstasy. Karen massaged the other foot and at the same time was slowly getting through the second bottle of wine.

"Now your turn, Karen." Chau left the lounge and went to her room. She opened a small chest of drawers and took out a smallish bottle and returned to the lounge.

"OK, Karen, now I give you special Vietnamese massage. You do as I say and you enjoy very much. I promise."

Karen was slightly tipsy now and replied, slurring her words a little: "Great, I'm all yours."

She laid back on the sofa as Chau sat very close to her. She gently undid the first button on Karen's blouse and then the next and the next, until eventually they were all undone and Chau slipped the blouse off. She looked enviously and admiringly at Karen's full pert breasts.

"I wish my breasts like that," she muttered sadly. "Mine like pancakes."

Karen stirred. "Don't worry about it. You are a gorgeous, beautiful woman."

Chau then slipped Karen's skirt off so she was left in matching black knickers and bra. She then stretched round Karen's back and undid the bra and took it off. Karen's naked breasts were exposed in all their glory.

"Lie on stomach please Karen."

Karen did as she was told and turned over. Chau opened the small bottle and tipped some oil into her palms and then started at the shoulders, gently massaging her skin and muscles.

"Oh thash goosh," slurred Karen.

"I know you like Karen, is very nice yes?"

"Yeshh, very nishe and relaxshing indeed."

Chau massaged gently and then more firmly as she worked her way down Karen's back. She then pulled her knickers down a little more, revealing her arse cheeks and crack. She massaged oil into her arse and Karen was loving every minute of it. Eventually Chau worked her way down Karen's legs, finishing with her feet.

"Turn over."

Karen followed the instruction and turned. Her breasts flattened out due to gravity, but they still looked fabulous. Chau took more oil and started to massage Karen's breasts. The nipples stood out firm and erect as Chau gently ran her hands over her mammary flesh. She continued massaging down and over her belly button. She again folded the knickers down to reveal that Karen's pubic area was very smooth. Chau massaged a little bit more and then got to the legs and eventually to her feet.

"I finish Karen. Was good for you?" she said, laughing.

Karen was also laughing, and she had sobered up a bit. "Oh, it was good for me alright. Are there any men about? I could do with one."

Karen thought for a second back to when Placido had given her a massage on her last visit to Spain. It had been good, but Chau's massage was better, without question. The English woman then decided to take a shower and disappeared into her room to get ready for bed. Chau was watching television when she heard the shower come on.

After a few minutes, Chau stood up and went towards her room. Karen came out of the bathroom with a towel wrapped round her at the same time and was standing in front of Chau. The tiny woman giggled and grabbed the bottom of the towel and pulled.

It came away, leaving Karen stark naked. Karen screamed and ran towards her room, closely followed by Chau. Karen jumped on her bed and lay with her head on the headboard, Chau was close behind her and launched herself onto the bed as well. Karen kicked her legs in the air to push Chau back and unwittingly revealed her pussy. Chau noticed but then quickly retreated to the end of the bed and giggled.

"Now you win Miss Karen," she challenged playfully. "But next time, I get you!"

Chau went to have her own shower and then got ready for bed. She was very tired after the long trip and all the excitement. Karen made sure all the windows and doors were locked, stuck her head into Chau's doorway and said goodnight.

Much later, Karen lifted her head from the pillow. She could hear screaming from Chau's room. She grabbed her gun and forgetting she was naked, rushed out of her door and into Chau's room. There was no one there, but Chau was apparently having a terrible nightmare, shouting and screaming in her sleep. Karen rushed across and sat on the side of the bed, took Chau in her arms and gently stroked her hair.

"It's OK Chau. Karen is here to look after you, shhhh baby, shhhhh."

Chau opened her eyes and then moved to the side of the single bed. She held her hand out and Karen took it and climbed in beside her. Karen felt Chau's nakedness under the covers as they looked into each other's eyes.

Karen turned over away from Chau. Chau immediately cuddled up to Karen's back and moulded herself to her body. They were both tired and Karen started drifting off to sleep. But not before she felt Chau's tiny hands gently caress her breasts and then move down much lower. She didn't mind.

It was a wonderful way to fall asleep.

CHAPTER 22

Paul had finally done it. He had called Lexi and invited her to have dinner with him at The Den. Lexi had said she would be delighted and they agreed to meet on the next Saturday night at 8 p.m.

Lexi had spent a long time deciding on what she was going to wear, but very little time on her make-up. She was a naturally beautiful young woman and heavy make-up belonged very much to her past, to the days when she had been working as a lap dancer.

Paul was both excited and concerned. He was excited because he knew what an incredibly sexy woman Lexi was, and concerned because of all the memories associated with Lexi and Emma, and their intimate threesomes. Paul had decided to meet her anyway, and if anything was going to happen between them, then it would have to happen slowly.

Lexi was fashionably fifteen minutes late and was looking stunning. She was wearing a plain black minidress with a bright orange coat. Paul was taken aback as he suddenly realised that he could easily develop deep feelings for this girl. Because Lexi was a sort of modern-day Grace Kelly: tall graceful and looking so serene most of the time.

They started the meal with best quality expensive chilled Prosecco. Paul gave a quick thought to Emma as the wine touched his lips. He admired Lexi as she sipped her drink. Food was pretty traditional at The Den; they offered excellent steaks cooked to perfection, with all the trimmings, which was what they both ordered.

"So Lexi, are you glad to be out of the Club Scene?" Paul asked her.

"Paul, I won't lie to you. I was young and wild, it was fun for a time but in the end, all those ghastly old men dribbling as I danced was awful. I decided, no thanks."

"Did you save any money?"

Lexi's face lit up. "Paul, I made a fortune! Some weeks I made three or four thousand pounds."

"Wow! That's good money for dancing."

Paul and Lexi were suddenly quiet for a few seconds.

"Poor Emma. I'm so sorry Paul. Are you getting over it?"

"Yes I am, I still have bad moments but it's getting easier."

"If there's anything I can do, you know, you just have to ask."

"Thank you Lexi." Paul nodded. "I'm feeling a lot stronger now, but I can't say it didn't hit me hard."

Paul and Lexi talked about opera, football, shopping and all sorts of other things.

She looked at him thoughtfully. "Whatever happened to that moron Ryder, the manager at the Starlight?"

Paul had to gather his thoughts quickly. "I heard he went abroad—Spain I think."

"Good riddance, what a horrible man. Have you still got the video tapes?"

"What tapes?"

Lexi thought, *Shit! Now what have I said!* She was silent for a few moments.

"Lexi, what tapes?" Paul was now more than a little interested and worried.

"Oh Christ Paul. Remember the time we were, err, all together in the upstairs room? You, me and Emma?"

"Go on."

"Ryder taped it all on numerous hidden cameras."

"He fucking what! Are you telling me there are tapes of the three of us?"

"Yes there are," Lexi answered miserably. "I thought he must have given them to you. I'd assumed you had asked him to film it."

"No I did not. So I wonder where on earth the films are now."

"I expect Ryder's got them with him in Spain or wherever he is."

Paul knew full well that Ryder wasn't in Spain: he was buried in cement in Bermondsey.

So, he wondered frantically, *what had the bastard done with the tapes?"*

Paul could hardly concentrate for five minutes. Sex tapes of him, Emma and Lexi! Jesus! *Could it get any worse*, he thought?

"Paul?"

"Sorry Lexi, I was miles away."

"No problem Paul. So what plans have you got for the future?"

"Well, business wise, I'm going legit. We have a couple of businesses to get rid of and then we can concentrate on building up the clubs."

"I'm so pleased to hear that Paul. You don't need all that aggro. When you're legit, you can stop looking over your shoulder all the time."

Lexi had been brought up in a happy family that believed strongly in Christian values. She may have gone off the rails a bit during her 'lap dancing phase', but she didn't hurt anyone and her dancing had always been merely a means to an end and strictly short-term. She was what could best be described as a 'good daughter'. She never forgot her weekly phone call home and her monthly visits. She loved going back home to Camberley for a traditional Sunday lunch. Her mum's roast potatoes were to die for, followed by delicious creamy bread-and-butter pudding.

The ex-dancer had one sister who was a year her senior. She hadn't seen her for over two years, since she lived on a commune in North Wales and was very reclusive. Lexi's dad would soon be retiring, having spent forty years working for Surrey Heath Borough Council in the Planning Services Department.

Lexi was more than a little interested in Paul but was conscious that she would have to play it very slowly because Emma's death had been so recent. She decided that she would leave all the running to Paul. However she would, of course, make it plain that she was interested but didn't want to rush things, which, without question, might well backfire.

They finished dinner and Lexi asked Paul to dance. It was a slow Lionel Ritchie number. Paul took Lexi in his arms and held her very close. Paul could smell her perfume, there was something so familiar about it. Oh God, he thought, it's JOY by Jean Patou, *the same perfume that Emma used to wear.* Paul took a step back.

She was surprised at his change of mood. "What's wrong Paul?"

"Nothing. I'm sorry. It's just, are you wearing JOY perfume?"

"Yes someone gave me some for Christmas. It's usually far too expensive for me."

"It was Emma's favourite." He then pulled Lexi back into his arms. "It shows you have good taste as well as being beautiful."

"Thank you. That's the nicest thing you've ever said to me."

They continued to dance and stayed on the floor for the next one, which was another slow number. Paul eventually led Lexi to their table and ordered a bottle of Prosecco.

"I'd like to see you again Lexi," whispered Paul as he held Lexi's hand.

"That would be good Paul. I like you very much. And I understand how you feel. We can take things very slowly."

Paul smiled and kissed Lexi gently on the lips.

"Drink up and then I'll get someone to run you home."

He got one of his trusted security team to drive her home with orders to see her into the flat and to ensure she was safe before he left.

Paul felt that he could be getting serious about Lexi. He wanted to see her again already and she had only been gone ten minutes. Funny that, thought Paul. I fell in love with Emma very quickly too. Hmmm…

* * *

Later that day he was deep in conversation with his chief accountant, Roddy Newman.

"You know the plan to take the business legitimate?" Paul asked. "I want it pushed as hard as you can. How are you getting on with the list of people to approach about the sale of the brothels?"

"It's slow, to be honest, Paul. I can barely keep on top of the business as it is, there's just too much work and not enough people."

"Well, that's your fault. I've told you before, you cannot do everything. If you need to take on staff, do it and delegate," Paul told him.

"It's not that simple Paul—there's a lot of sensitive information. For a start, how much we put through the tills in the clubs. Secondly, we've never declared the brothel earnings and the big trouble is, once you start lying and cheating with HMRC, it's difficult to put things right without getting into a huge amount of trouble."

"I understand all that but I want the brothels sold," Paul insisted. "They must be worth a fortune to the right people. What about Bill Caddy? He's bound to be interested."

"Well, I haven't actually got hold of him yet."

"Jesus Roddy, come on mate! He's always looking for new investments." Paul was tired, and things were moving much too slowly for his liking. "Just get it done and send me a report on your progress next week."

Roddy left in a pretty pissed-off mood, determined to sort the brothel sales as soon as he could.

Paul rubbed his eyes. Video tapes of him Emma and Lexi! *God, could it get any worse*, he thought? Imagine if they surfaced on the internet at some time? Paul made a quick decision and called Angus, one of his most trusted lieutenants, and asked him to pop into his office. Angus arrived within five minutes and Paul explained the situation regarding the tapes.

"Where would I start Paul?" Angus asked reasonably. "They could be in a hundred places or with a hundred different people."

"Yes, I realise that, but I want those tapes. I don't care how long it takes. Drop everything else and concentrate on this. I also don't care what it costs. Just get me the tapes, Angus."

Angus could see that Paul was very serious and understood why. If the tapes were to surface, it would be horrendous, especially for Emma's family, if they ever found out or, God forbid, if they actually viewed them.

"I'll tidy up my loose ends and get started straight away."

"That's what I like to hear. Keep me updated with progress and give me only good news."

Angus made his way back to his office and thought that his latest assignment was going to be as difficult as looking for a needle in the proverbial haystack.

CHAPTER 23

Karen had left the Isle of Wight and was back in her small flat in Rotherhithe that was conveniently near the police station. She had had a great couple of days with Chau and although she felt that Chau was actually in love with her, it was not totally reciprocated. Karen was very fond of Chau and they had slept together for the time she was there, but Karen thought of it more as a sort of sisterly fondness.

However, they had played around a bit sexually, which was certainly a first for Karen and that was clearly not how sisters behaved. Karen had had to promise that she would visit Chau in two weeks' time for the weekend, which was another commitment she didn't really need at the moment. Karen was unhappy and depressed. As well as loving her visits to Spain, she now had another place she would rather be rather than shitty old Bermondsey, and that was the Isle of Wight.

She drew back the curtains and looked out of her window. Cars were roaring past, there were empty crisp packets and plastic coke bottles being swept across the road by a strong wind, an old couple were moving past her flat at a snail's pace, all wrapped up in thick coats and scarves: it was all so fucking depressing.

Karen once again thought of a permanent move to Spain. Placido had begged her to move out and join him in Torremolinos. She thought of the beaches, the permanent sunshine, it was really so very tempting. Just at that moment, she heard shouting and saw a group of teenagers kicking a football on the pavement. The ball flew through the air and smashed the window of a house across the road. She moved away from the window, shaking her head, and sat down wearily. The detective constable knew she was depressed because ordinarily, she would have rushed out and grabbed the kids and made sure they paid for the damage.

The investigation into the people traffickers had hit a brick wall. Yes they had achieved success because they had arrested the two men at the house in Kensal Rise, but Bujar Dushka was still at large and they had no leads as to his whereabouts. Dushka was the one Karen *really* wanted. He was the ringleader and had also killed the three officers at the train-tunnel shooting.

She went into the dingy kitchen and made another coffee, her fourth so far and it was only midday. *Jesus, I've got to snap out of this and get my act together*, she thought.

* * *

Bujar Dushka had not left the house in Hodford Road since he arrived there following the gunfight with the police. His friend Dejan went out to work every day, so Dushka was left alone for long periods. He was too scared to go out and spent most of every day drinking the vodka and whisky that Dejan bought for him.

He'd had a huge argument with Dejan the night before, about the girl Chau. Dushka was obsessed with her and was determined to get his revenge by either selling her to another brothel, or killing her. Dejan had said it was senseless to go after her and to forget her—after all they had no idea where she was. Bujar was sure the police would have done everything they could to keep Chau in the UK so that she could give evidence when Adrjana and Andrea went to court. That would mean they must have put her on the Witness Protection Scheme, and were keeping her somewhere safe, so all he had to do was find out where it was.

Dejan returned from work and Bushka poured him a large whisky, saying, "Dejan, let's not argue anymore about the girl, she's just one bitch, there are millions more."

Dushka's friend took the whisky and downed it in one. "That's funny because I have taken two weeks off work to help you find her."

The other man was surprised. "Are you serious Dejan?"

"Yes, I owe you big time for helping me all those years ago."

"Wonderful Dejan! I am very pleased." To celebrate, Dushka poured two huge glasses of whisky and handed one to Dejan. "Let's get drunk and then we can work out how to get our revenge on the bitch!"

* * *

Chau was lonely and fed up. She had fallen in love with Karen. She had been distraught when Karen had left to go back to the mainland and now she could not stop thinking about her.

The Chinese woman had never before had a relationship with a woman and couldn't believe what had happened between them. She did know that she was in a very delicate state and had been through hell. She recognised that Karen had shown an interest in her wellbeing and no one had done that for a very long time, so she supposed perhaps that was one reason why she had fallen for her. Chau missed her so much, particularly at night. Being tiny, with a flat chest, she was smitten with Karen's tall muscular body and her fabulous breasts. Chau had also started shaving between her legs. When she saw how smooth Karen's private parts were, she wanted to try it for herself. And she loved it.

The young woman who had suffered so much made sure that she went out every day to the shops, and she always cooked herself a freshly prepared meal every evening and spent a long time doing it, as she had nothing else to do. Karen had suggested she take up some hobbies, such as painting or sculpture and maybe even join a couple of groups of fellow enthusiasts on the island.

She was not normally a drinker but had started buying herself a bottle of wine every day. Chau would open it at lunchtime and drink it slowly throughout the day. The problem was that after a few days of doing this, it seemed that the wine was running out before the evening and she had had to open a new bottle, so that she was soon downing two bottles a day. The worst thing was, within a short time, she had stopped showering every morning and her personal hygiene went to pot.

Before she left, Karen had sat down with Chau and explained the security issues that she should be aware of. Karen explained that firstly she had nothing at all to worry about as no one, not even other police officers, knew where she was. Secondly, they had arrested two of the traffickers and the other one, Bujar Dushka, had disappeared.

Karen emphasised how important it was that she was to telephone no one at all, nor could she use her credit cards, and that she had to rely on the generous allowance that was put regularly into a local bank for her.

Finally, she showed Chau where the panic button was: on the side of the bedside lamp in her bedroom. She made it very clear that this was to be used only in an extreme emergency, as its use could blow her cover with the local police in Newport.

The panic button connected directly to the Isle of Wight police station at Newport. The Island police force formed part of the Hampshire Constabulary, and its members usually dealt with nothing more serious than lawnmower thefts and the odd rowdy holidaymaker who was causing trouble.

Chau didn't have a problem with not being allowed to contact anyone, as she only had one friend in the UK—this was an English girl called Sabrina, who had been kind, and helped her settle into the brothel at Peckham. Sabrina lived in Camberwell and was a very strong independent woman who didn't take shit from anyone. Chau had Sabrina's mobile phone number but had no reason to call her.

The Chinese woman had taken up Karen's suggestion to start a hobby and had bought a collection of painting equipment: an easel, paper, canvases, brushes and a set of oil paints were now hers, and she was ready to take up the challenge of learning to paint.

Her first subject was a vase of flowers, which, she thought, didn't turn out too badly. She then progressed to attempting to capture views from the window, which was a great deal more difficult. In the end, it turned out that Chau's habitual drinking meant that all her paintings were somewhat messy and amateurish.

* * *

Bujar and Dejan had sobered up and were discussing how they could locate the girl, Chau, on whom they had focused their hatred. Bujar was clever inasmuch as he was incredibly devious, and he was also very streetwise. He had also travelled the world and had forged relationships with various police forces in different countries.

The crafty Albanian knew that Chau would have been taken away from London, so could therefore be in Scotland, Cornwall, or indeed anywhere in the UK. He knew that the police would keep her location known only to very few specialist officers, so it was reasonable to assume that the people in charge of the case against Adrjana and Andrea would know where she was. It would be easy to find out who those officers were by speaking to the defence lawyer.

Another question was, who else did Chau know? Did she have any friends? They knew she had lived at the brothel in Peckham, so it was likely that over the period of time she had spent there, she would have made a friend or two, and such contacts could also be a route they could investigate.

* * *

It was Wednesday night of Chau's second week on the island. She had polished off two bottles of wine and had been painting a vase that was sitting on a chest of drawers. It had turned out disastrously, and Chau had thrown the painting on the floor, stamped on it and then proceeded to throw paint all over the place as well; the room was a mess.

She opened a third bottle and had one glass which took her over the edge into outright drunkenness. Karen was coming to see her on the Saturday morning, and the prospect of seeing her friend made Chau cry with happiness.

The poor girl desperately wanted to call Karen but knew she could not. So she sat in the lounge, feeling lonely, scared and needing someone, *anyone*. She stood up and went into the hallway, took a diary out of a table drawer, and opened it up to her 'contacts' page. Then she picked up the phone and dialled a number. It rang three times and was then answered, the voice saying, "Hello?"

Chau was crying. "This Chau. I need someone to talk to."

* * *

Bujar and Dejan had phoned Ted Frost, the evil character who used to manage the brothel at Peckham. They had asked him if Chau had had any close friends. Ted told them she only had one friend, and that was a girl called Sabrina. They asked Ted for the girl's address but Ted had prevaricated, mumbling that he might have it but that it would take time to find.

The Albanian was going to threaten him but then changed tack, saying, "Would two grand help you find it very quickly?"

Ted had what he wanted. "I'll call you back with the address in five minutes."

Sabrina lived in one of the numerous massive blocks of council flats in Camberwell. It was Thursday midday, and Bujar and Dejan were heading there to see if Chau's one-time friend and fellow call girl, was in.

* * *

Sabrina had worked at the brothel in Peckham for over a year and had saved a good bit of money, so when it closed she had decided to take a few months off and take it easy. She had no family and had been brought up by countless foster parents and spent time in local council childcare establishments, and this had affected her life immeasurably.

She was really enjoying her time off: it was so good to get up in the morning, knowing that you didn't have to service a load of smelly 'johns' to make a living. She also knew that she would go back to it eventually, because there was nothing else she was equipped to do that paid so well. What she really dreaded was getting to her fifties and still having to make a living on her back. Her life consisted of a procession of fat sweaty johns, accompanied by used condoms, wet wipes, tissues, talcum powder and breath freshener.

The doorbell rang. She wasn't expecting anyone. Perhaps it's the postman, she thought. She opened the door a crack and peeked out. Before she could react, the door was kicked violently, and she flew back into the narrow hallway, hitting her head on the side wall. Stunned, she looked up to see two big burly men come through the front door and shut it behind them. She seemed to recognise one of them, and then it came back to her: he was a pimp who had supplied girls to Ted Frost at Peckham.

"What the fuck do you want, you bastards?" she demanded.

Bujar just looked at her and then turned to Dejan, saying with a smirk: "This bitch needs to learn some manners."

Dejan bent down and grabbed Sabrina's long brown hair, twisting it tight. He then pulled her up and dragged her into the small lounge and threw her onto the grimy sofa.

Bujar was in no mood to take any shit from this bitch. "If you know what's good for you, keep your mouth shut and just answer the questions. Do you know a woman called Chau?"

So that was what they were after, Sabrina thought. She decided she wasn't going to help these bastards. "Never heard of anyone called that. Is it a bloke or a woman?"

Bujar gave her a long hard stare then spoke. "I'm going to give you one last chance to be honest with us or my friend here will start to hurt you. Now. Do you know anyone called Chau?"

"I told you I never fucking heard of anyone by that name."

Bujar looked at Dejan and nodded. Dejan grabbed Sabrina by the throat and squeezed. He then slapped her face with the back of his other hand four times, causing her to almost black out. She was having difficulty breathing but knew they would not kill her, not yet anyway, for they'd come for information. Dejan let go of her and she collapsed onto the sofa.

"Dejan, do you think this bitch is attractive?" Bujar asked.

"Not bad for an old slag I suppose."

"I wonder what she would look like after having a bottle of sulphuric acid thrown in her face?"

Bujar took a bottle out of his coat pocket. It was a brown vessel, the type used for storing medicines. Sabrina looked at the thing with terror in her eyes, for she had no doubt that he would use the acid on her. She began to panic.

"Do you know Chau?" Bujar repeated.

"There may have been someone at Peckham called that, I'm not sure."

"OK. So now we know you know her. Has she been in touch with you recently?"

"I haven't spoken to her since Peckham was closed down," Sabrina told him. "And that's the truth."

"I wonder why I don't believe you?"

Bujar was looking round the small room. He was after something and then he saw it on the dining table—a blackberry mobile phone. He took two steps and picked it up, saying, "Let's see what's on here shall we?" He pressed the phone icon followed by the 'all calls' button. A small list of numbers appeared on the screen. "You don't use your phone much, do you bitch?"

Sabrina was praying. She could see how this might unfold unless she was very lucky.

"Mostly London numbers. But there's one from a 01983 number. Where is that, bitch?"

"No idea. Could have been a wrong number for all I know."

"Hmm, well let's see shall we?" He pressed the call icon.

It was ringing.

"Hello?"

Bujar was shocked as he recognised the broken English voice in his ear. It was without doubt the Chinese girl, Chau. He put on his best English accent and said: "Can I speak to Mr Sean Dyke please?"

Chau replied in her broken English: "There is no one here with that name, you have wrong number."

"Oh I am so sorry, where is that I am ringing?"

"The Isle of Wight," replied Chau. Little did she realise how such an innocent reply was going to alter her life over the next few days.

"My apologies for bothering you. Good bye."

Bujar could not believe it had been so easy. He turned to Dejan and laughed. "Very good!"

Bujar looked at Sabrina. "So fetch us a drink then. What have you got?"

"Vodka and brandy."

"Good, because now the three of us are going to have a little party."

Sabrina fetched the bottles of booze and three glasses. She knew what was going to happen next and a good drink would lessen the pain for her.

Bujar and Dejan sat on the other two chairs in the lounge and sipped their drinks.

At last it started as Bujar said, "Bitch take your clothes off—we want to see you naked."

She stood up and began to move towards the bathroom. "I have to go for a pee first."

Bujar shouted, "No bitch! You do exactly as I say. Nothing more, you understand?"

"Yes."

Sabrina went into work mode, for she was used to doing what she was told and obeying customers' wishes came as second nature to her.

She took off her sweater followed by her jeans, leaving her in only her bra and knickers. The bra came off first, to reveal a still firm pert pair of breasts. Then she then slid her knickers down and threw them onto the sofa. She hadn't shaved her pussy for ages, so she knew it looked a bit untidy.

"So dance a bit then," Bujar told her. "Show us what you got."

Sabrina started swaying from side to side in a rhythmic dance movement.

"Put some music on."

Sabrina put a CD into the player, which turned out to be a compilation of Motown hits.

The two men were beginning to relax and enjoy themselves.

"Sit on the sofa and masturbate for us."

"I really need to pee."

"I'll tell you when you can pee. Now get the fuck on with it!"

Sabrina sat back on the sofa and lifted her legs apart and started to touch herself. She got no pleasure from it but thought that if she put on a good performance they might go easier on her, so she began to moan; she closed her eyes and worked her fingers faster and deeper.

Dejan was getting very excited, partly because he hadn't had a woman for months. Bujar could see in his eyes that his friend was dying for it and he wasn't surprised—she was a good looking bitch. Bujar looked across at Dejan and nodded.

Bujar's friend stood up and approached Sabrina, and she arched her back at him. He didn't want to take his time, he simply pulled his trousers and pants down in one swift movement, allowing his massive erect cock to jump out. He moved between Sabrina's thighs and entered her. She wrapped her legs round Dejan's back, hoping that if she held him tight and pushed, it would be over quicker.

Dejan was in heaven and started shouting: "That's good bitch!" He was slamming into her mercilessly, and after a short time he withdrew, grabbed the back of Sabrina's head, and pushed his cock between her lips and thrust deeply. He came almost immediately, a flood of semen pouring into Sabrina's mouth. She nearly gagged, but, thankfully managed to swallow all his cum. Dejan was delighted. He pulled his trousers up and sat down, then took a good slug of brandy and sat back with a satisfied smile on his face.

"The bitch is tasty. Have a go Bujar."

Sabrina also sat back and relaxed. She took a large gulp of neat vodka, which acted as an anaesthetic. She was now waiting for the second man to take his turn.

"Come and stand in the middle of the room bitch!" ordered Bujar.

Sabrina did as she was told. "Now spread your legs apart and squat a little. Good. Now you can pee."

Sabrina took it all in her stride. She had performed every imaginable perversion for punters at Peckham, and nothing fazed her. She started peeing, a stream of urine pouring out onto the threadbare carpet and splashing everywhere.

"Now play with yourself at the same time."

Sabrina complied as the urine was spraying further and soaking into the carpet and onto chairs. Eventually the stream slowed to a dribble and then stopped. Dejan had enjoyed the show and could feel another big erection developing in his pants.

"It's my turn now Dejan. But how about if we both enjoy her, eh?"

Bujar took hold of Sabrina, turned her round and pushed her down onto all fours. Sabrina knew what was coming next and that it was definitely going to hurt. Bujar climbed underneath her and got his cock out. He grabbed her arse cheeks and guided her down onto his erection. She felt good and Bujar moved slowly to start with and then quickened the pace as he rhythmically entered her.

He then motioned to Dejan and the other man knew straight away what Bujar wanted him to do. He lowered his trousers again and got behind Sabrina's arse. Bujar stopped thrusting while Dejan tried to enter Sabrina's anus—it was so tight and his cock so big that it was proving difficult. Eventually he made it, and Sabrina gasped with pain.

"You like that, don't you, bitch?" shouted Dejan. He then commenced thrusting into her arse while Bujar was pumping her pussy. The two of them got into a rhythm until they both exploded inside her. Then they pulled out.

"Good, bitch!" said Bujar, as though he was talking to a dog.

Sabrina prayed that it would be over soon as they all got to their feet and she sat down back on the sofa and had another large vodka. The two men continued to drink and then told Sabrina to get them something to eat. She made them some ham-and-mustard sandwiches, which was all she had to offer. They ate their sandwiches and drank more brandy until the bottle was empty.

Bujar had one more job for Sabrina.

"Come here bitch and sit on your knees," he ordered.

The two men stood up and got their cocks out and stuffed them both into Sabrina's mouth. They then took turns to be sucked off. Dejan came first followed by Bujar, then they both sat back down and looked at the woman they'd abused.

Bujar spoke: "Time for us to go." He picked up the bottle of acid and held it out in front of Sabrina's face.

"Now listen bitch. No one hears about this, you understand?"

"Yes, I understand."

"If we should have to see you again we will blind you and disfigure you with acid. Believe me, it would be worse than death."

"I've been round the block," Sabrina assured him. "I understand, I promise."

Bujar smiled at her. "Good." They made their way to the front door and left.

Sabrina took a deep breath and collapsed in a heap—the silent prayers had worked. She cried and thanked God for saving her life. She had thought they would kill her. And they were correct in one of their assumptions: she had no intention of telling anyone about what had just happened.

"So Bujar, what next?" Dushka asked his friend as they walked back to the car.

Bujar threw the brown medicine bottle of water into a bin. "What next? We are going to the Isle of Wight of course. Saturday morning, we get the ferry."

* * *

Karen left Rotherhithe early on the Saturday. She wasn't sure if she actually wanted to see Chau. If Michael, who was the head of Rotherhithe CID, ever found out she had visited the vulnerable girl, she would be in deep shit. She hadn't even dared to tell Jeff, her partner, who certainly would have told her it was a big mistake, but of course he wouldn't 'shop' her to their superiors.

It was seventy-five miles to Portsmouth and should take two hours and five minutes, according to the satnav. She was booked on the 11 a.m. ferry and had left at 8 a.m. just in case there were traffic delays. Karen shot past Bermondsey Tube station and was soon at the Elephant and Castle. She hoped the whole journey would be as clear as this part.

It then seemed to be a succession of driving past underground stations: Stockwell, Balham, Tooting Bec, Colliers Wood and South Wimbledon. But it was then a clear run down the A3 onto the M275 super highway and there was the sign to Portsmouth & the Ferry Terminal: a great run.

She looked at the dash to see the time: 9.51 a.m., so it had taken under two hours—a good result. At the Ferry Terminal the traffic marshals directed Karen to one of the lines where she found herself second from the front. First-on last-off, she said to herself, shaking her head. She then locked the car and made for the on-site cafeteria. A mug of steaming hot coffee and a chocolate croissant were just what she needed and she relaxed with the *Vogue* magazine she had brought with her.

It was 10.30 a.m. when Bujar and Dejan pulled into the queue at the Ferry Terminal. They were near the back of one of the queues, and Bujar laughed. "You see," he commented, "it is our lucky day Dejan—last-on first-off!"

Bujar looked at his watch. "Quickly, go and get some coffees Dejan."

Dejan dashed off towards the cafeteria and was there in three minutes. As he passed beside the tables towards the serving counter, he noticed an attractive woman in tight jeans and a white shirt with the cuffs rolled up. An image of Sabrina flashed through his mind, and he looked at the woman again and wished that he could do the same with her as he had done with that bitch. He licked his lips, savouring the memory.

Karen glanced at Dejan as he passed her table. She may have smiled if the man had been handsome, but he certainly wasn't, so she buried her head in the magazine again.

Dejan left with his two coffees and returned to where Bujar was waiting. Karen glanced at her watch: it was time to go. She stood up and made her way back to her car and waited in line to drive onto the ferry.

Once the ferry set sail, Bujar and Dejan quickly found the bar, ordered two beers and found a place to relax for the short journey.

Karen found a comfy chair with a sea view and settled down with her latest read, *Alchemist* by Peter James, a story about a pharmaceutical company that was up to no good. The crossing was over in no time at all and the tannoy system announced that passengers should go back to their vehicles and wait to disembark for Ryde.

Dejan's silver Ford Mondeo was the fifth car to roll down the ramp. He drove for thirty yards and pulled over into a layby and the two Albanians sat there and began to talk about how they were going to find Chau. Bujar was all for visiting post offices and enquiring after an oriental woman who was a good friend of theirs. Dejan said there must be a hundred post offices and that they could never get round them all in a few days. Dejan was in the middle of talking when he suddenly moved closer to the window and watched a mini that was approaching.

"Bujar, take a look at this bitch, she's very sexy," Dejan said, leering at her. "I saw her in the café at the Terminal."

Bujar turned and casually glanced out of the window at the mini which was almost on top of them. He could not believe his eyes.

"JESUS!" he shouted and ducked down quickly. "That's the fucking copper I saw when they took Adrjana and Andrea. She must be going to see Chau. Quick Dejan, don't lose her!"

The driver turned the ignition key, but nothing happened. "Not now for fuck's sake!" he shouted angrily. He turned it again and the engine spluttered and coughed and then a cloud of smoke enveloped the car as the engine finally started and he revved up. They were a couple of vehicles behind Karen's mini, which was an ideal position to be in for them.

"Dejan, I'm keeping low," he said urgently. "I don't want her to see me or the game's up. I can't believe our luck! Seriously, God or someone is on our side today."

Dejan laughed. He was thinking of fucking the copper. Oh how he would enjoy that—fucking a fucking copper!

Karen took the Cowes road and began to look forward to seeing Chau. She was crawling along and did not notice the Ford Mondeo following her. She soon pulled up outside number 32, Baring Road and looked up at the bungalow.

Suddenly, the door opened and Chau came running up the path towards her, shouting, "Karen! Karen!"

Karen got out of the car and, before she knew it, Chau had launched herself at her, throwing her arms round her neck and nearly knocking her over. The Chinese girl grabbed hold of Karen's hand and almost dragged her down the path towards the front door.

"Karen, how have you been?" she asked eagerly. "Did you have good journey? I cook nice meal for us. Did you bring any wine?"

"Chau stop talking for one minute please!" Karen told her.

"Sorry. Just I please to see you, I lonely here, you know."

They entered the front door and Chau gave Karen one of her little-lost-girl looks and Karen couldn't help but smile. The police officer then shocked herself—she pulled Chau in close to her and kissed her passionately on the lips. After a minute she stopped and Chau was in shock.

"That is very nice Karen, I looking forward to you coming. Come and tell me all your news." She pulled Karen into the lounge and they plonked themselves down on the sofa.

The Mondeo moved past the bungalow. Bujar was ducked down in the front so that no one could see him. "What number is it Dejan?" he asked.

"Thirty-two."

"Now, all we do is wait for the police bitch to leave and we take the other one. Let's find somewhere to stay and get a meal and some drinks inside us." Bujar was in a very good mood and could not believe how lucky they had been.

The detective was telling Chau about life as a copper and Chau was looking at her, spellbound. Chau didn't have much to say to her, as life on the Island was boring for her, apart from her new-found hobby of painting.

"Karen, you go get stuff from car, have shower, I get dinner ready."

Chau had prepared a fabulous meal of Sichuan style 'gong bao chicken' which was chicken with a sticky sweet-and-sour chilli sauce and peanuts. She had also prepared some special fried rice and dumplings to go with the feast.

Karen showered and dressed in a beige coloured kaftan, which was comfortable to relax in. Chau was in one of the blue Chinese trouser suits she normally wore, which made her look even more petite than she was.

"Miss Karen, how long you be on Island?" she asked.

"The honest answer is, I don't know. The two men we arrested are being put through the court procedures as quickly as we can, but justice grinds at a very slow pace I'm afraid."

Chau relaxed and for that moment was in heaven. "Anyway Karen, I am happy you here and I will enjoy your company very much."

"Hmm, that sounds interesting," said Karen, with a big grin on her face.

Chau stood up from the sofa and reached her hand to Karen's cheek and gently touched her. Karen took the hand in hers, stood up too and kissed her passionately.

"Why do you still call me 'Miss Karen' sometimes?" the detective asked.

"Oh I like sound of it. You no mind, do you?"

"No, not at all. I quite like it actually. Look you'd better go and do dinner or we may never eat."

Chau skipped into the kitchen, singing some obscure Chinese song, which Karen found delightful. Soon, dinner was ready and Karen opened a bottle of chilled Chardonnay and they both sipped at their drinks whilst enjoying the scrumptious food.

Eventually they finished the meal, went back into the lounge and sat on the sofa. Karen opened another bottle of wine and poured two large glasses.

"Are you going to get me drunk and then, and how you say it, take the advantage of me?" said the tiny woman, smiling.

"I don't think I have to get you drunk to do that, do I?"

"No, you don't"

Chau leaned over and kissed Karen full on the lips, while her hands went to the hem of Karen's kaftan, lifting it up slowly to her waist. Karen was not wearing knickers, and Chau kissed Karen's tummy and then made her way south to the spot she knew instinctively that Karen loved to have licked.

Karen was in ecstasy and couldn't believe that she was now having sensual sex with a woman. There was no doubt that a woman knew where to stick her tongue for maximum effect, whereas men were more like bulls in china shops. Karen was losing herself in the moment but felt she should reciprocate the pleasure. So she sat up and lifted Chau's top off and nuzzled her small nipples and then kissed her neck. Chau always smelt so sexy, Karen thought: it had to be some sort of oriental perfume.

"Karen I have surprise for you!" Chau pulled away, jumped up and went out of the room. She returned a minute later with her hands behind her back. "Guess what I got Miss Karen?"

The other woman moved to grab Chau's arm but she turned away.

Karen was now very interested. "So what is it then, Chau?"

Chau brought her hands from behind her back and Karen gasped. "Oh my gosh!"

The Chinese girl was holding a huge black double-headed dildo.

"Gosh!" Karen was astonished. "What is that? Oh my God! I don't believe this is real, Chau! Where the hell did you get that thing from?"

"I order from China. Twenty-one pounds. Is very nice, no?"

"Wow, I don't know what to say. You're unbelievable! Fill my glass up. Bloody hell!" Karen was shaking her head and as she held her glass out to be filled.

Chau took off her trousers and straddled Karen's lap. "You like to try it now Miss Karen? It give you and me good pleasure together."

Karen took it in her hand, staring at it. "We need some oil."

Chau jumped off and went to her room to fetch some massage oil. She came back and handed the bottle to Karen. The bigger woman poured some of the lubricant onto her hand and began to rub it along the shaft of the dildo. She then turned it upside down and commenced applying oil to its other end.

"God, I'm getting horny just doing this," she said as her breathing increased rapidly.

Karen then spread Chau's legs apart and gently touched her with the dildo. Chau shut her eyes and quietly moaned. Karen then slowly and gently inserted the dildo inside her. Chau let out a long moan of sheer pleasure as Karen pushed the dildo in further and further. Karen then spread her own legs and tucked in close to Chau. She then inserted the other end of the dildo into herself, pushing hard and firmly.

She relaxed for a minute and then whispered to Chau: "Move slowly forward and backwards, but do not let it come out."

Karen did the same, and after a few strokes they were soon pushing in and out in unison, grinding into each other, building up the speed and the pressure.

"It's too big for me!" gasped Chau, panting.

"Keep going. It will get easier." Karen was thrusting her pelvis hard and Chau was desperately trying to match her, stroke for stroke.

"Oh God, yes!" Karen moaned. "I'm nearly there!"

Karen was indeed nearing an orgasm.

"Yes Chau! Yes Chau! Push! AHHHHHHHHHHH!" She reached her climax in an explosion of shockwaves that went through her whole body, leaving her shaking violently.

They both collapsed back onto the sofa.

"Sorry Chau," Karen apologised. "You didn't finish, did you?"

She leaned over and started rubbing Chau in the special place that had already been awakened. It didn't take long before Chau too reached a shuddering orgasm and fell backwards, truly satisfied at last.

"What's on telly then?" asked Karen, as she held out her arms for Chau to join her.

"See channels."

Karen started switching channels. "OK. Here's the tennis."

"No, No," said Chau. "Press button again, please."

"Oh, how about *You've Been Framed*?"

"No, No, No, Miss Karen."

"Do you like *Come dine with me*?"

"Yes, Yes," said Chau, laughing excitedly. "I like that. Sometimes cooking they show very bad."

They settled back on the sofa arm in arm, and watched Steve from Bracknell, cooking beef in beer. They watched telly for a couple of hours until Karen fell asleep. Chau left the sofa and went round the bungalow, checking that all the windows and doors were shut and locked. Once she had done that, she went back to gently shake Karen awake and said it was bedtime. Karen woke and stumbled into the bedroom and took off her kaftan, then she slipped into the cold sheets, naked. She then felt a warm body curl up behind her and a whisper in her ear, "Goodnight my darling Miss Karen."

Sunday was a good and a bad day for Chau. Good because she had made love to Karen in the morning and then had her company until 5 p.m. But it was bad that she would then have to leave to catch the ferry back to the mainland.

Karen would have liked to have stayed longer, but it was a great couple of days, and far away from the grime of Bermondsey. The couple enjoyed a traditional Sunday roast at the local pub. But soon after that it was time for Karen to leave.

Chau had said a tearful goodbye at the bungalow and then went back inside, feeling very dejected and upset, crying bucketloads of tears.

Karen drove to the ferry terminal and boarded the boat at ten minutes to five.

What she hadn't seen was the two men in the Ford Mondeo watching her leave.

Bujar and Dejan were sitting in their car with evil grins on their faces. They turned to each and smiled, as though to say *now the fun begins*.

CHAPTER 24

Tony Bolton was still languishing in Broadmoor Psychiatric Hospital. The only good aspect of life for Tony was his weekly bunk-up with the insatiable Dr Sharon Travis.

For a man who had roamed free like a lion for most of his life, being caged up in Broadmoor was a living nightmare. He had stopped taking all the medication thrown at him and was trying desperately to hold himself together, both physically and mentally. There were a lot of men who couldn't take the pressure of Broadmoor. Sometimes their craziness was exacerbated, and sometimes inmates even killed themselves—hanging was the usual method they chose.

Tony however, had no intention of losing his marbles and stimulated his brain as much as he could, making sure he did daily crossword puzzles, read the papers and had meaningful conversations on many different topics with anyone who was capable of responding in kind.

The psychpathic killer had lost weight—now he was about three stone lighter, and this upset him, because he felt he didn't look quite so scary any more.

One thing he did stick to was making sure he spent time in the gym. He may not have been as bulky as he once was, but what he did have was solid muscle—something that Dr Sharon Travis appreciated.

He hadn't made any real friends as such in the prison, but he was keeping an eye out for anybody he thought could join him in breaking out of Broadmoor. One idea he spent many hours planning and thinking about was the possibility of getting the lovely Sharon Travis to help him get out of the nuthouse.

* * *

Richard Philips was stuck in HM High Security Prison Long Lartin, in Evesham, Worcestershire. The prison was located in the strangely named 'Shine Hill Lane' in the village of South Littleton.

As a high-profile prisoner who was recorded as being an escape risk, he was forced to wear a bright orange jacket that stuck out like a sore thumb anywhere. He was also under intense scrutiny, and had his cell searched every other day at different times. The only good thing he found when he arrived was that all prisoners each had their own individual cell.

Richard kept as busy as he could—he did weight training twice during the week, once in the evening and twice at the weekend, which was the maximum allowed. He also worked, assembling plumbing equipment for an outside company, which gave him a few extra quid a week. On top of these activities, he was learning computer skills and cookery. He'd chosen cookery thinking he might be able to nick extra food, and that proved possible on most occasions.

Since Richard was serving a life sentence, and had no idea what the future held, he wanted to be regarded as a 'model prisoner'. To this end he enrolled on two further classroom courses which were: CSCP, an acronym for 'Self change programme' and CALM which stood for 'Controlling anger and learning to manage it'.

It was all bollocks as far as he was concerned, but it looked good on his record file. Richard had a plan, and the first part of it was to lose the 'Escape Risk' badge he had been given. This would take time, but he had plenty of that. As soon as he was seen as a model prisoner, he would look for some help and break out as quickly as he could.

CHAPTER 25

Paul Bolton's trusted employee, Angus, had been given what he considered to be a very difficult task. Trying to locate the Paul, Emma and Lexi sex tapes was like looking for a needle in a haystack. Ryder, the scumbag who'd secretly made the tapes, was in Millwall Park in Bermondsey, encased in cement, so that was the first and most obvious source gone before he even started. Angus was clever—he had been there and got most of the tee shirts—but this kind of job was something new to him, and he wasn't particularly looking forward to it.

He started by simply making a list of locations that Ryder could have left or securely deposited the tapes. First on the list was the Starlight Club, but that was an extremely unlikely possibility, but he would check anyway. Next had to be Ryder's flat in Albany Road next to Burgess Park, near the Elephant and Castle.

Next to be added to the list was a safety deposit box in a bank or depository. He would check with Roddy to see which bank Ryder's wages had been paid into. Another idea could be a firm of solicitors. People sometimes used solicitors' premises as a repository for various things, prior to them being sent to someone or disposed of in a certain way should the depositor die or have an accident.

The last idea that Angus considered was the tapes being held by a family member or a friend. Angus would have to locate Ryder's contacts, but that could stir up a hornet's nest, what with Ryder being underneath the soil of Millwall Park in a concrete overcoat.

Angus spent a day at the Starlight Club, speaking to all the staff and combing the whole building for any secret safes or hideaways. There was a safe in Ryder's old office but there was nothing in that and if there had been it would have been found when the new manager had taken over.

He spent a long time in the wet rooms upstairs, but common sense told him that since these rooms were where the filming actually took place, it was an unlikely choice for keeping them hidden. He did notice that the cameras were still in place, and made a mental note to check with Paul as to what purpose he wanted them used for.

The flat in Albany Street was a bit of a problem. It had eventually been repossessed due to mortgage arrears, and had then been auctioned off on the cheap to get rid of it quickly. Angus checked the electoral register and found out that Bruce Reynolds and Catherine Gardner jointly owned the property.

He visited the Albany Street flat early one morning on a stake-out.

A man and a woman, presumably owners Bruce and Catherine, left on bicycles at seven forty-five, heading towards the city. Angus then broke into the flat and searched it again thoroughly for any hidden safes, but there were none. The visit had reminded him to find out where all of Ryder's belongings had gone, as it was possible that the tapes could be amongst his stuff.

Ryder's personal belongings had gone to his widowed mother, who had retired to a small two-bedroom bungalow in Eastbourne. Angus put a note in his diary to go down to Eastbourne and search, but he didn't hold out much hope that the video tapes would be there.

He then spoke to Roddy and found out that Ryder banked with Barclays at 260, Walworth Road. Angus paid the bank a visit and enquired if a safety deposit box could be rented. The answer was no, they did not offer that service. It was possible that Ryder might have a safety deposit box somewhere else, but for some reason, instinct told Angus that it was unlikely.

Next on the list was Ryder's solicitor and Roddy confirmed that he did have a lawyer and the firm was Madements Solicitors of Fetter Road, London, EC4. Madements were specialists in defending those accused of serious crimes. Angus decided to delay contacting Madements, since he knew solicitor-client confidentially would be invoked if he started asking questions.

Ryder's mother, in Eastbourne was where Angus went next. He caught the 9.47 a.m. train from Victoria and arrived in Eastbourne at 11.13 a.m. He took a taxi to 22 Acacia Road, where Edna Burridge lived. Angus walked up the small front garden path and rang the doorbell. The chime seemed to go on forever and eventually, a frail elderly lady opened the door on a lock chain.

"Hello Mrs Burridge," Angus began, using all his charm. "I'm very sorry to come unannounced but I used to work in London with Ryder, and I wanted to have a chat with you."

"Chat about what exactly?" The elderly lady asked cautiously.

"Well, I wanted to see if you had any idea when Ryder might be coming back to work. He's a key person in our organisation and we really miss him."

"I suppose you can come in then." Mrs Burridge took the chain off and opened the door. "Would you like a nice cup of tea and a biscuit?"

"That would be lovely, thank you," Angus replied as she took him into the living room.

"Take a seat—I won't be five minutes," The elderly lady said.

Five minutes later, Mrs Burridge came back with a tray laden with an old fashioned teapot and a saucer with biscuits. She placed the tray on a side table between them.

"So did you know my son well, Mr err—?

"Fraser. But please call me Angus."

"Well in that case you may call me Edna."

"Thank you Edna. Yes I knew Ryder well. I worked in London with him."

"Do you know where he is?"

"I'm afraid not, but there is a strong rumour that he went off to Spain with a lady friend."

"Hmm. Very delicately put Angus." They both smiled and Angus was encouraged that the meeting was going well.

"Well," Angus explained, "the reason I'm here is to ask if you had heard from your son."

"Goodness me, I haven't heard a dickey bow from him for a very long time."

"What on earth did he do with all his stuff before he went?"

"He didn't do anything with it. I had to deal with it all and I can tell you it was quite a job!"

"My goodness Edna, that was kind of you to sort things out for him."

"Well it was pretty easy really. I just got a house clearance man round and he took the lot. Mind, I didn't get much for it."

"Everything went well, good, so it was nice and easy."

"Yes," the woman agreed. "The only thing I had to do on top of that, was to send some packages to an address in London, and that was it."

Angus's heart rate quickened. "Were they something special then?"

"I've no idea. But they were all boxed up and they looked important so I posted them. I didn't want anyone to lose out just because my son had absconded."

"Edna, do you have any old video tapes in the house?"

"Yes, some family ones." She stood up and walked across to a desk and pointed to a drawer. "They're in here. Why?"

"Oh, nothing important." Angus got up, opened the drawer and looked in at a large collection of video tapes. He took one out and held it up to show to Edna.

"Would you say the packages were that sort of size?" he asked.

Edna took it in her hand and felt the size and weight. "Yes I think it could well have been tapes that were in the packages I sent."

"Do you remember anything about the address Edna? Think now, it could be very helpful?"

"Nothing at all except that I had to pay for the postage to London."

"How many packages exactly? Do you remember?"

"Three. I remember very clearly it was three."

Now that he had the information, Angus wanted to get away as quickly as possible.

"Well, the tea was lovely, thank you so much Edna," he said, shaking her hand.

"Oh, it was no trouble. I'm sorry I can't be any more help, Angus."

"Believe me, you have been very helpful. Thank you very much."

Angus left, got into his car and immediately got on the phone to Paul, saying, "Paul, I may have some news but I need you to check something with Lexi. How many tapes did she see that Ryder had?"

After Paul said he'd check and get back to him, Angus sat still in the car and waited. Five minutes later, the mobile rang. It was Paul.

"Hi Angus. Three. The answer's three."

"I'm on my way back, Paul. See you later at The Den."

So, Angus thought. *I know now the tapes were sent to London. But where exactly in London?"*

CHAPTER 26

Paul had been working really hard to find new clubs to buy and to get rid of the brothels. There were always clubs for sale but the cost had become completely crazy, especially if you wanted to buy the freehold. Paul had seen clubs to die for but if he had paid the asking price, they wouldn't make a profit for about ten years which was out of the question, considering the huge capital outlay.

He had at last got hold of Bill Caddy and had received a warmish response to the idea of Caddy buying some of the remaining brothels. A meeting had been set up and Paul was very hopeful that he could make progress.

The relationship with Lexi had progressed with a visit to the Adelphi Theatre to see *The Bodyguard* which they had both thoroughly enjoyed. Afterwards, they crossed over the road to the Savoy for a late supper. Paul was still unsure where to take the relationship but he enjoyed seeing Lexi so much, and he really wanted to find out where it would lead. Paul tried really hard to keep Emma out of conversations but his ex-girlfriend always seemed to crop up one way or the other.

Paul had arranged for Duke to drop Lexi home before he headed back to the flat at Chelsea Harbour, where he poured himself a large whisky and sank onto the sofa. He sipped the drink until the glass was empty. He then put the opera *Madame Butterfly* on his sound system and poured himself another whisky. 'Vogliatemi Bene', the haunting vocal duet from Act 1—the title translating to 'Love me, please'—echoed throughout the flat.

The lonely man thought back to when he had met Emma in the Thomas A Becket pub down the Old Kent Road; it seemed a lifetime ago. His mind then wandered to the first time they had made love—at the Holiday Inn on Epsom Downs. He could still smell her perfume and see that beautiful smile as he gulped the whisky down, burning his throat. The tears poured down his cheeks.

Then he thought of Fifi and things got even worse. In his mind, he saw Tony dragging Fifi in front of him, her face shattering with the impact of the machine-gun bullets. Paul buried his head into the sofa cushions. "Emma!" he shouted. "Emma, why did you have to go?"

* * *

It wasn't only Paul who was suffering from the loss of Emma. Her family had lost both daughters: Emma and Fifi. Peter Miller had never returned to work and spent his days gardening and drinking red wine. He used alcohol to try desperately to deaden the pain but it didn't matter how much he drank, the demons would never go away. Worst of all was the guilt that he had not been there to protect his girls.

Mary Miller was still receiving counselling and was taking 40 mg of the 'happy pill' Fluoxetine, daily. Peter and Mary seldom spoke and their marriage was on the brink of collapse.

Emma and Fifi's brother Ian had gone off to Israel and was working on a kibbutz. He was just about holding himself together and had met a German woman, Annaliese Kruger, who was helping him get through the family tragedy.

Then there were the aunties and uncles, cousins, friends, the list went on forever. Fifi's school friends had still not recovered from the shock. Her best friend Trixie was still at home and virtually lived in her bedroom and was also receiving counselling. Two of the worst hit were Sophie and Mel, Emma's best friends, whom she had grown up with. Both the girls were hit hard, all they ever did was spend time at each other's houses, and neither of them had been able to go near a club or pub since it had happened.

Lexi was in a dilemma. She wanted to get very close to Paul and to help him get over the loss of Emma, but she didn't want to scare him off. She remembered the first time she had seen Paul and Emma at the club. She knew that they had watched her perform for the Chinese group but had not seen or spoken to them on that occasion.

Then Ryder had asked her to do a private show for Paul and Emma and to make it really good, because they had asked him to film it. That was when Emma joined her on the stage and all three of them had ended up naked. Emma had then asked Lexi to visit the flat at Chelsea Harbour, and the visit had turned into a drunken orgy.

Lexi was extremely sorry that Emma had gone but couldn't help thinking that somehow it was all karma, so that she would ultimately end up with Paul. The one thing she did know was that she would go at Paul's pace. They'd seen each other a few times now but Paul had not made a move on her yet, and she was desperate to give herself to him.

Paul had asked her to go to the *Phantom of the Opera* for their next date, a show she had always wanted to see. It was some time away but Lexi was happy they were keeping in contact. She was sure that Paul felt something for her but that he was scared to show it because it would seem like a slap in the face to Emma's memory.

Lexi just prayed that if she was sensible, things would work out in the end.

CHAPTER 27

Bujar and Dejan were sitting in the bar at the Roseglen Hotel in Palmerston Road, Shanklin. They had seen Karen leave the Island and were in good humour as they discussed what to do with the Chinese girl, Chau.

"The neat vodka is good, eh Dejan?" Bujar said to his friend.

"The little Chinese bitch will taste sweeter I'm sure," leered Dejan.

Bujar laughed, for he was in an ebullient mood. He could picture the policewoman's face when she was told her precious bitch had been taken. He could taste her sorrow, her disappointment, her terror at what was happening to the girl; oh it was a glorious time to be alive!

Dejan put his vodka down. "What are we going to do with the bitch?"

"I've been giving it some thought. We are on an island so have to plan carefully. If we get stuck here, there will be nowhere to go and we are fucked. I think we should drug her and take her back to the mainland in the boot of the car. What do you think?"

"You want to keep her alive? What for?"

"The bitch is still worth money. This is personal, Dejan. Nobody fucks me over, I want a return on my investment."

"Better just to fuck her for hours and then kill her."

"No. You can have her as much as you want but the bitch stays alive and we take her back to the mainland."

"As you wish, Bujar." Dejan held his glass up and they clinked glasses to seal the deal.

"Tomorrow is Monday, a quiet day of the week, especially over here, out of holiday season. We will take her tomorrow morning, have some fun, and then decide when to get the ferry."

They continued knocking back neat vodka and thinking about the fun they were going to have the next day with the Chinese girl.

CHAPTER 28

It was Monday morning following Karen's weekend on the Isle of Wight. She rolled into the CID office at Rotherhithe Nick at 10 a.m.

"What sort of time do you call this Karen?" her friend and colleague Detective Constable Jeff Swan asked.

"I suppose you were in at 6 a. m., were you?"

"Seven actually."

"Are you sure?"

"OK Detective you caught me out." Jeff smiled. "Eight-thirty, I swear, and that's the truth."

"Yeah alright, I believe you."

"So, how was your weekend then?" Jeff asked.

"Quiet. Read my new Peter James novel *Alchemist*, most of the time."

"Hmm, I detect we're not in the best of moods this morning?" said Jeff sarcastically.

"If you must know, I'm having a very heavy period."

Jeff's mouth turned down and he shifted uncomfortably in his seat. "Too much information, thank you."

Karen knew that would shut him up. Mention periods and for some reason, men go quiet very quickly.

"I need a coffee." Karen turned to go back out of the door.

"Erm Karen, haven't you forgotten something?"

"What's that, Jeff?"

"Yes, I'd love a coffee. Thank you for asking."

Karen kept walking. "Jesus, give it a rest, Jeff."

Jeff had never seen Karen like this and was concerned, but when she returned she was holding two coffees.

"OK, there was no point asking if you wanted a coffee because I knew you would say yes so I was going to get it anyway." said Karen, placing a large latte in front of Jeff.

"Thank you, most appreciated." He took the lid off the coffee and added two sugar sachets. "On a serious note, what's wrong? And for goodness' sake don't mention you-know-what again—makes me feel queasy."

Karen shook her head miserably as she sat down at her desk. "Do you ever get that feeling that everything's against you? You know something Jeff? I just feel like a worthless piece of shit at the moment, that's all."

There was a note of real concern in Jeff's voice as he replied: "Yes I understand. But why now? At this precise moment in time?"

"If I knew why I could do something about it. But I can't put my finger on it. Anyway, what's happening here, anything exciting?"

"Nothing," Jeff grunted gloomily. "Interviews with those two Albanian shitbags are a complete waste of time, they just repeat 'no understand' all the time. We got a translator in and he left after two minutes because they said when they got out they would cut his penis off and shove it down his throat. Nice eh? It's not important though. They'll be going to prison for a very long time, trust me."

"I hope so. Any sign of that bastard Bujar Dushka?"

"No. Brick walls everywhere we go."

"Pity, I want to meet him again as soon as possible." Then after a while, she added: "Look Jeff, I don't think I can work today. Seriously."

"Go home then, relax, take it easy. If Michael asks, I'll say you've gone home sick."

"OK, thanks Jeff." Karen left quickly in case Michael saw her. She was soon home and lying in a hot bath. She had a very quiet relaxing day, eating well and laying off the booze.

It was late in the afternoon when it happened. Nothing could have prepared her for it.

Her mobile phone rang at 4.23 p.m.

She answered it to hear a frantic voice: "This is Hampshire Police on the Isle of Wight. We're informing you that an emergency alarm has been triggered at a property in Baring Road, Cowes. A patrol arrived there five minutes after the alarm call to find the property empty. The bungalow was in a state of disrepair. I understand that your people were hiding someone there under the Witness Protection Scheme."

Karen thought quickly. "Have you sealed off the ferry and airport?"

"Yes. Who are we looking for?"

"A single young Chinese woman, five-feet-two, very slim, her name is Chau. She could have been taken by one or two Albanian criminals, one of whom is likely to be a man called Bujar Dushka. He's armed and has already killed three police officers over here."

"Jesus! We better get the armed teams out."

"Do it. He's armed and he'll not hesitate to shoot to kill. I'll be on the next available chopper flight—make sure every vehicle leaving the Island is thoroughly checked, and I don't give a shit what the ferry companies say, do it properly."

Karen was in shock. She'd stressed to Chau that the alarm button was a last resort. She managed to snap into professional mode, ignoring her emotions as she called Jeff.

"Jeff, I need your help right now," she began. "Chau has been taken—it must have been that bastard Dushka."

"Wait there. I'll be with you in five."

Karen grabbed a small holdall and stuffed it with a toothbrush, toothpaste some soap and deodorant. She grabbed some clean knickers, a pair of jeans and a couple of shirts—she was travelling light.

When Jeff arrived at Karen's flat he wasted no time, saying, "What's the plan Karen?"

"I've already asked Michael to get us a chopper. It's on its way."

"Where is it landing?"

"Across the road in Southwark Park in front of the Sports Complex." She collected up the few things she was taking and headed for the door. She looked at her watch: it was 4.38 p.m. "Let's go Jeff, we haven't got a minute to lose."

CHAPTER 29

Bujar and Dejan drove away from the Roseglen Hotel in Shanklin and made their way across the Island to Cowes. It was 11 a.m., the journey was swift, and they soon parked up in Crossfield Avenue, at the back of Baring Road, with the nine-hole Cowes Golf Course in between. They sat in the car for a few minutes. As usual, Bujar had no plan.

"What are we going to do with the bitch, Bujar?" Dejan asked.

"We have some fun today and then take her off the Island tonight and go back to your place."

Dejan was throbbing with anticipation at the prospect of fucking the Chinese bitch. He had never had an oriental woman and imagined her to be very petite with a small tight pussy. He was very pleased with how things were panning out: he had two bottles of vodka with him and couldn't wait to see what the Chinese girl was like.

* * *

Chau had slept late and eventually surfaced at about 10.30 a.m. She had a leisurely breakfast of coffee and a croissant while enjoying the stunning sea view across the Solent. It was a slightly windy day but she was used to the fluctuating weather of the Isle of Wight and it didn't bother her now. She was sad that Karen had gone but she had made a promise to come back as soon as was possible. Chau had also begun to think of home and wished her family were with her, like in the old days. She finished her breakfast, cleared the table and went to the bathroom to take a shower.

The water cascaded over her as she luxuriated in the hot water and foaming bath gel. She reached up to the curtain rail to take her towel.

She screamed as the shower curtain was pulled down viciously. And there, before her eyes, was the devil himself—Bujar Dushka.

"Hello once again bitch!"

Bujar grabbed her round the throat and lifted her out of the bath and pushed her into the arms of Dejan, telling him to: "Take the bitch to one of the bedrooms."

Chau could not walk, as the big ugly man carried her, feet suspended above the ground.

Yet Karen had promised her she was safe! She couldn't understand what was happening. She let out another loud scream. Dejan smashed her in the face with the back of his hand. She went quiet, whimpering and sobbing. Dejan kicked open the door with his foot and threw her onto the bed in the room Karen had slept in.

Dejan then surveyed the oriental girl and he was impressed with what he saw. It was going to be wonderful fucking this little bitch in all her holes, he thought. Bujar entered with the vodka and three glasses and set them down on the bedside table.

"Let's have a party!" he shouted and started to pour neat vodka into the three glasses.

Chau was hunched up in a ball at the top of the bed. Bujar handed her a glass of vodka. She shook her head. He roared: "Take it or we'll force you! Now knock it back in one go!"

The terrified woman took the glass and put it to her mouth—it didn't seem to smell of anything and she took a sip. It didn't taste of much either. Then she lifted the glass and drank it down quickly. As it flowed down her throat, she coughed and spluttered. She could feel the heat burning her insides, and knew that it was a strong liquor.

She assessed her captors. They were two big, ugly and heavily muscled thugs. Chau knew that she was in for a rough time and welcomed the warm glow that the vodka had given her. She held out her empty glass. Bujar laughed and filled it up to the brim and she drank and didn't stop until the glass was empty.

They had sex with her, taking turns. Then they both raped her at the same time. They were both big, well endowed, men and her delicate parts were ripped as they double-penetrated her. Blood was everywhere, which at least put a dampener on the Albanian men's perverted idea of fun.

Later, Dejan was sent out to get food and soon came back with a large bucket of fried chicken and chips. Bujar and Dejan went to the dining table and stuffed their faces with the food and finished off their meal with vodka.

Chau was awake and listening to the rapist pigs talking. It seemed that they were going to take her off the Island that night and head back to London.

She knew that her only hope was getting to the emergency alarm in the other bedroom. Her heart was pounding. Calm down, calm down, she said to herself, breathing in and out slowly.

And then she was faced with a choice: she could either run into the other room and press the alarm. Or she could ask to go in there using the pretext of wanting to clean herself up. She decided on the latter idea.

"Mr!" she called to the two thugs.

She heard Bujar reply, "What do you want, bitch?"

"I clean up and repair myself. Stuff I need in other bedroom."

"OK, go then!"

She limped very painfully out into the hallway. The two men were watching her. She forced herself to smile and say: "You two teach me how to be woman."

Bujar and Dejan look at each other in surprise and laughed. Then they picked up their drinks and clinked glasses.

Men are so stupid sometimes, thought Chau.

She entered her own room and suddenly heard Bujar shout, "Leave the door wide open!"

Chau didn't mind doing so. She smiled to herself and sat on her bed. Her lower abdomen was on fire, it hurt so much, and she was certain they'd done serious damage, but she was alive, and that was all that mattered.

Next, she stretched her arms out and, for a split-second, enjoyed the delicious awareness that she was going to fight back. She could see the alarm, and it was a beautiful moment to know that she could press it whenever she felt like it.

What's more, Chau calculated that the longer she could keep them at the bungalow after she had pressed the alarm the better her chances. Help would come very quickly, so even if they killed her, at least they would be caught and spend years in prison. The thought of that made her smile.

Slowly, Chau inched towards the alarm. She touched it gently at first and then pushed hard. At first it didn't seem like anything had happened and she prayed it was working properly. She then went out of the room and asked the Albanian rapists if she could use the bathroom.

"Yes you can," Bujar told her. "But leave the door wide open!"

Bujar and Dejan had relaxed. They were satiated with vodka and fried chicken and their endless couplings with the tiny Chinese girl.

Chau slowly walked into the bathroom. Now was the time to do it.

She slammed the door shut and turned the lock. Bujar heard the door slam and the lock turn. He was up in a second. "You fucking bitch! I told you to keep the fucking door open!"

"Please Mr, me doing woman stuff, don't like you see."

"Open the fucking door, Bitch!"

Chau was beyond fear, so high on adrenalin that she was almost enjoying the situation: "You in trouble now Mr, you in big trouble!"

Bujar knew something had changed: the bitch seemed happy. She must have had done something in the other bedroom.

"Dejan, check the other room with me, quick!"

They rushed into bedroom two and started looking around. Bujar told his friend: "We're looking for some sort of alarm button." The worry came across in his words.

Dejan ran his fingers along the side of the bed. His eyes were darting everywhere, and then he saw a red button on the side of the lamp by the bed. "Bujar, what's this?" he asked.

"That, my friend, is a panic button and the cops will be here very soon. MOVE!"

Then he stopped and held out his hand to stop Dejan. "Smash that fucking bathroom door down and bring that fucking bitch out! She's going to pay for this!"

Dejan rushed out of the bedroom, tensed and charged the bathroom door. The crash reverberated loudly but the panel did not give. Chau was now screaming for help.

"Again Dejan!" bawled Bujar. "And this fucking time, make it count!"

Dejan moved back further to get a better run at it, charged full pelt, and smashed his shoulder against the door, which came off its hinges and crashed to the floor.

"Bring her!" shouted Bujar with venom. Dejan grabbed Chau. She scratched and spat at him as he dragged her out of the bathroom.

"Fuck! We don't have time for this." Bujar stepped across to Chau and punched her full on the jaw, and she went out like a light.

"Carry her to the car and put her in the boot. Quickly!" Bujar ordered, looking at his watch: it was 4.17 p.m.

They piled the unconscious woman into the boot and locked it. Then they ran round, jumped into the car and Dejan started the engine and pressed the accelerator hard: they flew forwards up Crossfield Road.

"Stop!" shouted Bujar. "They'll be at the house in a couple of minutes, and they will soon close off all exits from the Island! We are in deep shit, Dejan."

Dejan didn't look or sound too worried. "Do not worry Bujar. I have had a good life. We must take as many of them with us as we can."

"You're right Dejan. Head away from Ryde Ferry Terminal. We will soon find out just how tough the Isle of Wight police can be."

Dejan took a succession of small country roads until they ended going up Tuttons Hill, past the Portland Inn Pub and then straight on into Church Road. They got to the end of it, took a right into Lower Church Road and two minutes later were in Marsh Road. They took a left and were on a very long straight road called Rew Street. The driver then put his foot down and they surged up to 60 mph and they relaxed, for they were back in control. They passed Sunnycott Caravan Park, drove for ten minutes and then Bujar directed Dejan to turn right into Rolls Hill.

"It is all trees here, very nice," Bujar said, looking through the car window. "I'm looking for something."

"What?" asked Dejan, his eyes glued to the road. Bujar did not reply, he just kept looking around.

They continued on Rolls Hill and then into Whitehouse Road. Bujar was still scanning the area on either side of them. Suddenly he shouted and pointed: "Turn left down Colman's Lane there. Yes, that dirt track!" Bujar had seen something in the trees which would suit them perfectly.

There was a sign to Parkhurst Forest. Then Dejan saw the house tucked away in a secluded spot that could hardly be seen from the road and, even better, it was completely detached, in a field on its own. It was a beautiful house, with a timber-framed facade.

"Park right outside the front door—we are not going to fuck around," said Bujar.

Having done so, the pair grabbed their Uzi machine guns, got out of the car, marched up to the front door and rang the bell. A few seconds later, a woman in her thirties opened the door.

"Hello, can I help you?" She smiled.

Bujar stepped into the hall and lifted his weapon. The woman's face drained of colour and her eyes were alive with fear.

Bujar pushed her to the floor. "Who else is in the house, bitch?" he demanded.

The lady of the house, Amanda Ferry, was terrified. She had never encountered bestial scum like this before, and was hardly aware that such animals existed.

Bujar stuck his face close to Amanda's and shouted. "Who else is in the fucking house?" His breath stank of stale chicken and booze.

Just then, a boy of about ten appeared at the top of the stairs. "Mum! What's happening?" he called out. Then he saw the two men and the guns and turned to run back up onto the landing.

Amanda shouted, "Run David! Run!"

But Dejan was up the stairs in a flash. David was caught and dragged back downstairs. "Now stand there and be quiet and you won't get hurt," Dejan told the crying youngster, releasing him.

"This will be the last time I ask." Bujar levelled the gun at Amanda's face. "Who else is in the house?"

"Just the two of us." Amanda was shaking with terror, especially as the thugs now had her son.

"Where's Dad then?"

Amanda didn't answer straight away. Bujar looked at Dejan, saying, "I think you need to let this bitch know what happens if she doesn't answer me quickly."

Dejan strode over to the woman and slapped her hard twice in the mouth. The boy moved to protect his mother. "Sit down sonny before I break your legs!" he snarled. Blood was trickling down Amanda's face.

"So, where is Daddy?" Bujar demanded.

"He's on his way home from work," replied Amanda, whimpering.

"What time will he be here?"

"About 6.30."

"Are you preparing a meal?"

"Yes."

"Prepare for three extra." He turned to Dejan. "Dejan, fetch the Chinese bitch."

Within a few minutes, Dejan returned, dragging Chau by the neck. She was still groggy from when Bujar had punched her and from being locked in the car's boot. Amanda saw the poor little Chinese girl with the swollen face, covered in blood. Dejan dropped Chau on the floor in a heap.

Amanda heard herself asking, "Can I clean her up?" She looked at the two men.

"Shut up you, fucking bitch, and speak only when you are spoken to!" Bujar took a step forward and kicked her in the stomach.

"Ahhhhhhh!" She screamed and doubled over on the floor, clutching her stomach. David was now crying loudly.

"Shut the fuck up! Now!" Bujar shouted and glared at him threateningly. The boy managed to calm down a little. He looked petrified.

Amanda was terrified. She was scared to death for herself, for her son and for her husband Brian, who was on his way home. How could she warn him? She looked at the two men, realising that they would be lucky to get away with their lives.

Chau was waking up and looking around her, confused. Who were these new people, she wondered? She had not seen them before. Still feeling very weak, she managed to sit upright, looking around the room to get her bearings and to see what was happening.

"Go to the kitchen, woman, and prepare food, and put some wine on the table!" commanded Bujar.

"Yes," whispered Amanda as she made her way painfully to the kitchen.

"Dejan, collect any mobile phones and cut the house phone wires."

Dejan went upstairs and after a while, returned with two mobiles, and he also found one more in the lounge. Then he smashed the three phones into pieces.

* * *

It was 6.10 p.m. as the helicopter landed at Cowes Golf Club. Jeff and Karen jumped off and, ducking down beneath the wind from the propeller blades, made their way towards the welcoming committee in front of the clubhouse.

A tall, straight-backed, stern-looking police officer stepped forward.

"I'm Commander Baker," he told them. "You must be Foster and Swan. Welcome to the Island."

"Thank you Commander," said Jeff as they shook hands. "Any news at all?"

"Not yet. We have plenty of DNA and fingerprints at the house in Baring Road and—"

"We need to go to the property right now," Karen interrupted.

"Right you are. Vehicles are behind us in the car park." The commander turned and strode towards that place. "I understand the suspects are armed and dangerous?" he asked.

"If it is who we think it is, then they are the most vicious dangerous criminals you could ever meet," said Jeff. "They shot and killed three police officers a short time ago. We have to shoot to kill because they will not hesitate to use their own guns!"

They were outside the Baring Road bungalow in three minutes. Karen marched up the path, telling herself: *I am a police officer and I must focus on that, I am a police officer and I must...*

The bungalow was teeming with crime-scene technicians, taking prints and swabs. Karen and Jeff were introduced to the team leader, Nathan Ellis.

"What have you got?" asked Karen, fixing Nathan with a steely look.

"By the looks of the prints, two men and one woman were in the premises. We have plenty of DNA from blood droplets, semen, saliva and hair."

Karen shuddered when she heard blood and semen.

"How much blood?"

"Very small drops, so certainly not a life-threatening wound, not even a serious one I would guess. There are bottles of vodka and, coupled with the semen, that would indicate a sex party or something of that nature."

"Yes, well, I think it's more accurate to call it a serious case of rape rather than a party," said Karen, giving Nathan a hard stare.

Jeff said, "Get the DNA and prints back to London as quickly as possible and match them against what we have on the Albanians. We're pretty sure it's them but we'd better make certain."

Karen wandered slowly around the lounge, thinking of poor Chau, looking and wondering what had happened. Jeff disappeared into the Chinese girl's bedroom: the room looked quite tidy at first, and then he stopped dead.

Jeff was looking at the bedside table, on top of which was a book. He looked closely at the title: *Alchemist* by Peter James. He then slowly moved into the other bedroom: it was a mess and he could tell immediately this was where the so-called 'party' had taken place—vodka, smashed glasses, messed-up bed and bloodstains on the sheets.

The detective had trouble controlling his anger. One of the two must be Bujar

Dushka. What an animal that man was. He was determined that the Albanian creature had to die, and he prayed that it could be him who delivered the fatal bullet to his head.

"So Commander, what progress have you made?" Jeff asked the officer in charge of the Isle of Wight police contingent.

"Ryde, Fishbourne and Yarmouth Ferries—oh, and the Ryde Hovercraft—have all been locked down," Baker replied decisively. "I also have a team at the airport, so no worries there."

"So they must still be on the Island and we've got to flush them out somehow," said Jeff. "Have you got enough armed officers here to deal with this? These men have machine guns, not single-shot pistols, and they enjoy using them."

"We have two teams of armed-response officers, one in Newport and one in Shanklin. I've already asked for more officers from the mainland who are on their way as we speak."

* * *

Bujar and Dejan took most of the food that Amanda had provided and ate like pigs. They left the dregs for the others who, understandably, were not remotely hungry. However, Chau knew the importance of keeping her strength up, so she tried to force down as much as she could.

Amanda was getting more and more worried as she looked at the clock. It was 6.20 p.m. and her husband Brian would be home soon.

"Dejan, wait in the garage for the Daddy," Bujar gave Dejan a meaningful look. "We must welcome him home."

Suddenly, everyone at the table tensed. A car could be heard pulling into the drive and stopping. The driver got out and looked towards the house, mystified, wondering why the garage door was not open. They saw him shake his head as he opened it up. He returned to the car and drove slowly into the garage.

They heard the engine shut down and the clang as the garage door was closed from the inside. Three minutes later Dejan returned to the table and nodded once at Bujar.

Amanda was fraught with worry and screamed at Dejan: "Where is my husband? What have you done to him, you bastard?"

"He is having a nap, do not worry," Dejan replied calmly. "Now shut the fuck up before I get pissed off with you!"

"You're just animals!" Amanda spat at Dejan and the saliva hit him in the face.

"Bastards!" she yelled, then rose from the table and made towards Dejan with hate in her eyes.

Dejan looked at Bujar, who raised his eyes towards the stairs. Amanda lifted a hand to scratch at Dejan's face but she stood no chance. The Albanian killer grabbed her hair tightly, simultaneously kicking the legs from under her.

She collapsed onto the floor and Dejan grabbed her wrist and started dragging her towards the stairs. He picked her up and they reached the landing and Dejan kicked open the first door to reveal a bedroom. He pulled her inside and threw her onto the double bed and began to rip off her clothes, starting with her top.

He slapped her face and pushed her back down on the bed as she struggled to get off it. Next, he undid the belt on her jeans and tried to yank them off, but Amanda lifted her head and pulled them back up. Dejan gave her a vicious slap to the face that rocked her backwards.

Soon the jeans were off and Dejan's eyes raked over her body—it was a nice body: maybe a few pounds overweight but the extra flesh gave you something to get hold of, he thought. He leaned over and grabbed her knickers and pulled. Amanda sat up again and went to punch Dejan, but another hard slap stopped her in her tracks. Her knickers and bra were now off and he was loving the feeling of being in control. He took hold of her knees and yanked them apart to reveal his prize.

He slowly lowered his trousers, feeling the growth of his massive erection. He climbed on the bed and lay down on top of Amanda. Then he entered her with brutal force and heard her gasp painfully. He rocked on top of her, thrusting and withdrawing with force.

"Take that, Bitch!" he snarled. "Not so mouthy now, are you?" He pounded away, getting progressively faster and pushing harder. "You like it Bitch?" He was nearly there. At the penultimate moment he withdrew his penis, shifted position, then grabbed Amanda's hair and pulled her mouth onto his cock. He held the back of her head firmly and was thrusting into her mouth fast and hard.

Through her welter of horror, Amanda was aware of him ramming his penis in and out of her mouth. She was groggy from the beatings but her pure undiluted hatred gave her the courage to get her own back.

He was pushing so hard that he was making her gag. Then she felt him stiffen and stop moving, and knew that he was about to come.

As she tasted the first drop of semen, she clamped her teeth down hard onto his cock and bit down for all she was worth.

Bujar, Chau and David looked up as they heard an agonising scream from upstairs. The little boy started crying loudly. It was obviously a man's scream, and the only man it could be was Dejan.

The rapist's friend sprinted up the stairs and flung the bedroom door open. He was met with an incredible sight. Amanda's teeth were still clamped around Dejan's cock and, judging by the sight of it and Dejan's screaming, it looked like she might actually have bitten clean through it.

Dejan had his hands round Amanda's throat and was attempting to strangle her. Bujar immediately crashed the butt of his Uzi onto the top of Amanda's head and she fell back, her jaw slackened, releasing her attacker.

"Shut up Dejan!" Bujar yelled as Dejan carried on howling with the searing pain, with his hands over his severed cock. Blood was pouring down his legs, and Bujar turned away from the sight of the dangling lump of bloody flesh.

Dejan rolled onto the bed, still clutching his cock. "FUCKING BITCH! FUCKING BITCH!" He was shouting as he rolled from side to side. He calmed down slightly and looked closely at the state of his cock.

"Jesus!" he said. Although everything was covered in blood, the thing looked terminally damaged. "I need to see a doctor quickly, the bitch!"

So saying, he picked up the bedside lamp and felt how heavy it was. Then he tore off the shade, smashed the bulb against the floor and rammed the jagged glass edges into Amanda's face. He lifted it up and smashed it again, but this time he held it by the stem, swinging the heavy base into the side of her head. Then he leaned back, breathing hard and whimpering with pain.

Bujar looked at Amanda and felt for a pulse, and after a moment pronounced: "She's dead."

Dejan was happy.

"Good," said Dejan. "The bitch got off lightly."

"Dejan, stay here," Bujar told him. I'll send the other bitch up to see what she can do for you."

Bujar went down and told Chau to go upstairs and see if she could help with Dejan's wound. He sat down and then suddenly he screamed. "BITCH!" He shouted at Chau. "Where is he? Where's the fucking boy?"

A few moments previously, when they'd heard the scream from upstairs, Chau had realised that it was their opportunity. She had looked at the boy, saying, "David go and get help! Run as fast as you can, get help, do you understand? We need the police. Go now, quickly!"

David was ten, old enough to knew exactly what to do and he was through the front door and gone in a second. Chau sat back and prayed that the boy would get away and bring help, knowing that the longer that bastard Dushka was upstairs the better. She was counting one and two and three and four and five... He had been gone for at least two minutes when Bujar came back downstairs.

When Bujar realised the boy had gone, Chau started praying silently.

He rushed to the front door, yanked it open and rushed outside, scanning left and right, but the boy had disappeared. He ran back inside the house. "Dejan?" he called upstairs. "We are leaving NOW! Hurry!"

Dejan hobbled downstairs. He was in excruciating pain, blood soaking the crotch of his trousers and cascading down one of the legs. He grabbed Chau by the arm and dragged her out to the car.

"Hurry Dejan! We need to get as far away as possible." Bujar was already in the driver's seat, revving the engine.

* * *

David ran as fast as he could and for as long as he could before he got an itch on his left foot, due to grit in his trainers, that slowed him down a bit. Eventually, he reached Whitehouse Road and flagged down the first vehicle, which was a truck. The driver, a big burly man in his forties, stopped by the curb where David was standing and wound down his window. He was surprised to see that the young boy was all alone, and tears were streaming down his face.

"Hey boy! What's wrong with you?"

David was breathless as he gabbled away: "Police! Please call the police and ambulance, my parents are in trouble!"

"Where? Who?" While waiting for answers, the lorry driver was quickly grabbing his mobile and dialling 999. It was 7.30 p.m.

A local squad car that had been driving along Forest Road rushed to the scene and arrived at 7.42 p.m. David was put into the police car and he directed them to his house.

They pulled up outside and got out of the car. The house was eerily quiet, the wind was sweeping leaves across the ground, causing a whispering noise.

The officers knew that something didn't seem right. Suddenly there was a bang as the front door slammed shut and immediately opened again. The male officer asked his female colleague to wait with the boy while he investigated.

The boy had told him that his father had been in the garage, so he firstly lifted open the door and went in. He groped in the darkness for the light switch and flicked it on. Light flooded the garage and PC Groves walked around the car, then he saw it: the body of a man lying on the floor. He knelt down and failed to find a pulse, concluding that the man was dead. He gently turned the corpse and saw that his head had been caved in, probably with the car jack that was lying next to him. Around the head there was a huge puddle of blood.

He phoned in his report immediately and requested backup, saying that he had already found one dead body and there could be more. He then went through into the main house, and noted that the lounge was in a mess.

Then he heard a noise from upstairs. He took out his truncheon, flipped it open, and tiptoed up the stairs, worried that he was unarmed. He heard a pitiful moan, which sounded like it came from a woman. Groves moved towards the room the noise was coming from, pushed the door and looked in.

"Oh God!" he gasped. There was a naked woman lying on the bed, and the sheets were crumpled and covered in blood. But it was her face that was the most shocking—it was a mass of hanging flesh.

He rushed in and leaned over the woman. "My name's Peter Groves, I'm a police officer," he reassured her, talking gently. "Help is on the way."

The woman whispered, "Mmm my... son... David—"

Groves leaned closer, as he could hardly hear her. "Sorry, say that again?"

"Mm—my son... David!"

"He's fine." The officer then remembered the name the boy had told her. "He's fine Amanda, David is fine. He is with us, he's not hurt."

PC Groves then heard voices and an ambulance crew came into the room. They took control and kept telling Amanda she was going to be OK and that she would be in St Mary's Hospital in ten minutes. Amanda was strapped to a stretcher and carried down to the ambulance. David saw his mother and opened the police car door and ran to her crying, "Mummy, Mummy,

Mummy!"

The woman officer came out of the car and followed him.

Amanda heard David's voice and called weakly, "David, David come here."

The men carrying the stretcher stopped when they saw David. The boy reached the stretcher and turned away when he saw her face, but he quickly turned back, staying calm, and placed his hands in hers and said, "Don't worry Mummy. Everything will be alright, I love you."

Amanda whispered through tears. "I love you David, I love you so much."

The policewoman put her arm around the boy and gently led him back to the car.

* * *

Jeff and Karen were drinking coffee in the golf course café when word came in that a man had been murdered and his wife brutally assaulted near Parkhurst Forest. A young boy had escaped and reported that two men with foreign accents had attacked his father and tortured his mother.

The mother—Amanda Ferry—was in St Mary's Hospital in a critical condition and would be severely facially disfigured, but was likely to survive. The boy had also mentioned a Chinese girl, but was vague about her role in the incident. Jeff and Karen knew immediately that the perpetrators were the Albanians and that the girl was Chau.

Jeff, Karen and two cars full of armed police were soon on the A3020 Newport Road driving at full speed. Cars from all over the island were converging on the Parkhurst Forest area to try and trap the Albanian killers.

* * *

Bujar and Dejan had again bundled Chau into the boot of the car and had driven off with screeching tyres and a trail of dust. They were on Whitehouse Road in seconds and hit the junction with Forest Road.

"Turn Left!" shouted Bujar as he saw a sign to Newport. They bombed down Forest Road and hit the A3020 Medina Way and turned right to Newport. Little did they know that Jeff and Karen were only two minutes behind them on the same road. They passed the Isle of Wight College and were heading into a built up area.

"Good, this is more our kind of scenery," said Bujar. They continued and could only go in one direction as they hit the Newport one-way system. They forked left into Fairlee Road and up past the cemetery.

Bujar shouted again: "Pull into the Texaco petrol station, fill her up quickly!"

Dejan filled the tank and drove off back onto Fairlee Road without paying. The attendant in the shop immediately called the police and reported the theft. This information was passed through to Jeff and Karen, who were in Newport town centre, considering what to do next.

"We have to gamble it's them," Jeff said, studying a map of the Island. "Let's get after them! What do you think, Commander?"

"They don't know the Island so they'll be driving randomly," Commander Baker replied. "If I was them, I would do one of two things: either head into the interior and find another house to hide in, or I would drive towards the coast and look for a boat."

"Let's go after them along the Fairlee Road and then decide which direction to take," suggested Jeff.

* * *

"Dejan, I have a plan," Bujar said to his friend. "We will see if the police can keep up with us." Bujar was concentrating on the route, then he saw the sign saying 'DC Engineering'. "Fork left!" he told him. They drove onto East Cowes Road up past the Island Cheap Skip Depot and then came to the main A3021 junction. "Turn Left."

"We are going back to Cowes?" asked Dejan looking confused.

"Yes, I'm hoping it will throw them off us and give us a bit of time."

Dejan continued driving at a sensible speed along the A3021, which became Whippingham Road, on past St Mildred's Church then past Queens Gate Primary School. Bujar was scanning both sides of the road. Past Osbourne Petrol Station, Bujar noticed the change of road name to York Avenue. *Why do they change road names halfway along,* he wondered.

It was a long straight road and they were making good progress, and soon they were passing the Jubilee Recreation Ground on their left. Dejan didn't know it, but Bujar was following signs towards the East Cowes Ferry.

"Turn left here into Ferry Road."

"Ferry?" queried Dejan.

"Yes. I think it will take us back over to the Cowes side that we know."

The floating bridge ferry was there bang in front of them as they saw the water of the River Medina.

"Excellent!" cried Bujar. "I wonder where our police friends are?"

* * *

The truth was that the police were charging all over the Island in a panic. They had never before had a situation of lunatic gunmen being loose on the Island killing people.

Jeff and Karen had both been studying the maps in the car. They had driven past the A3021 turn-off to East Cowes and were speeding up Lushington Hill towards Fishbourne Ferry Services, and further on to the Island Hovercraft Service.

"You don't think they could have gone back to Cowes, do you?" asked Karen anxiously.

"God knows," Commander Baker, who was in the back of the car, answered.

"That Bujar is a crafty, evil animal," Jeff added. "I just don't know. Tell you what, let's split. Radio the car behind to continue to Fishbourne. I've got a funny feeling they may be going back to somewhere they already know a little—Cowes."

They turned the car round and headed back to the A3021 turn-off and were there in five minutes and then charged down towards East Cowes Floating Bridge Ferry at 100 mph.

"Commander, can you organise a reception committee on the West Cowes side just in case we are lucky and catch them out for a change?" Jeff asked. He was feeling optimistic that the bastards would be nabbed soon.

* * *

Bujar and Dejan were on the ferry and crossing the River Medina, which only took a few minutes and were soon pulling off the craft onto the Cowes side. They then drove down Medina Road, passing a huge collection of boats in the Shepherds Wharf Marina.

They continued round the corner past the Duke of York Pub and York Road on the left, and as they joined Mill Hill Road, Dejan shouted angrily, "Road block! Fuck! Now we're stuck, there's nowhere to go!"

The police had set up a stop point just round the corner, so that once you turned, you could not avoid being checked.

But the two police officers who had set up the road block were unarmed. Bujar was thinking they could do a U turn. However, he realised that doing so would just trap them back at the ferry point.

"Drive on the other side of the road and go straight through," Bujar ordered.

Dejan pressed his accelerator foot to the ground and the car screeched forward. The two policemen heard the roar of the car before they saw it. One of the officers stepped out in front of it and held up his hand, but Dejan hit him full-on at 65 mph.

The officer crashed onto the windscreen and bounced up over onto the roof and hit the road with a horrendous thud. Dejan continued at 95 mph. The other policeman frantically radioed in, reporting the roadblock car crash and the injured officer. Jeff and Karen heard the news forty seconds later.

"The bastards are on the other side! Get that fucking ferry moving!" shouted Jeff.

The ferry the police took might have been only five minutes behind the criminals' boat, but a car travelling at over 90 mph can go one hell of a distance in that time. Police cars were converging on the Cowes area in force. Dejan continued speeding up Mill Hill Road.

An armed-response vehicle was being driven at high speed, aiming for Cowes: they didn't want to miss all the fun. What made them even more determined was that they had heard that the officer hit by the car had died.

They were bombing down the A3020 Newport Road, sirens blazing and lights flashing. With a screech of tyres, burnt rubber smoke shooting into the sky, they turned left into Mill Hill Lane.

Bujar and Dejan heard the siren and then saw the police car. They had no alternative but to take the next sharp left turn down St Faith's Road.

But they knew the net was drawing in on them.

Jeff and Karen were now on the Mill Hill Road, fast approaching the St Faith's turning.

"Take the next right!" shouted Bujar. Dejan screeched into Arnold Road.

"Pull into the third house, number 6. As soon as we stop, get the bitch out and take her into it. I'll watch your back."

They pulled in to the kerb. Dejan leapt out, opened the boot and dragged Chau out and towards the side door.

The police car stopped at the junction of St Faith's Road and Arnold Road, not sure where the Mondeo was. Then one of the officers spotted the car and pointed. "Over there!"

The officers jumped out of the car while the driver radioed in the news about the location of the Albanians on Arnold Road. A few seconds later Jeff, Karen and their team arrived at St Faith's Road. The Armed Response Unit was sent forward to the junction of Arnold Road and Shamblers Road. The former only had twelve houses in total, six on each side, all of them in close proximity.

The Albanian killers, dragging Chau along with them, pushed through the side gate leading to the rear of the house and tried the back door handle. It was locked so Bujar smashed the window and unlocked it from the inside. There didn't seem to be anyone in. The men then shut the door, and went into the lounge, pulling Chau with them. Dejan threw her onto the sofa and quickly looked around the room then saw what he wanted.

He grabbed a bottle of whisky off the sideboard, opened it, threw the cap on the floor and then took a long pull from the bottle. After gulping down about half the contents, he held it out to Bujar. Bujar took it, swigged a small amount and put the bottle down. He wanted to be alert for what was going to happen in the next hour or so.

More police arrived and surrounded the area. They started by evacuating occupants out of properties in Arnold Road and the surrounding streets. Jeff and Karen were pleased that at last it looked as if there could be no escape for the Albanian killers.

Bujar went to the back of the house and looked out of the back door. There was a garden which backed onto another garden, separated by a four-foot high flimsy wooden fence. He knew the police would already be staking out the roads around the house and he made a quick decision. He strode back into the lounge.

"Dejan, it is time for us to part company." He took hold of Dejan's hand and shook it warmly. "I will take as many as I can with me, brother." Bujar kissed his friend on the cheek, grabbed Chau by the neck and pulled her up and headed for the back door. Outside, he turned right, stopping at the small fence that separated this property from the next.

Bujar kicked at the fence until it broke and then he forced his way through the gap, dragging Chau behind him. He was on the patio of the adjoining property.

Suddenly the back door of the house opened and a big man came out, shouting, "What the hell are you—"

Bujar pistol-whipped him, knocking out his front teeth, and also smashing his jaw and nose. The man fell to the ground, holding his face and howling in agony. Bujar moved along the patio towards the next house, reaching a brick wall.

Bujar lifted Chau in the air and threw her over the wall into the adjacent back garden. He heard her land on something soft and guessed that it was grass. He then hauled himself onto and over the wall, landing on a flower bed. He pulled Chau up.

"Move!," he yelled. "I haven't finished with you yet, bitch!"

Chau was more alert now, surreptitiously looking around for any avenue of escape. Bujar tried the back door of this new house: it was locked. He pulled his sleeve over his hand and smashed the window and then reached in and turned the key in the lock, opening it and finding himself in a kitchen.

He heard the voice of an elderly woman calling from another downstairs room: "Is that you Mavis?"

Bujar quickly clamped a hand over Chau's mouth and hissed, "Sit on the floor and do not fucking move." To make his point he shoved the gun right close to Chau's mouth and gave her an evil look. He walked silently into the lounge. Chau heard a thud and a whimper and then there was silence. He returned to the kitchen and pulled the blinds down on the windows.

"Find some bread and make a sandwich and strong coffee."

Chau stood up and made for the kettle, which was next to the microwave. She took the kettle, filled it with water at the sink, put it back and switched it on. She noticed a rack of kitchen knives set back in the corner by the sink.

* * *

Meanwhile, Dejan had seen numerous police marksmen taking up positions at the front of the property and decided it was time to make a move. He ran up the stairs and went into the front bedroom, which afforded an excellent view of the road and surrounding area.

He opened the window carefully and poked his Uzi through the gap and opened fire, spraying bullets indiscriminately into the street. Car windows were shattering, and policemen were running for their lives as bullets ricocheted in every direction.

After the police had got over the initial shock, they started to return fire and the bedroom window came under a hail of lead. Dejan stepped to the side and then backed to the door and out onto the landing. He took up position facing the stairs, so that anybody stupid enough to come up would be mowed down in a second.

Bujar had heard all the shooting and said a quick prayer, asking that Dejan would be able to kill as many people as possible before he went to meet his maker. The truth was, Bujar knew his time was up and there was simply no way out. He decided that he would kill as many as he could, shoot the bitch, and then shoot himself.

Ten minutes had passed without sight nor sound from the house where Dejar was waiting.

"We need to go in," said Jeff to Commander Baker.

"Easy to say. But it's my men who will get the worst of it."

"Let's go in with smoke and firecrackers?" persisted Jeff. "You know they'll not hesitate to kill the hostage, don't you? We've got to act as soon as possible."

"Yeah, I agree," said Karen, raring to go.

"OK. We go in." The commander called together the team leaders of the Armed Response Units.

"We go in through the back and the front at the same time," he ordered. "Use smoke, shoot to kill, and try and save the hostage if possible."

Dejan was waiting and waiting. He knew that he would be dead in the next ten or so minutes. He knew also that he deserved to die for the hideous things he had done throughout his life. He heard noises downstairs—they were here, it would end soon.

The armed officers, wearing full body armour, had entered through the front and rear doors. They had secured downstairs and knew that the killers were upstairs waiting for them. Smoke grenades were thrown up the stairs, and one rolled back down and was hastily kicked into one of the rooms and the door shut after it.

Dejan was desperately trying to see through the smoke but it was blinding him and he had to retreat into the front bedroom. He decided to go out in a blaze of action. He stepped in front of the middle of the window and opened up with his Uzi, spraying bullets at anything in the street. One second later, his face was blown apart by multiple bullets. He fell to the floor.

For the vicious rapist killer it was all over.

The armed team arrived in the bedroom and located Dejan's corpse. They searched the rest of the house and reported that one body had been found, one of the killers was still missing, and the hostage was nowhere to be found.

Jeff and Karen were shocked. Where the hell had Bujar disappeared to with Chau?

"He's here close by," said Karen, looking worried. "He couldn't have got far without us seeing him."

Jeff frowned, anxiousness make him talk fast. "He must be in one of the other houses. This is getting trickier by the minute." He turned to the commander. "Commander we need to search every house, starting with the ones on either side of number 6."

"I'll get the teams on it straight away."

"Jeff, I'm going to help. I must find Chau." Karen was scared and agitated.

"I know where you spent the weekend," Jeff said to her quietly.

"How the hell—"

"It doesn't matter how I know. Remember, Dushka is a born killer Karen, you must be prepared for the worst. And you shouldn't get personally involved."

"I don't care! I must go too. After all, I'm responsible for leading those bastards to Chau. I have to do what I can."

Jeff could see that Karen was determined to go, whatever he said.

"OK, but stay with the teams, they're the professionals. I'll be following right behind you in a minute."

Karen went to the boot of the car and took out a handgun, checked it was loaded and clicked off the safety catch. She could see the two teams of armed officers being briefed. *Jesus! Why don't they just get on with it?* she thought.

She couldn't wait for them. Karen decided she would start at number 8 and move up the road from there. She crouched and ran along the wall in front of the house. Then she got to the front path and shot round the corner and backed up against the side of the front door.

So far so good, she thought.

Karen turned the front door handle, but found it was locked. She elbowed out a small pane of the glass and opened the door from the inside and kicked it open.

She was aware that if Bujar Dushka was in the house, he would have heard her, so she had nothing to lose by making her presence felt, calling out: "This is the police! Come out with your hands in the air!"

Karen waited for a few seconds "This is the police! Throw down your weapon and come out where I can see you! Now!"

She held her gun out in front of her as she squeezed through the front door sideways. Her hands began to shake and she could feel sweat running down the side of her face. She jumped into the hall, turning quickly in all directions, ready to shoot at anything that moved.

There was silence. He could be above, she thought, just waiting for her to ascend the stairs. She checked the lounge, dining room and kitchen. Everywhere was tidy, there were no signs that any intruder had been in the house.

She knew that she had to go up the stairs and the prospect terrified her. If he suddenly appeared, then she was dead meat. She started to climb, her hands were shaking again and she tightened her grip on the gun to steady them. When she was near the top, she shouted and jumped up the final two stairs, ready to shoot.

But there was no one there. She checked all the bedrooms, finding that all the rooms were tidy and she surmised that Bujar Dushka and Chau had never been inside this house.

Karen lowered her gun and sat on a bedroom chair. She wiped her face with the bed eiderdown and drew in a deep breath. She was wondering whether to wait for the other armed officers before proceeding, but then the thought of Chau compelled her up and back downstairs. She wanted to get to number 10 next door.

She went to check outside the back of the house and noticed the wall Dushka and Chau had scaled a few minutes before. Deciding it would be safer to go over the wall than to go out to the front door, she climbed up onto it and jumped over into the next garden. She landed on the grass and glanced up at the house.

The kitchen window blinds were drawn. *Odd that,* she thought. She held her gun aloft and moved to the back door. She put her ear to it, thought could make out some noise and reasoned that there must be someone in the kitchen. She wondered if the house had been properly evacuated—whether the noise was coming from residents.

Meanwhile, Bujar had heard and seen Karen scrambling over the wall. He told Chau to stand still by the sink while he crouched down opposite the door, ready to shoot Karen when she entered. Chau was in a panic—she knew Karen was going to come in and unless she did something, the animal would shoot her dead.

Karen pushed her shaking right hand towards the back door handle and held it tight. Her hand stopped shaking. She turned the handle very slowly.

Inside the kitchen, Bujar and Chau watched as the back door handle moved slowly. Bujar stiffened and took aim at the centre of the door.

Chau slipped her left hand behind her and felt for the wooden knife stand. She touched it. Fingers slid along. And then her hand felt a knife handle. She pulled the knife out slowly and held it to her side. It was a five-inch vegetable knife.

The door handle turned and then stopped. Dushka shut one eye and aimed at the door, which kept moving very slowly.

Chau screamed, "KAREN LOOK OUT!" She dived towards Dushka, stabbing him in the shoulder with the knife. The man gasped and fired a round which hit the wall as he fell to the floor. Chau pulled the knife out and held it above her head ready to plunge it down into him again but he grabbed her wrist and held it tight. He pushed her away from him, dug his fingers into her wrist very hard. And the knife clattered to the floor.

Karen heard the warning and ducked just in time as she heard the shot slam into the door. She crashed into the kitchen and rolled on the floor. She saw Chau and the evil bastard Dushka lying on the floor. Karen raised her gun but he had got hold of the knife and was holding it at Chau's throat as he pinned her tightly against him.

"PUT THE GUN DOWN, YOU BITCH POLICE OFFICER!" he bawled. "Put it down or I'll slice her in a second!"

Karen was scared for Chau. She quickly dropped the gun and sat back.

"Now Bitch, it's your turn to suffer," Bujar said as he sank the knife into Chau's neck. She screamed and gurgled as blood began to spurt. Bujar tried to pull the knife out to slice at her again, but the blade was stuck: it was so blunt it had got caught in hard tissue and would not move.

The detective seized the opportunity to leap at him, sinking her nails into his face and viciously scratching down hard. Dushka stood up and threw Karen against the oven. She hit her head and saw stars, but she managed to jump back up and desperately looked around for a weapon. She saw the knife-holder by the sink. Grabbed one of the knives and rushed at him.

The Albanian was bending down to pick up Karen's gun but Karen got to him first and plunged the knife into his back He screamed as she withdrew it and brought it down again into his soft flesh. Undeterred, Dushka was still scrambling for the gun and almost got it, but at that instant, Chau hurled herself at him, holding the vegetable knife two handed and thrusting it deep into his neck. He fell back in agony, clutching the wound. Chau pulled the knife out and plunged it back deep into his throat, causing jets of bright red blood to fly in every direction.

Karen joined in the bloody fray as she screamed with burning rage and drove her knife very deep into his thigh. "DIE, YOU FUCKING BASTARD!" she shouted.

"Kill him Karen! Kill him!" screamed Chau as she continued to plunge her knife into Dushka's body. He appeared lifeless as he lay sprawled on the floor. His blood was everywhere, but the two women carried on with their frenetic attack.

Then it stopped and there was silence. The only sound was that of Karen and Chau as they breathed heavily from the exertion. They sat back on the floor, covered in blood and gore. Incredibly, the killer was still alive, moaning in agony but not moving. They knew he might still be hanging on to life by a thread, despite the multiple stabbings.

He managed to open his blood-covered, swollen eyes slightly and whispered hoarsely: "You fucking bitches! When I get out I'll be visiting you two!"

Chau was shocked and scared. "Get out?" she repeated. The thought of him going to prison and then being let out again was inconceivable to her.

"Karen kill him! Kill him for me! Please kill him!" She screamed again and again.

"I can't, not like this," apologised the other woman. "He might not even survive this—look at him. But if he does, he has to stand trial."

"No he doesn't," Jeff said as he walked in the back door. He put his pistol against the killer's head and pulled the trigger. It exploded into blood and bits of flesh that landed on Karen and Chau.

Chau wiped her face and looked at the blood-covered bits of flesh that had landed near her foot. She almost vomited when she realised that amongst them was an eyeball. She screamed and scrambled away from the bloody mess, then sat back on the floor, with her back against the wall, whimpering and breathing heavily from exhaustion and shock. Fortunately the wound to her neck had looked worse than it was, the blunt knife had only succeeded in making a flesh wound.

"Is over now, thank God," Chau said to Karen. And she started to shake and cry loudly.

CHAPTER 30

Paul and Lexi were coming out of Her Majesty's Theatre, having seen *Phantom of the Opera*.

"Paul," Lexi began, "that is the best show I have ever seen, incredible—better than *The Bodyguard*."

"I agree. I thought it was superb, the only thing I didn't like were the seats—too small and not enough leg room," Paul answered. "They should move it to a more modern theatre."

"What? You're not serious! That theatre is part of our history!"

"Put it in a museum then," he said, laughing.

She tucked her arm into his and they strolled down Haymarket towards Trafalgar Square. It was a pleasant evening and she was really enjoying some prime time with Paul, which didn't happen that often. They reached Trafalgar Square and as usual, there were people milling around, listening to one or two people on soapboxes who were shouting out messages. A magician and a clown were entertaining tourists and there was a general atmosphere of life being good.

They moved away from the Square and towards the Strand. They nipped into the Costa Coffee Shop. Paul led Lexi to a table then went to the bar and ordered two lattes and two pieces of carrot cake. He carried the orders to their table and sat opposite Lexi.

"It's been a lovely night, hasn't it?" he said.

"Paul, I've enjoyed it *so* much. I wish we could do it more often."

"Yeah, so do I, but the business won't run itself. But hey, there's no reason why we can't get out a bit more and enjoy ourselves."

"I'd like that Paul." She held his hand and squeezed it. "You do know I want to spend time with you, don't you?"

Paul wanted to say: *Let's get a room in a hotel and make mad passionate love*, but something was holding him back. Instead he said, "Let's finish our coffee and stroll down to the Savoy. We can have a cocktail in the American Bar."

Lexi slurped on her coffee, laughing. "Great, I love a nice cocktail. Let's go."

The walk down the Strand was wonderful. Crowds were coming out of the Adelphi and Vaudeville Theatres. Some of the theatregoers were taking rickshaws up and down the Strand; many were going to Charing Cross Station to catch trains back to the suburbs. The sun was still out, the weather was warm, encouraging more people to mill around or walk at a leisurely pace, chattering and laughing.

It happened very quickly and Paul was not ready for it.

A young man knocked into Lexi as he was walking by and nearly knocked her over. He continued walking without so much as a glance in her direction.

Paul turned and called out to him: "Oi! Watch where you're going!" The young man, who was about eighteen, and had long greasy hair, turned and stuck his middle finger up at Paul and kept walking. Paul was infuriated and would like to have taught the yob a lesson, but decided to leave it.

They continued walking until five seconds later Paul heard his name being called. He turned round to see Duke approaching, holding the greasy-haired yob by his collar and showing something to Paul in his other hand. Lexi caught sight of Duke and just looked at Paul in surprise. Then she was gobsmacked when she noticed that the object in Duke's hand was her purse!

"That's my purse!" she said as she gratefully retrieved it from Duke's hand.

"What the hell?" Paul stared, almost too surprised to speak.

"Paul," Duke explained, "this toerag nicked Lexi's purse when he bumped into her."

Paul looked at the young man. He appeared to be a typical dropout with nothing better to do than go around nicking things when opportunities presented themselves.

Lexi tucked her purse away securely into her shoulder bag then spat at the yob: "You bastard! Get a fucking job and stop nicking purses!"

The yob looked sullen but defiant, trying but failing to wriggle out of Duke's grasp.

"What do you want me to do with him Paul?" he asked.

Lexi butted in angrily: "Call the police and have him arrested of course!"

Paul was thinking, looking the yob in the eyes. "What's your name, Sonny?"

"I'm not your Sonny, mate."

Duke lifted the youth up onto his toes. "Show a little respect to the gentleman when he's talking to you, you slimeball!"

"OK, let's try again. What's your name please?"

"Charlie."

"OK Charlie, this is important, so listen. Have you got a job?"

"No, I'm resting at the moment."

Paul looked at Duke and they almost laughed. They both remembered that was exactly what Duke had told Paul when they met at the Millwall Leeds match months ago.

Paul then rummaged in his coat pocket and brought out a card and gave it to Charlie.

"Come and see me in the next couple of days and I might give you a job."

"What?" Charlie looked down at the card in his hand and then looked at Paul suspiciously. "Why would you want do that?"

"Because I'm able to, that's why."

Paul turned and took Lexi's arm and they headed down to the Savoy.

Duke looked at Charlie. "It's your lucky day. Now get lost!"

"And how come Duke just suddenly appeared?" Lexi asked when they were on their own. "I didn't know he was following us." Lexi was still thinking about the incident.

"Duke is always with me. You may not see him but he is always there for me and for whoever is with me."

They reached the Savoy and made straight for the American Bar.

"Lexi, have you been here before?"

"No, why?"

"No particular reason. It's just that it's one of the most famous bars in London."

"Really? Why?"

"Hmm, well it's one of the first American bars in London serving American cocktails; there are not many like it left now. What would you like?"

"Surprise me."

They stood at the bar and Paul spoke to the barman. "Good Evening Erik. Can we have a White Lady, and a Dry Martini for me please."

"Certainly Mr Bolton; and how are you, sir?"

"Very well thank you Erik, and you?"

"Never better, thank you, sir."

"We'll be sitting in the corner. Thank you."

When they were settled in their seats Lexi said to him: "Well, you must have been in here quite a few times if he knows your name."

"Yes I have, Lexi. I love the history of the place. So many famous people have been here, have maybe sat in this exact spot."

Lexi acted suitably impressed although in reality, she would have been just as happy to be in the local café. Soon, their drinks were brought over.

"Hmm, this White Lady is delicious," she said enthusiastically. "Can I taste your Martini?"

"Yes of course." Paul passed his drink to her. She took a sip and nodded appreciatively. "That's delicious as well. I could get used to this." Then she took another sip.

Paul smiled and held out his hand. "Thank you."

CHAPTER 31

"Tony, I'm so pleased. You seem to be improving all the time."

Dr Gary Thompson was leaning forward in his chair smiling at Tony Bolton as he began their meeting.

"So Tony," he continued, "I think we can give you a pat on the back and actually improve your situation here. Dr Travis is also very pleased with your progress and speaks very highly of you now, which is surprising, considering your little spat when you first met her. I'm delighted you are now getting on so well."

Tony was laughing inside, thinking: if only this prat of a doctor had any idea of how well I'm getting on with Dr Travis, he'd have a heart attack.

"Dr Travis is very helpful to me," Tony replied with a straight face. "I don't know what I would do without her. I'm feeling so much better about everything. It's wonderful."

Dr Thompson patted Tony on the knee. "Great! So look, in view of your progress, we can give you a bit more freedom in the grounds—how does that sound?"

"Oh Doc, that would be truly amazing! I've got so much to thank you for."

Dr Thompson was grinning and basking in the glory of his new relationship with Tony Bolton.

"Well Tony, as I've told you so often before, this is a two-way street: you be good to us and we will be good to you."

Tony was smiling from ear to ear and acting like the cat that got the cream.

"Dr Thompson, how will I ever be able to pay you back for all the help you have given me?"

"Just to see you getting better is the only payback I need."

Tony was still smiling as he thought that the lessons Dr Sharon Travis had given him in 'how to be the perfect patient' were working.

Dr Thompson continued: "I hear you're now attending church services regularly. That is wonderful Tony."

Tony looked thoughtful before he answered slowly: "It has made me more peaceful in myself." He looked sincerely at Dr Thompson and added seriously, "I have given myself to God and he has answered me and opened the door for me to enter His company."

Dr Thompson almost fell off his chair. His immediate thought was that he would become even more sought after than he was now, once he had published his new thesis. Because the specialist treatment was obviously working and, coupled with his medication, he had turned Tony into almost the perfect patient. He was desperate to get back to his office and re-run the tapes of the meeting. He would then add it to his thesis entitled "Treatment – Mr T Bolton".

"I've got to get off now Tony. What are you going to do with the rest of the day?"

"I'm reading a really good self-help book so I'll get myself a nice cup of tea and then curl up on the sofa with it."

"That sounds like a wonderful idea. See you soon, eh?" Then the doctor scurried off back to his office, content that he had changed Tony Bolton from being a psychopath to being a law abiding person.

Tony grabbed himself a cup of tea and strolled back to the day room. He sat on the sofa and he chuckled to himself as a huge beaming smile appeared on his face.

His only thought right now was breaking out of the hospital and getting even with his brother Paul. He was sure Paul had set up the 'referee incident' at the Lancaster Hotel, knowing full well that he would go berserk. Yes, he decided. Paul should suffer for that.

Tony had not yet broached the subject of escape with Dr Sharon Travis but the time for doing so was getting close. Dr Travis had proclaimed her love for Tony and was besotted with him. Anything he wanted she got for him, but he knew he had to be very careful to keep her sweet, as getting her help could well be the only opportunity he'd ever get to break out of the hospital, so he was not going to blow it.

The next thing he needed was a map of the hospital showing the roads, and the various buildings' entrances and exits, and it had to be in detail. That was to be Dr Travis's next assignment.

Dr Sharon Travis was sitting in her small flat, which was provided by the hospital. She was having a cup of tea and thinking about Tony Bolton. Even by her own standards, she was appalled at her behaviour with the monster. But she had always been a highly sexual animal, and that was the root cause of her getting involved with him in the first place.

However, now that she had placed herself in a position of weakness, Bolton could blackmail her for anything he wanted—not that he had asked for anything substantial yet. She couldn't get him out of her mind and thought more and more about how they could extend their weekly sexual encounters.

She also thought the answer could be to leave the job—just hand her notice in and leave the same day. But she realised that she could not do that because she was in love with him. Whenever she used that word 'love', she would shake her head, thinking she must be crazy and ought to book herself into the hospital as a patient.

Sharon therefore decided to continue working at the hospital and to enjoy her relationship with Tony Bolton until it ran its course.

"Sharon, I need you to do me a favour."

Tony and Sharon Travis were sitting in the reading room, talking in low tones. There were other patients and staff dotted around in the area, all chatting quietly.

"What favour is that Tony?" Sharon asked.

"I need a map of the hospital and the surrounding area."

Sharon didn't like the sound of this.

"And what do you want a map *for* exactly?"

"I'm interested in the place," he lied. "You have to admit it's an interesting establishment, isn't it?"

Sharon looked thoughtful and then said carefully, "It's a sackable offence to give you a map. I mean, you might want to use it to plan an escape." She regarded Tony carefully to gauge his reaction to her words.

Tony laughed and leaned closer, so that for a moment his mouth was almost pressed to her ear and whispered: "If I was outside, I could fuck you all day and every day. That would be good, wouldn't it?"

Dr Travis smiled. "Yes that would be very nice Tony but there is no way you will get out of here for years, if ever."

Tony was not stupid, he knew full well that he would never be allowed out. After all, he had killed three people in the past twelve months, one of them a policeman. He knew he would rot in the hospital for the rest of his life. So, it was time to take a gamble.

"Look Sharon, we have a great relationship. I think the world of you. Why shouldn't we have a chance at happiness like any other couple? I'm in love with you."

Sharon thought of those words: 'happiness like any other couple'. *Oh yes*, she thought, *if only... But I want to be happy, I deserve some happiness, I am owed some happiness.* "What are you suggesting Tony?"

"It's very simple, my love. I want you to help me get out of here so we can be together."

Sharon was overcome: he did love her and wanted to make her happy, but of course he couldn't do that while he was in here. She couldn't speak for a second and Tony continued:

"We could get a little cottage somewhere, a love nest for the two of us, somewhere near the sea with fabulous views; it would be wonderful. And in time, we could start a family."

Sharon was dreaming: the baby was asleep upstairs, and she was in the kitchen cooking a delicious meal for when Tony came home from work. Happiness beckoned and she was not going to let it get away.

"You'll love me and look after me?" she asked. "And treasure me for ever?"

"Oh yes, nothing would give me more pleasure than that," said Tony earnestly.

Sharon took a deep breath and said, "In that case, what is a woman to do if she does not help her man? I'll do anything you want. Just tell me and I'll do it."

"Oh Sharon, you have made me so happy!" It was all he could do to stop himself reaching out and holding her hand.

"Tony, I'm going to start looking for somewhere beautiful for us to live. Oh my love, we will be together soon."

CHAPTER 32

DC Karen Foster and Chau had been taken to St Mary's Hospital in Newport. Karen was suffering from shock and Chau had a deep wound in her throat. Fortunately, the knife had miraculously missed vital nerves and the wound was not life threatening.

Chau had been crying for an hour after the battle in the house at Arnold Road and was in a state of complete mental and physical shock and exhaustion. Now that she was ensconced in St Helen's ward, she had recovered a bit and was resting. Karen was in the bed next to her, which had helped tremendously in calming her after all her horrendous experiences.

Karen was pleased to be alive and was over the moon that the animal Bujar Dushka was dead, and would not trouble either of them again. She had been shocked but very pleased that Jeff had taken the illegal decision to blow the bastard's head off, rather than allowing doctors to patch up his horrendous stab wounds so that he could face justice. Jeff's justice made much more sense to her.

The detective constable was mainly interested in a quick recovery, getting out of the hospital and going home. She was also thinking of what was going to happen to Chau. Allowing the Chinese girl to remain on the Isle of Wight was out of the question, since her cover was blown. She also wondered if Chau might still need protection. Bujar and Dejan, the main threats, were gone, and the two other traffickers were in prison, awaiting trial, so Chau was not in immediate danger.

Karen was also unsure of her personal feelings towards Chau. She felt such a need to protect her, but was that enough for any kind of relationship? Was it actually love? She glanced over at the petite Chau, so innocent and beautiful; she just wanted to go and get in bed with her and cuddle her.

"Chau, good day to you," she called across. "How are you, lovely woman?"

Chau looked over at Karen. "Miss Karen, I so happy you here, here near me. I think of you in my dream."

"Oh Chau, I'm so sorry. I'm really sorry. It was my fault those animals found you. I'm so happy they are dead and that they'll not trouble you ever again."

"But you tell me that before, Miss Karen. Maybe they have friends, maybe they watch hospital now, waiting to take me again?" Chau was beginning to shake and had become agitated. "They may be here soon, and they will kill me next time. No escape for me next time." She started crying.

"Chau listen! I won't leave you! I never ever will leave you again. I promise." Karen was also becoming emotional. "Chau, don't worry, you will come and live with me, OK?"

"You sure Karen? Please? Are you very sure?"

"I have never been sure of anything more in my life. Say you will come please? You'll make me so happy."

Chau was silent for a few seconds and then said, "Yes, I come Miss Karen and I will live with you. I love you. I want to spend my life with you."

Karen closed her eyes with relief. She leaned over towards Chau's bed. "We will go home soon and I will look after you. Chau I love you too."

Karen left the hospital before Chau and was able to get the flat in Rotherhithe ready for when Chau was discharged. It was really a case of a good clean, plus some new cushions and curtains in the lounge, and some new bed sheets.

As soon as Chau was ready to leave, Karen went back to the Isle of Wight to pick her up and brought her back to the flat in Rotherhithe. It was a very moving experience for both of them and they continually told each other they were in love and very happy. They slept together and began life as a couple. Karen lost all interest in men and had not even given a thought to Placido in Spain.

It was the beginning of a new life for Karen and Chau.

CHAPTER 33

Richard Philips still couldn't understand why he'd been labelled as a high risk escape prisoner and transferred to HM Prison Long Lartin.

There was no way either Ed Spencer, Matt Collins or Peter Clarke would have snitched on him, for they were all on the payroll. Who the hell else could it have been? Nobody else even knew about his escape plans. He was racking his brains to see if he had inadvertently let something slip. Who had he seen and spoken with just before the transfer?

The only person he had seen was Paul Bolton. *Hmm*, he thought, *could it have been him? Think, think. What did we talk about?*

Then it hit him. Oh God! Now I remember, he thought. I said I'd see him soon— that must be it. He must have put two-and-two together and came up with four. *How stupid of me*, he thought angrily. *How absolutely, fucking, stupid of me!* Paul Bolton must be laughing at me now, thinking he's saved himself a few million quid. Well, he'll find out what happens when someone crosses Richard Philips.

Richard was trying to lose the brightly coloured jacket he had to wear because he was classified as a high-risk inmate. The only way he could do that was to knuckle down and become the 'model prisoner'. He'd been assured that after a good three months keeping his nose clean, he could lose the jacket. The three months were nearly up and then he could start seriously planning to get out. He could also start cooking some of his own meals, which was a new initiative by the prison authorities.

HM Prison Long Lartin had originally been a Category C men's training prison and had first opened in 1971. It had been regularly updated over the years to Category A. In April 1990, prisoners attempted to break out en masse: thirty prisoners had barricaded themselves on a landing after security staff foiled the escape bid. Now all prisoners in Long Lartin were serving a minimum four-year sentence, although they also held Category A prisoners on remand, prior to appearing in court.

Just as he had done at The Scrubs, Richard had begun to cultivate friendships with other prisoners who, he thought, would prove useful in his escape bid. He had already found the muscle he wanted, a brick shit-house called Marty, who dealt in the dark arts of violence.

Long Lartin prison was a very modern establishment compared to the old Victorian prisons that were still in service. Cells were far superior to somewhere like The Scrubs and the whole regime was more conducive to helpful rehabilitation rather than straight old-fashioned Victorian-style punishment.

But time still had to be served, and Richard felt like a lion in a cage, pacing up and down, resenting his lack of freedom, and unable to escape. Doing a year or two was a picnic—the minimum sentence of anyone at Long Lartin was four years, but with good behaviour, that could mean serving two or even less.

Richard had been given life with a minimum of twenty years. That was a lifetime and he had decided that if he couldn't get out, he would rather kill himself than rot in prison. You had to be in a prison to understand everything, for instant the constant smells: disinfectant, sweat, stale food, cigarette smoke.

Then there were the constant noises: doors clanging, keys jangling and the clattering of locks being opened, guards shouting, prisoners shouting and whispering and time, *the dreaded time*, standing still as though it was going at half the speed of the time in the outside world.

There were, of course, moments of excitement: fights between different gang members, very occasionally somebody would get stabbed with a rusty old shank, where the possibility of infection was sometimes more dangerous than the actual wound.

One of the more interesting facts about prison was the large number of different kinds of people that you met. One minute you might be talking to an illiterate labourer who was involved in an armed robbery, and the next you'd be chatting to a very savvy accountant who had embezzled a million pounds. And of course as was inevitable, you made friends with people who were dishonest, violent and sometimes, complete psychopaths.

Richard could cope with prison as long as he had goals and he definitely had those, the first being to get out of prison as soon as possible. The second was to make Paul Bolton pay for both stealing his business and then getting him sent to Long Lartin. Oh yes, Paul Bolton would pay alright.

He'd pay with his life.

Richard served his three months and, as promised, was allowed to remove his brightly coloured jacket. He no longer stood out from the crowd.

So now was the time for him to seriously plan how to get out and back into the real world.

CHAPTER 34

They had gone over the plan a hundred times. Dr Sharon Travis was in love and had become totally besotted and obsessed with Tony Bolton, the multiple murderer.

She was prepared to do anything he asked of her. Her dream of a cottage in the country, and looking after her man, was finally going to happen and she couldn't have been happier.

Tony was not in love with Sharon Travis but he did like fucking her.

She had sucked him off, let him have her in the arse and was happy to do anything he wanted, sexually. The only bugbear was that she constantly wanted him to tell her that he loved her. Well, he thought, if that was the price for getting out, he was willing to pay it.

He knew her needs and how to provide for them. He asked her to think about what wallpaper she would like in the lounge and how she would like to decorate the nursery for their children. Sharon, in fact, was herself mentally unbalanced, and perhaps her interest in psychiatry had stemmed from a desire to understand her own problems. However, the one thing she wasn't, was violent. She just needed to have the constant reassurance that she was loved and cared for.

Broadmoor was going through a redevelopment and there were massive building works going on right next to the existing hospital. A brand new 234-bed high-security psychiatric facility to replace the entire current building was due to open in the spring of 2017. The old site would then have 400 new homes built on it. Broadmoor was surrounded by a huge twelve-foot-high wall that was topped by razor wire.

The site was comprised of a number of individual secure buildings, so there were multiple problems in attempted escapes throughout the whole of Broadmoor. Nobody had escaped from the secure hospital since 1993 and security was felt to be the best it had ever been. There were even plans to reduce the number of the special 'prisoner has escaped' sirens in the local community, from thirteen to six.

Tony was convinced that he could not get out without the help of someone on the inside and he now had Dr Sharon Travis, who fitted the bill perfectly.

It was another day of their usual weekly meetings and Dr Gary Thompson was again pleased with Tony Bolton's progress. He was using Tony as a guinea pig for certain new methods of treatment which he was going to present to a conference of Psychiatric Doctors in Blackpool in a couple of months' time. Pressure of time meant that it was imperative to him that Tony's treatment was all kept on schedule, and that was one of the reasons he allowed Sharon Travis and Tony to spend so much time together. Sharon had cleverly used a double bluff, telling the senior medic that she wasn't very keen on the idea, but would do it in the interests of research and to help her new mentor, Dr Thompson. Meetings between Dr Davis and Tony were therefore taking place all the time.

"Hello Tony, and how are you on this bright Tuesday morning?" asked Thompson.

"Great thanks Doc, yeah, really good," Tony replied cheerfully. "I always find that when I've had a good sleep I do feel better in the mornings."

"Of course you do. How often have I stressed the importance of getting a good night's sleep?" The doctor oozed bonhomie. "Tea or coffee for you, Tony?"

"Tea please thanks, Doc. Is Dr Travis joining us today?"

"Yes, she'll be along shortly. How are you getting on with Dr Travis?"

"Very well indeed. You know she's really helping me, Doc. I'm very happy with all the help you're both giving me."

Dr Thompson smirked, holding his hands up as he said, "That's why we are here Tony, to *help people* and it is so gratifying when patients join us in that healing process."

The door opened and Sharon Travis strolled in with a loud 'Good morning' to Dr Thompson and Tony.

"Ah Dr Travis," the self-important doctor fussed up to her. "We were just discussing Tony's progress and how we're all so happy with it."

Sharon smiled at Dr Thompson. "Doctor, I have to say it's all really down to Tony. He's working so hard to improve, it's a joy to see."

She turned to Tony and smiled, their eyes sending out signals to each other. Her message was simple: *Tony I love you,* while his own message was, *God, I'd like to rip your knickers off and fuck you right now.*

"So, as to looking forward, Dr Travis, what do you feel we need to do next to help Tony?" Thompson waffled on.

"In fact I have been giving that a lot of thought," said Dr Travis seriously. "And I really do believe it's time for us to reward Tony for all the good work he has done."

Dr Thompson scratched his chin, deep in thought. "Hmm, well yes, I can see the need for maybe, some kind of a reward. What did you have in mind?"

"Tony has expressed a wish to stroll in the grounds—of course under supervision. He wants to walk on the grass, see the trees and smell the flowers."

Dr Thompson turned to Tony. "Is that what you want Tony?"

"Doc," Tony leaned forward, speaking passionately and sincerely. "If I could do that for just one hour, I would be so happy. Surround me with ten bodyguards if you like but, yes, a spell out in the fresh are is what I would really like."

Dr Thompson was imagining himself at the lectern giving his speech to the two thousand delegates, advocating the need for 'rewards' in treatment. He laughed. "Ten bodyguards won't be necessary Tony. Dr Travis and I will accompany you. Gracious, it will be a moment for us all to savour."

Dr Travis looked at Tony out of the corner of her eye and was delighted that the plan was working.

"Oh thank you so much Doc. I can't wait." Tony was all smiles and was also delighted with their progress. "That's given me a goal—something to look forward to."

"Good. So look, I'll talk with Dr Travis and we'll agree a date and let you know. How does that sound, Tony?"

Tony looked at Sharon first and then at Dr Thompson. "Marvellous Doc, thank you so much."

"No Tony, thank *you* so much." Dr Thompson then got up to leave. "Are you coming Dr Travis?"

"I just need to go over something with Tony for five minutes and then, if I may, I'll join you in your office."

"Super. See you in a minute then."

Dr Thompson had totally disregarded the rules by letting Sharon remain in a room alone with a male patient, but he had been swept up in the *bonhomie* of it all.

As soon as the door shut Tony grabbed Sharon and kissed her. He then grabbed her breasts, ripping two buttons off her shirt. He began to fondle the ripe melons that lay inside.

"No Tony, we'll get caught, it's not worth the risk! Stop it!" She pulled away from him. "Very soon you can have me whenever you like, but you need to calm down now."

Tony took his erect cock out of his trousers. "Please Sharon! At least give me a quick handjob. I'm ready to burst already."

Sharon wasn't keen on these quick sexual moments, but she recognised that Tony had needs and she had promised to do whatever he wanted within reason. She took his cock in her hand and moved the skin up and down. Tony moaned. "That's good my darling. You take such good care of me."

It didn't take long and was soon over. Sharon cleared the mess off the floor with a tissue, which she put into her handbag.

"It's working Tony," she whispered delightedly. "It's really going to work."

"Yes Sharon, we will soon be together for ever."

She kissed him on the lips and then opened the door and left.

Tony stood for a moment thinking: *women are so fucking stupid it's unbelievable.*

CHAPTER 35

Charlie, the young man who had nicked Lexi's purse at the Strand, had turned up at the club two days later, asking Paul for a job. Paul had lectured him about how he needed to knuckle down and do something with his life, then had set him to work in the Catering and Bars department. Word reached him after a couple of weeks that the new boy was working hard and doing a good job. He was delighted and asked to be kept informed about his progress; there was something about the lad that had reminded Paul of himself when he was that age.

Paul and Lexi were now a couple and saw each other regularly. They still hadn't made love and Lexi was upset about that, but she didn't want to rush Paul if he wasn't ready. They went to the theatre, the cinema and had numerous meals in top-notch restaurants. Paul had decided he needed a few days' break and had asked Lexi to accompany him to Cornwall for a long weekend. She had said yes immediately and was so excited to get Paul on his own for a whole weekend, even though his minder, Duke, would be around as well.

The brother of killer Tony had booked a double room in a small 46-room place called the Harbour Hotel and Spa in St Ives in Cornwall. He had made sure that the double room had a sea view over the Porthminster Bay. It also had a balcony where you could sit and have your coffee whilst enjoying the stunning views.

It was a long drive down but of course, Paul and Lexi didn't need to consider that, since Duke was driving as usual. Duke was pleased because he had family in Cornwall, meaning he could drop Paul and Lexi off and then go to visit them.

They were getting close to the hotel and Lexi was wondering to herself if they were to be sharing a double; she was praying that Paul had only booked one room, which would mean that they'd be sleeping together at last.

The hotel was lovely, and they said their goodbyes to Duke and checked in. Lexi was so happy when she heard they were sharing a double room and then was over the moon when she saw the views and the balcony.

"Oh Paul, it's lovely, I'm so happy!" She threw her arms round Paul's neck and gave him a huge kiss on the lips.

Paul looked out of the window. "Wow! It's so quiet and lovely here. This is going to be a wonderful, relaxing weekend."

Yes Paul, said Lexi to herself. *Believe me, you're going to enjoy this weekend!* She had bought new erotic underwear and was in a very provocative and sexy mood.

"So, what's on the agenda for tonight, handsome?" she asked as she pulled him close.

Paul nuzzled his face in her hair. "Well, first, dinner out in a fabulous restaurant, lots of fabulous wine and then whatever we feel like doing later on."

"Sounds good to me. How long before we go out?"

"About an hour. Can you get ready in that time?"

"'Course I can! I can shower, do my make-up and get dressed in forty minutes tops."

"Great, you do that while I go and have a look around the hotel."

Lexi was disappointed. She had wanted to undress in front of Paul so that he could see what a gorgeous body she had. "Okay, see you in a bit."

In fact Paul *had* wanted to stay in the room and watch Lexi undress: he knew she had the sexiest body in the world from the time when the three of them had had fun together, but there was just something holding him back, and he knew that something was Emma. The thought of Emma kept stopping him crossing the physical barrier with Lexi. *Am I betraying Emma?* he kept asking himself...

He went downstairs and wandered around the hotel and had a good walk outside. He then enquired if there was a really first-class fish restaurant and was pointed in the direction of the Mermaid Seafood Restaurant.

After about twenty minutes, he went back up to the room and found Lexi was just finishing doing her make-up.

"We're going to a fabulous fish restaurant," he announced.

"Sounds very good, I'm starving." *And not just for the fish*, she thought.

"OK, go downstairs, have a look at the spa, and I'll be down in ten minutes."

Lexi was a bit confused but then understood that he wanted to take a shower in private.

"Spa? Wow, that sounds good," she enthused. "OK Paul, I'll meet you in reception."

Paul had a quick shower then put a clean shirt on and was down in reception in twelve minutes. He waited five more and Lexi walked in. He noticed two men standing by the entrance door immediately gave her the once-over, and he could tell they were impressed. She did look beautiful: a simple belted white lace dress clung to her curves, as if it had been made just for her. A little make-up and she really did look good enough to eat.

He took her hand and they went out to the taxi that he had called. They laughed as they spotted that the restaurant was in Fish Street. After arriving at the Mermaid Fish Restaurant, they grabbed a table for two, near the back.

Paul ordered a cold San Miguel while Lexi had a glass of house white wine. They looked at the menu and Paul decided on the speciality: 'Bowl of Seafood'. On enquiring what exactly was in the bowl, he was informed that it was a large container of steamed mussels, baby squid, scallops, tiger prawns and John Dory.

Lexi chose the whole baked sea bass. Paul ordered a bottle of Sancerre Premier 2004, since he knew it would complement the fish perfectly. They were both hungry and tucked into the delicious plates of steaming food the moment it was placed in front of them. The bottle of Sancerre didn't last very long, so Paul ordered another. Lexi was drinking her fair share and was fast becoming happily tipsy.

"Paul, I love this restaurant. Let's come back tomorrow?" Lexi rubbed her leg against Paul's and leaned across the table for a kiss, and Paul immediately complied.

"We can come back if you like, but there are loads of great fish restaurants in St Ives," he explained. "It might be nice to try somewhere new."

"I don't mind as long as I'm with you Paul," she answered quietly. "You do realise how much I'm in love with you?"

"How much is that, Lexi?" said Paul, laughing.

Lexi spread her arms as wide as she could. "That much or even more."

"That's a lot, Lexi."

Lexi became serious. "I love you so much, Paul. But you, you don't want to..."

Paul took her hand in his and spoke gently: "Lexi, you are a wonderful, gorgeous, beautiful woman. Of course I'm in love with you. Please, just take things at my pace and we will make it, I promise you." He kissed her hand tenderly.

Lexi was close to tears. "Emma was a—"

"Let's not talk about Emma tonight," Paul cut in quickly. "If she's looking down at us now I know she would be very happy for us."

"Oh Paul!" Lexi hugged him close and kissed his cheek several times.

"So, what are we going to do now big boss?" She smiled teasingly.

"Well, let's pay the bill and go down to the marina. I like looking at the boats."

"Sounds good to me."

They ordered a taxi and were on the seafront in five minutes.

The area was so picturesque, just like a picture postcard.

"I love it here Paul—everything's so quaint and old-worldy."

Paul was more interested in looking at the boats. "Do you like the sea, Lexi?"

"It scares me, Paul. The thought of being at sea in a small boat terrifies me."

"But you like a pleasure cruise up the Thames?"

Lexi laughed. "Yes, but the Thames is not the sea. I like to see land at all times, so yeah, the river's OK." They were holding hands and acting like a couple of newlyweds on their honeymoon, especially Lexi. They looked at all the boats and there was a cool wind coming in off the sea.

"Shall we go back to the hotel?"

"Yes Paul, let's do that," smiled Lexi, holding him close.

Another taxi and a few minutes later and they were ensconced in the Harbour Hotel bar. They chatted with a couple of locals about the demise of the fishing fleet, the weather and the cost of bread. They polished off another bottle of white wine and soon it was midnight. Lexi leaned over and whispered in Paul's ear: "Why don't we go up to the room? I'm tired." *But not that tired*, she thought.

"Yeah, you go up and I'll join you in five minutes." Paul turned and started speaking to one of the other guests. Lexi was mortified and left and went to the room. She brushed her teeth, washed her face, undressed and got straight into the double bed. As she started to nod off, she heard the door open and Paul entered and shut the door and went into the en-suite bathroom. She could hear him brushing his teeth and later flushing the lavatory, then he turned the lights out and came back into the bedroom.

He sat on the edge of the bed and took his clothes off. He got into the bed and stayed over on his side with no sign of movement. There was a terrible silence for what seemed an eternity, but was probably only two or three minutes. Lexi moved her legs across the bed and rolled over all in one movement. Her feet touched Paul's and he moved his feet away quickly. Lexi was about to cry when Paul's feet came back and started stroking Lexi's legs very slowly and tenderly.

"Paul, please kiss me," she whispered.

She heard and felt him move towards her and she quickly moved as well and they met in the middle of the bed. She could feel his huge erection against her tummy. She put her arms around him and hugged him as hard as she could, pushing her breasts into his chest. She ran her hands through his hair while stroking and kissing his face gently.

"Paul, Paul, Paul, I love you," she whispered and nibbled at his ear then she stopped.

Something was wrong.

He was crying. "Lexi I'm sorry I'm so sorry I loved her so much and the baby," he spluttered through the tears and uncontrolled sobbing. He buried his face into her shoulder as his body shuddered with emotion. Lexi was now crying and stroking his hair and face.

"I know Paul. She was a beautiful, kind lovely girl." She pulled him closer in a tight embrace. "I'm sorry Paul, I'm so sorry." They continued like this for some time and eventually Paul stopped shaking and then, suddenly, he kissed her hard on the lips, probing and pushing with his tongue.

Lexi didn't understand. "Paul stop it," she said. "Don't do it like this. Not now."

Paul grabbed Lexi in a vice-like grip and pushed her down onto her back on the bed, still kissing her. Although she was trying to stop him he made his way down her tummy and was soon kissing and licking her most erogenous area.

Lexi could feel her passion rising. She was ruffling his hair as he continued to kiss her. Suddenly he stopped and went back up to lie close to her, face to face.

He then kissed her gently on the lips and then her neck. He looked her in the eyes. "Lexi I love you and want you to be my woman for ever." He had said it and was happy. He kissed her long and hard on the lips again and she responded eagerly. Their tongues were entwined in a frenzy of licking and kissing that drove them both to the heights of passion.

She reached for his cock, it was still erect and very hard indeed. She touched it gently, then gave it a hard stroking.

Paul was out of control. He quickly straddled her and she opened her legs to let him slide between them. He looked into her eyes and smiled as he gently entered her. She closed her eyelids and enjoyed the wonderful feeling of him filling her. She had never been happier in her life.

It was 10 a.m. when Lexi woke up. She looked across at Paul, who was still asleep. She looked at him closely, studying his ears, his nose, and all the lines and creases on his handsome face. She then regarded his muscular arms and flat stomach.

Then she gently lifted the sheet to look at his cock, which had now shrunk. She marvelled at how huge it had been last night. She touched it gently then quickly withdrew her hand.

But it seemed to suddenly come alive. She was fascinated and touched it again, then started to stroke it gently and rhythmically, up and down. After a few moments it became fully erect and hard. Suddenly, Paul moaned and stretched. And impulsively, she took the cock between her lips and started to suck. Paul moaned and pushed it further into her mouth.

Paul felt the wonderful warm stirring in his groin and slowly opened his eyes. He opened and closed them and then opened them once again. *Yes*, he thought, *it's definitely Lexi giving me an early morning blow job and boy, it feels so good.*

"And a good morning to you Lexi," he panted, realising she couldn't reply.

She raised her eyebrows in a gesture of hello and continued to suck on his cock. He lay back and enjoyed the intense feelings as he built up to ejaculation. He slowly started pushing further and further into her mouth, faster and faster, until he was moaning loudly, "Yes! Yes!" Then he released his load into Lexi's mouth. He continued to shudder and push until he was completely spent. But she continued to suck until he was totally flaccid. Then she sat up and smiled at Paul.

He opened his eyes and laughed. "Did you enjoy your breakfast then?"

"Loved it," she said, licking her lips. "Can't wait for the next course."

He grabbed her and gave her a big cuddle. "I'm starving, let's go and get a huge, full-English breakfast. What do you say?"

But she was looking at Paul's cock. "Do we have to? I could do with that again. And you can put it anywhere you like." And she smiled, raising her eyebrows.

"Hmm, that's tempting," Paul answered. "Tell you what, we go down, have a huge feast and then come back to bed." He stuck his tongue out and wiggled it.

"Well, seeing as how you put it like that, then OK, it's a deal." She then jumped up and skipped to the bathroom. "If you want to join me, you're welcome."

Paul smiled as he looked at her beautiful arse and followed her in.

The weekend had been a fantastic success and Lexi was ecstatic. They had made love endlessly and she had adored every minute of it. Then they left and went back to their respective homes, with Paul promising to take her out on the next Saturday.

CHAPTER 36

Duke was driving at a leisurely fifty miles per hour down the A12 towards Chelmsford. They had just gone past Brentwood and were heading towards Mountnessing and Ingatestone, two small Essex villages. Paul and Angus, the man he'd asked to try and trace the sex tapes, were sitting in the back, discussing various issues about the clubs and the businesses.

"I can't accept that we have come to a dead end." Paul was frowning, and he was well pissed-off. "There has to be something we can do to find those fucking tapes."

"Paul, listen," Angus told him. "Ryder's mum sent the tapes to someone, somewhere in London. I have tried everything; I've even been to the Mount Pleasant Post Sorting Office in London to see if they had any lost packages. Do you know what they said? They didn't have *any*, not *one fucking lost or undelivered parcel!* I nearly called him a lying cunt, but thought better of it."

As soon as Angus said 'cunt', Paul looked at him. Everybody knew that the word reminded him of his brother Tony, since he was in the habit of saying it so much. Angus made a mental note not to use that word again if he could help it.

"Angus, so what are you saying?" Paul resumed. "You've given up? Is that what you're saying?" Paul turned away with a disgusted look on his face.

"Jesus, Paul, I can't perform miracles."

"Don't worry Angus, I'll find someone who can." Paul continued to look out of the window, signifying that the discussion was over.

There was an awkward silence in the car as they drove on through Margeretting and on to the outskirts of Chelmsford. Angus was now unhappy. He didn't want Paul to find someone else to look for the tapes. Doing that would mean Angus being dropped for the job, and he didn't like that, because Paul was a very generous boss. *I'll have to try again about those damn tapes*, he thought.

"I think Mary lives near the County Cricket Club."

"I know where I'm going," said Duke in a rather angry tone.

Paul looked out of the window again. *Better to keep quiet than talk anymore*, he thought.

"New London Road, isn't it Duke?"

"YES, I know that." Duke pulled into New London Road and looked for number

23. It was a huge house and very impressive. Duke parked the car and they all got out. Duke looked up at the house and whistled. "Wow! This is some gaff."

Paul was already heading to the front door but before he got there, it was opened by Peter, the bodyguard. "Welcome," he said to all of them as Paul strode into the house without acknowledging him, followed by Angus and Duke.

Peter raised his eyebrows at Paul and looked at Duke, who also walked past him. "Don't even go there," Duke said in a friendly low tone.

"Paul! So nice of you to come down and visit." Mary Coombs had appeared in the hallway and was looking radiant.

"Wow Mary, you look great! Peter and the team must be looking after you really well."

"I can't complain Paul, nobody listens even if I do, so there is no point." She smiled.

Angus and Duke had followed Paul into the hall. Paul turned to them. "You guys, go and find yourselves a cup of tea or something."

Paul and Mary went into the lounge and made themselves comfortable.

"Mary, you are looking very well and I'm so pleased."

Mary ran her fingers down her cheek. "Yes, the external scars are healing but the ones inside, it's not quite so easy to get rid of them I'm afraid. I still have nightmares. My poor Jack. I'll never get over it completely."

"Of course you won't Mary. But life goes on. How are the roses coming along?"

Mary threw her head back and laughed. "Paul, you have never seen such beautiful flowers! Perhaps you could spare a minute to see them?"

"Mary, I would love to."

"Good. Well, let's have a cup of tea and a cake first, then I'll show you."

She disappeared and came back five minutes later with a trolley of delicious looking cakes and a pot of tea.

Paul leaned forward to get a good look at the cakes. "Hmm, rich fruit cake. Looks scrummy."

"Homemade of course," said Mary proudly as she scooped a big slice onto a plate and gave it to Paul.

"I gave your chaps some tea and cakes in the kitchen."

"Yeah well, they're not in my good books at the moment—you shouldn't have bothered"

"Paul, that's very unlike you! Usually you're full of nothing but praise for your chaps."

He always had to stop himself from laughing when Mary called his minders 'chaps'.

"Yes, well, I've got a few issues and we are having some difficulties sorting them out."

Mary began to pour the tea. "Well you know, if there is ever anything I can do to help, you only have to ask."

"Thank you Mary, I do appreciate that."

They drank the tea, ate the cake and then strolled down the garden.

"Mary, if you don't mind me asking, where did Jack—"

"I had the shed where it happened removed. Couldn't bear to look at it."

Paul decided to change the subject. "Oh wow! Look at those roses!"

Mary was beaming from ear to ear. "Yes, they are rather lovely aren't they?"

They admired the flowerbeds that were full of a rainbow coloured collection of the most beautiful roses.

"The smell Mary, it's just incredible!"

"You see Paul, I always remember the BT advert phrase: 'It's good to talk'. Well I talk to my flowers all the time!"

"Perhaps you should talk to some of my staff!"

Mary laughed.

"Right, as much as I would like to stay," Paul apologised, "I have a business to run."

They began to walk back up the garden path and Paul imagined the carnage on that fateful day when Jack was killed and Mary nearly died herself.

"Well Mary, I'll see you in a few months. I'm not coming in. Can you send those Herberts in the kitchen out to the car please?"

"Of course. Thank you so much for visiting, Paul. You've been very kind. Bye."

Paul had done his duty and was delighted that Mary was looking so well after all she'd been through—she deserved nothing less.

They were back in the Range Rover and heading back to London. Paul was still not talking to Angus.

"Paul, I'll go back over everything and make sure I have not missed anything," said Angus sheepishly.

Paul turned back from looking out of the window. "Now, Angus, that's more like it. And make sure you're very thorough this time around. I will not relax until those tapes are found."

Paul turned back to the window, still thinking about the tapes. Ever since he learned about the existence of the tapes and the thought of the things being out in the world somewhere, gave him a headache. He was terrified someone could blackmail him or worse, that they might go viral on the internet.

Emma's family would be mortified if they ever had to watch what was in essence a porn film, showing Emma, Lexi and himself. He shook his head, realising he never should have trusted that snake Ryder. He racked his brains to think of where Ryder could have sent the damned things.

He had learned many years ago to always put himself in his enemy's shoes. If it was me, he thought, I would put them somewhere they would be safe until I could use them. Ryder was unaware that he was going to be killed, so he could easily have put them in a safe deposit box somewhere. But, according to Angus, he had posted them to someone for safekeeping. Who did Ryder know that they had missed? A family member? A friend? There must be someone, and it was Angus's job to find that person.

"Angus, I want you to concentrate on Ryder's family and friends. Someone has received those tapes. They probably don't even know what's on them, but have just been asked to look after them until Ryder went to retrieve them. Angus, I want them found by any means you can. Make no mistake, this is top priority, OK?"

"Sure Paul, I'm on it already." Angus was only too eager to begin the search again—he'd do anything to remain on Paul's payroll.

Paul now turned his thoughts to the sale of the brothels. His first meeting with Bill Caddy had gone well and he had gone away to think over what sort of offer to make. The big problem was that Bill knew Paul was desperate to get rid of the sex houses, and would therefore lower any offer he was going to make.

There was no such thing as a secret in the world of clubs and brothels in

London. Shit, thought Paul, whatever he offers, as long as it's reasonable, I'll accept. He had spent a long time with his finance man Roddy, working out a valuation. When they had finished, and Roddy told Paul what the brothels were worth, he was dumbstruck.

"How did you arrive at that figure, Roddy?"

"Simple. Six times annual profits plus goodwill. Seventy million is not an outrageous price, Paul."

"So, it will be interesting to see what Bill offers."

"I'm afraid he will think he has you by the balls. Word is out that you want rid of them, so he's going to offer you a shit price and see what happens."

"Well, I'm not giving them away."

Roddy said after a while: "Look you want to sell, he wants to buy. There's a deal to be done as long as both parties are sensible."

"What do you think is the lowest price I should go?"

"It's not for me to say Paul, but if you knocked off the goodwill and gave him a twenty per cent discount, you're looking at forty-eight million."

"Christ! You've just knocked off twenty-two mill! Shit!"

"It's a buyer's market. Let's not guess. He'll be in touch when he's ready."

CHAPTER 37

Tony was looking round the recreation room at the other patients, or what he preferred to call them: nutters. He could not understand why so many nutters self-harmed. At least, seventy per cent of them had cuts, abrasions, burns and all sorts of small injuries. There were several men who had deep scars on their wrists where they had tried to end a life of misery. Depression was the norm in the hospital: everybody was on medication. Some of them were on low doses, while others were prescribed large amounts.

Drugs were a problem for the authorities just as they were in prisons. Cigarettes were traded and bartered, and booze was like gold dust. Mobile phones were the currency of the rich, and available if you could afford one. Tony thought he was perfectly normal mentally, and that it was everybody else who had the real problems, and were without question, completely insane.

Because it happened very slowly, Tony had not noticed the change in his appearance; the main change was his weight loss. He had been a big muscular man, but now a lot of that muscle had turned to fat and his face had become drawn and pudgy. The other very noticeable difference was his colour. His skin usually had a healthy glow, but months inside Broadmoor had given it a slightly grey pallor.

None of this however seemed to bother Dr Sharon Travis, who was still besotted with Tony. Any mention of love, children, curtains or carpet colours brought her out in a blaze of adulation for Tony Bolton, murderer and career criminal.

The escape plan had been completed and Sharon had got Tony to promise that nobody would be hurt in the execution of it, but Tony still carried a knife that he had made from a sharpened toothbrush that would be a lethal weapon in the right hands. The plan was audacious and bold and would require Tony and Sharon to have nerves of steel.

***

It was Saturday morning at 11 a.m., staff were thin on the ground as it was a weekend, but even more so on this particular day: food poisoning had hit the staff canteen on the Thursday and Friday. Tony was as usual, sitting in the recreation room on his favourite sofa, reading one of his gangster crime thrillers that he loved so much.

He had commandeered the sofa as his own and only one person had dared to sit on it while Tony was there. Tony had leaned over to the man and spoke slowly into his ear, saying: "If you don't fuck off right now, I'm going to take your head off and piss in the fucking hole." The guy had moved very quickly and had never ever even looked at Tony again.

The recreation room was a big area with high ceilings and old Victorian comfy chairs arranged on the threadbare grey carpet. There were also a few old tables in the reading section. Tony actually liked the room, and especially enjoyed the feeling of space, a welcome relief from his tiny cell or 'room', as the staff liked to call it. Tony was scanning the space continuously, looking to see how many staff there were. He also got up and went to the window to see what was happening in the grounds. *Nothing much happening there*, he thought.

That morning there were about thirty-odd patients in the room and all was quiet. Dead on eleven-thirty, Dr Sharon Travis appeared and made her way over to where Tony was sitting.

"Good morning Tony. How are you?" She smiled and winked.

"Very well thanks Doc, kind of you to ask."

"Time for your special treat today."

"Oh good, I've been looking forward to it, Doc.

The two of them headed towards the door. Halfway there, Tony turned and winked at one of the other patients, who gave a slight nod. Tony and Sharon left the room and walked slowly down a very long corridor, Tony's shoes making a loud slapping noise every time they stepped on the concrete floor. The corridor seemed to go on forever until they came to a small mini entrance hall with numerous corridors leading into the hospital. There was also a guarded door, that led out to the grounds. Dr Thompson was waiting for them.

"Tony, how are you? Are you looking forward to a bit of fresh air?"

"Can't wait Doc. It's very good of you indeed to arrange all this."

The three of them approached the exit door and Dr Thompson signed a book, entering all the details of who was going out, at what time, and their destination.

The weather was pleasant, and leaves were scattered all across the driveway as Tony, Sharon and Dr Thompson made their way slowly down the gravel drive.

Tony was taking deep breaths of fresh air and admiring the trees and flowers in the borders. He was secretly scanning the area and could see the hospital's main entrance, about three hundred yards away down the long winding drive.

"This is so nice," Sharon said, trying to make small talk. She was beginning to tense up.

Doc Thompson turned to Tony. "Tony, we can do this more often you know, if you keep up your improvement."

"You and Dr Travis have been so helpful to me and I'm very grateful."

Tony wanted to get as close as he could to the main entrance, which was now one hundred yards away.

Dr Thompson suddenly stopped. "I think that's far enough for today Tony." He turned round.

"Oh Dr Thompson, just five more minutes! I'm sure Tony would appreciate that," pleaded Sharon.

"Well OK then, but only five minutes, then we go back. I have a busy day ahead of me."

Tony walked slowly down the drive, picking up leaves and sticks and throwing them into the air, laughing. He straightened up and looked around casually. The entrance was fifty yards away.

Now was the time.

He lifted both arms into the air and started doing some exercises. Dr Thompson gave him a quizzical look. The patient standing by the window in the recreation room saw the movement outside. He nodded to another patient and suddenly all hell broke loose.

Furniture was thrown through windows, fighting broke out, and guards were attacked. The alarm was sounded immediately and guards ran to the recreation room from all directions.

Dr Thompson froze, for the alarm going off signalled a major disturbance. "Jesus!" he shouted, looking alarmed. "Let's head back, quickly!"

"But wouldn't it be safer to wait in the main entrance till it's under control?" asked Sharon.

Dr Thompson looked confused. "Eh? Yes, good idea." He agreed that going back and getting involved would be pointless.

"Let's get to the safety of the main gate then," said Sharon, leading the way.

As they neared the main entrance, two security guards ran past them, heading towards the recreation room. A guard saw their approach and came out to meet them.

"Dr Thompson, what's happening?" he asked.

"There's a riot in the recreation room in C Block. How many men have you got here still?"

"Three others and me. Who are these with you?"

"Dr Travis and this is a patient—Tony Bolton."

The chief guard ushered Tony to one side. "Stand there please, sir."

He turned and called out. "Steve! Come here please!"

A third guard came out of the main entrance door and approached the group. Tony was judging the timing and taking note of where everybody was standing. He took two steps and suddenly grabbed Dr Thompson by the arm. He then took the toothbrush out of his pocked and held it tightly to Dr Thompson's neck, scratching it and drawing blood. He started dragging him towards the entrance.

"MOVE AWAY YOU CUNTS OR I'LL RIP HIS NECK TO SHREDS!" he yelled.

The two guards were unsure what to do and followed from a short distance. One of them tried to pull Sharon back but she resisted and carried on walking behind Tony and his captive. The noise had brought the other two guards out from the entrance to see what the commotion was. One rushed back and pressed the 'prisoner escaping' warning bells.

Sirens started blaring in the hospital and thirteen other locations surrounding Broadmoor, warning local residents that a prisoner had escaped. Tony continued to drag Dr Thompson with him, and finally went into the entrance reception area. He pushed Thompson into a chair and continued to hold the toothbrush knife to his throat. Tony looked out of the window and, in that instant, one of the guards jumped on him and knocked the sharp toothbrush away from Dr Thompson's neck and it fell to the floor.

"SHIT!" shouted Tony as he tried to grapple with the guard and to retrieve the weapon. Thompson, who was now on his feet, was looking on spellbound as the other guards rushed to help.

"Give me the knife!" Tony shouted, still struggling with the guards.

Dr Thompson did not understand. Who was he asking to give him the knife?

He was then taken aback when he saw Dr Travis bend down and quickly pick the knife up from the floor and hand it to the prisoner. Thompson stared, mouth agape, unable to speak. He couldn't believe his eyes! Did he just see Dr

Travis give the knife to that madman Tony?

Without stopping a beat, Tony then attacked the guard closest to him with the weapon, plunging it into his throat and causing jets of blood to fly through the air. Dr Thompson collapsed to the floor in shock while the other guards attacked Tony with truncheons.

Suddenly, a door crashed open and four muscular, hard-looking thugs entered the room. They raised their guns and started shooting. Two of the guards were killed instantly in a hail of bullets, while the other one crouched beside his colleague who was bleeding to death. He held his hands up, shaking and looking up at the gunmen in terror.

Sharon Travis was in shock. All she could think of was that Tony had said nobody would be injured. But now there was blood everywhere, and it had a foul metallic smell. There was groaning from the injured guard and Dr Thompson was still on the ground, ashen faced.

The thugs were rushing for the door, pulling Tony along with them. Sharon shouted, "What about me?" Nobody paid her any attention as they left the building and jumped into a huge Jaguar car. Tony was pushed into the back and sat in the middle of two of the gang. Sharon rushed outside after them and ran right up to the car, banging wildly on the side of the window, looking at Tony

"Tony, Tony don't leave me, Tony please!"

She was screaming and crying and clawing at the window as the car started and pulled away. She dropped to her knees, still yelling at the departing car. Then she suddenly saw it stop and reverse towards her. The back door opened, a head stuck out and yelled, "Hurry up and get in the motor!"

Sharon was up like a shot. She hurtled to the car and scrambled into the back seat, and a hand reached across her and slammed the door shut. "Go!" shouted one of the men.

The lady doctor looked sideways at Tony, who smiled at her. She stretched across the man next to her and threw her arms around her lover. "We did it, we did it!" she said, laughing and crying.

The Jaguar roared away, screeching down Upper Broadmoor Road and on into Duke's Ride and then turned into the East Berkshire Golf Club entrance. Hidden in some thickets was a white van with 'Fred's Fruit and Veg' printed on the side, with pictures of potatoes, sprouts and all other sorts of vegetables.

"What the fuck is this?" Tony was looking at the van, aghast. "You sure this will get us back to London?"

One of the thugs got out of the Jaguar and got into the driver's seat in the van, inserted and turned the key. The engine started immediately, with a smooth humming sound. He reversed out of the thicket and stopped. He then opened the side door to reveal a space that had been created inside hundreds of boxes of fresh vegetables.

"Tony, you and the lady in please," he ordered.

Tony and Sharon climbed in and sat on the floor of the van and then the driver pulled back some boxes, covering the gap they'd climbed through, and locked the door.

The mad killer felt the van start moving and pick up speed. He looked at Sharon and they burst out laughing. Tony picked an apple out of one of the boxes and took a huge bite, announcing cheerfully: "Good plan wasn't it?"

Sharon thought about the guards and the bloodbath. "But people died Tony. You said that—"

"Yeah, but all that matters is that we're together," he interrupted. Then he threw the apple down and took her by the arm and she moved and sat on his lap.

She was still thinking about that awful moment at the hospital, when they drove off in the car, apparently leaving her behind. "But Tony," she asked him. "Why did you let them drive off in the car back at the hospital? I thought you were going to leave me behind!" Her voice shook with emotion.

"Oh, that! The driver didn't know you were coming with us. Well, I set him straight and we went back for you, didn't we?" He squeezed her tightly. "Anyway, we're together now, nothing else matters. Nothing!" Tony was looking into her eyes and could see he had won her over as usual. She smiled and held him tightly.

"Now we have a long journey," he said. "And there'll be no interruptions. So what do you say we—" He kissed her full on the lips and she melted. He then took her hand and placed it on his erect cock.

The van pulled into a lock-up in Lewisham Way and they transferred to a small Vauxhall Corsa.

"Shit! When are we going to drive in something decent for God's sake?" Tony demanded.

"Tony, these motors are very popular, and we want to melt into the background. This is perfect."

"Yeah well, if you say so. Where are we going now?"

"We've got a very nice little house in Brockley Road, five minutes away."

"Good, we need a shower, some good food and a bottle of Scotch."

Sharon was touched when she heard the word 'we'. Any traces of doubt in her mind about Tony's concern for her had now vanished. They got to the house and disappeared inside quickly. The street was deserted, so nobody had seen them. The driver said his goodbyes and told Tony he would come back in two days—that would give them time to recuperate and rest.

Tony went into the kitchen and started opening cupboards—they were stacked with food of all descriptions. He opened the fridge, which was full of milk, cheese, ham and some delicious looking steaks. There were potatoes and vegetables, bottles of wine and at last he found the whisky. He opened it and took a large swig and shook his head.

"Better go easy on that, you haven't had much recently," Sharon cautioned.

Tony smiled happily and he took another swig. "Let's grab a shower and then you can cook some steaks. We'll have a drink and then we'll feel like human beings again."

"Good idea." They went upstairs to the bathroom.

About two hours later, they were both sprawled on the sofa, holding hands and looking relaxed after a satisfying meal that Sharon had rustled up. They were now enjoying their after-dinner drinks, Tony his usual whisky and Sharon with her white wine.

Sharon had turned out to be a surprisingly dab hand in the kitchen, and she had cooked the steaks with some vegetables, and they had enjoyed the meal very much. Then she had cleared and washed up. They had then turned the TV on and seen the news about the escape from Broadmoor: of Tony and the female staff doctor who had been kidnapped by him and his gang of thugs. They turned it off quickly—they'd heard enough.

"I've been thinking," she said, as she nestled into him.

Tony looked at her and waited for her to continue.

"This is all going to be very difficult because you are so recognisable. The fact is Tony, we have to change your appearance and change it dramatically. You've already lost weight so that will help, but we need to change your hairstyle and colour, and your face, as much as we can. Then change what you wear."

"I could put a dog collar on, that would be fun," Tony laughed and added mockingly, placing his hands on her head, "Bless you my daughter." Then looking serious, he asked, "Anyway what about you?"

"Don't worry about me. By the time I've finished, even *you* won't recognise me."

She wrote out a list of what she needed and gave it to the 'gofer'—the general helper in the team—when he came back a couple of days later. It was a long list. The gear arrived in two large shopping bags, which Sharon tipped out onto the coffee table in the lounge.

"Wow! There's a lot of stuff." Tony was picking through the items and then held up a brown coloured wig.

"Is this for me?"

"No silly, its mine." Sharon moved a couple of items aside and picked up a black wig. "This is yours, try it on."

Tony had never worn a wig in his life. "This is horrible and I bet it's going to itch," he complained.

"Stop moaning Tony, this will keep you safe." She put the wig on his head and adjusted it into place and then took a step back and admired it.

"Tony, it looks really good on you! Go on, look in the mirror."

He went to the bathroom and Sharon heard him say, "Wow! Not bad!" He reappeared smiling. "It looks good. I'm surprised."

"Wigs have come on a lot in the past few years. The expensive ones are made from real hair."

Sharon readjusted and fluffed out the wig slightly. "You know what Tony? With a bushy moustache, designer stubble, your eyebrows done maybe, nobody would recognise you in a month of Sundays. We change your clothes to smart casual, something like an arty yuppy sort of person might wear. Seriously, no one will recognise you *ever*. Imagine, you can stroll down to the shops and buy the paper, and you'll be safe as houses."

"Yeah, I think it'll work. Let's see you in your wig then."

Sharon put the brown, long-haired wig on and it looked really good.

"Corr! I could almost fancy you like that," he joked.

Tony made a playful grab for her but she ducked away. He cornered her and got her hands behind her, and pushed her back up against the wall. He then kissed her and moved his hands onto her breasts, then stopped suddenly and looked at her gravely.

"Look Sharon, I'm glad you're here but as you know, you'll have to live as a wanted person. It'll be difficult. Maybe one day we can move abroad. But I've got plenty of money and a very big payday coming, as soon as I sort my fucking brother out."

"What's going to happen with you and Paul?"

"First of all he's going to give me a very large amount of money."

"Oh yeah?"

"And then I am going to kill him."

Sharon looked shocked. "Killing? Violence? Is that how we're going to have to live?"

"Once I've sorted Paul out, we can go abroad and relax, travel the world, enjoy ourselves. Sharon, trust me. Have I ever let you down?"

* * *

Paul was sitting in his office at the Den Club, discussing the sale of the brothels with Roddy.

"That bastard Bill Caddy." Paul was shaking his head in disbelief. "Thirty fucking million he's offered for the brothels. "I can't sell them for that."

"Well, the good news is, there are no shareholders," Roddy told him. "If there were, then you're right, you couldn't sell them for that."

"Fucking hell! I desperately want to get rid of them but I'm not giving them away."

Suddenly the office door burst open and Angus stepped in, looking very worried.

Before he could speak Paul shouted at him. "Don't you fucking knock anymore?"

Angus just stood there, silent.

"Well it must be something important," Paul snapped. "What is it?"

"Tony's only gone and escaped from Broadmoor."

The blood drained from Paul's face. His mouth was agape as he stared at Angus in shock. He slumped back and buried his face in his hands for a few moments, then he slowly lifted his head and looked at Angus and Roddy. "Fucking Shit! That's all we need at the moment!"

There was silence in the office. You could hear a pin drop.

After what seemed like a long time, Paul spoke: "Both of you go. I need to think."

Paul knew that now Tony would come after him. He'd realised the depth of his brother's hatred after the scene at Broadmoor on the one occasion when he'd visited him. He knew Tony was insane and now that he'd escaped, it was inevitable that he would come after Paul.

His psychopathic brother had the money to get a team of guns together and it wouldn't be long before they came knocking at Paul's door. Paul was certain of one thing: he would have to be ready for him, or he would be dead.

CHAPTER 38

Rotherhithe Nick was still a bit of a dump but it was like home for Jeff and Karen and had been for a number of years. They loved the familiarity of the building: it was solid, dependable and historic. Life at the Nick had returned to normal. Jeff had sunk back into a state of lethargy and Karen was content to have some peace and quiet, at least for the time being, as things could always change unexpectedly.

The real bonus for Karen was having Chau at home, cleaning, cooking meals and being very domesticated. Karen thought they were almost like a normal married couple with her going out to work while Chau stayed and looked after the house. Chau had taken to domesticity like a fish to water and loved every minute of it.

Karen would arrive home at about five-thirty or six, she would have a shower, come downstairs and a beautifully cooked meal would be waiting. They would have a couple of glasses of wine and then Chau would question Karen about her day. Karen liked the questions because it meant she was interested in her work. They would usually curl up on the sofa and watch a bit of telly and then go to bed at about eleven. They made love at least four times a week and Karen was learning how to enjoy Chau and her delicate touch.

Jeff had quizzed Karen on the relationship and rather than hide it Karen had told him that they were lovers. Jeff had done his best to keep it as quiet as possible because whatever anyone said about gay relationships being OK, such things were still frowned upon in The Force.

Karen had been put forward by Michael for promotion to Detective Sergeant but Karen had been upset that Jeff had not got the credit he deserved. She believed that the successful completion of the operations of the past few months, involving the Albanians and women trafficking, would not have been possible without Jeff's input and direction.

But Jeff was perfectly alright with the situation and tried to reassure her not to worry about it. She was about to go before a board and be interviewed as to her suitability, and Jeff had wholeheartedly wished her luck with it.

There were no new cases and nothing exciting happening until they heard that Tony Bolton had escaped from Broadmoor Hospital and was on the run, and had also, apparently, kidnapped a female doctor. Only God knows what has happened to that poor woman, thought Karen dismally.

"What are we going to do?" asked Karen.

"Why don't we pay Paul Bolton a visit and have a little chat with him?"

"Sounds good Jeff, I can't wait."

Jeff contacted the Den Club and made an appointment to see Paul in three days' time: on Thursday at 11 a.m.

On Thursday morning, Jeff and Karen were on their way to the Den Club.

"How come we've never met Paul Bolton before?" asked Karen, frowning.

"That's a good question, and the honest answer is because he's always covered his tracks."

They found the Den Club and parked in the nearby National Car Park.

Angus met Jeff and Karen in the reception area and he welcomed them to the club. He took them through the plush bar and dancing areas and into the executive suite of offices. He knocked on Paul's door and entered. Paul immediately got up from his chair.

"Mr Swan and Ms Foster. Good to meet you. Please, both of you, take a seat."

"Thank you Mr Bolton. And how are you today?" Karen asked.

"I'm good every day, have to be to keep on top. So what can I do for you?"

The two officers had agreed that Jeff would lead in most of the conversation, but Karen could butt in if she had something to contribute.

"We just wanted to have a chat," Jeff began. "You're obviously aware that your brother Tony has escaped from Broadmoor?"

"Yes. I did hear security at that place is shocking."

"Do you happen to know where he might be?"

Paul half laughed. "This is the last place he would come, believe me."

Karen interjected. "Oh, and why's that, Mr Bolton?"

"Well, this would be the first place you would look, isn't it?"

"Have you had any officers in touch at all?"

"No, you're the first."

"When did you last see Tony?"

Although Paul had visited Tony in Broadmoor, he certainly couldn't say that because he went in using a false identity.

"I haven't seen Tony since that awful day at the Lancaster Hotel."

"You haven't been to visit him? That's a bit strange, isn't it Mr Bolton?"

"I'm a very busy man."

They all sat in silence until Paul spoke: "Well if that's all then." He rose from his chair.

"I haven't finished, Mr Bolton," said Jeff, still sitting down.

"As I said, I'm very busy."

"We could continue this down at the station if you like."

Paul sat down. "OK, let's finish off now. That's a good idea, because it saves you coming back." He was getting a little fed up. "There's nothing I can tell you. I have no idea where Tony is."

Jeff looked thoughtful. "Does Tony own any other properties apart from the one in Bermondsey?"

"Not that I know of."

"What about this woman he's kidnapped?"

"What about her? I have no idea what is going on in that lunatic's head. I have no idea who she is or where he is."

Jeff turned to Karen. "Are there any questions you would like to ask Mr Bolton?"

"Judging by your last comment and the fact you've never visited Tony, is it fair to say you're not on the best of terms?"

Paul didn't want to say too much. "I really do feel that I've answered enough of your questions, now shall we—"

Paul was interrupted by two suited men who entered the office without knocking. One was short and the other was tall. The taller of the two, who appeared to be in charge, looked at Jeff and said: "My name is John Ferner. I'm a solicitor with Abbot and Gray. Mr Bolton will not be answering any more questions at this time."

Jeff knew of Abbot and Gray, they were the most popular law firm with criminals in London.

It was a no-win situation. "No problem," Jeff said. "If we need to see you again Mr Bolton, we'll invite you to our turf."

Jeff and Karen got up and left the office.

"What the hell are you two doing here?" asked Paul, looking at the two men in surprise.

"We were called by a Mr Angus."

"Yes, yes Angus. OK well, it was nothing really. They were just asking a few questions about Tony."

"Well, it has already cost you a great deal of money for us to come here at such short notice. Is there anything we can do for you?"

"As a matter of fact there is. I want you to go and lock yourselves in a room with Angus and talk to him about video tapes and then come and see me before you leave."

"Yes well, OK then, we will." They turned and left the office.

Paul sat back and exhaled. He had so many problems he didn't know where to start. Tony was on the loose and without question would be looking for trouble. The tapes were still out there somewhere and it looked like he might have to sell the brothels on the cheap. Hell! Some good news would be welcome.

There was a knock at the door. Duke entered and shut it behind him.

"Nobody else would come boss, sorry," he apologised.

Paul was getting more and more pissed-off by the second. "So, what the fuck is going on now?"

Duke seemed dumbfounded, but he just managed to speak. "It's Richard Philips."

"Yes? Spit it out man!" Paul was impatient.

"He's escaped from prison."

Paul couldn't say a word. He just slumped further into his chair and stared at Duke. Suddenly, he stood up and swept his desk with his arm, scattering piles of papers to the floor. He kicked at his chair viciously, sending it flying across the room.

Then he stopped and he looked at Duke. "So, Duke, I now have Richard Philips and Tony after my blood."

"No Paul, *we* have Richard Philips and Tony after *our* blood."

Paul went to Duke and put his hand on his shoulder. After a moment, Paul said quietly, "Get Angus, Dave, Pauly and Matt. Call in the teams and prepare for a Bermondsey war."

The End

The Author

Chris Ward lives in Epsom Surrey with wife Helen and two of their seven children. He has been Commercial Director of several food manufacturing companies and currently runs a food marketing business. Hobbies include WBA, Cooking, Wine, Reading and Travelling.

THE BERMONDSEY TRILOGY OF GANGSTER THRILLERS

"Bermondsey Prosecco" is the sequel to "Bermondsey Trifle" and the second book in the Bermondsey Trilogy.

I implore you to read both books as it will give you the full picture before you go onto read "Bermondsey The Final Act" which is the third and final book.

"Bermondsey The Final Act" takes us back to the heart of Bermondsey for a battle royale between Paul Bolton and his brother 'Mad Tony'.

Richard Philips has escaped from Long Lartin prison. Will he join forces with Mad Tony? Or will Paul pay him off to keep the peace?

DS Foster DC Swan are still chasing criminals and somehow get caught up in the mayhem caused by Paul and Tony.

The Final Act will be action all the way and a book you will not be able to put down for a second.

Follow the trilogy on Twitter @BermondseyT

And Facebook at http://facebook.com/BermondseyTrifle

Bermondsey Prosecco

Printed in Great Britain
by Amazon